All That Smolders

ONE BOOK, ONE ISLAND
WWW.NANTUCKETATHENEUM.ORG

ALL THAT SMOLDERS

A MYSTERY

JAMES SULZER

NEW YORK
LONDON • NASHVILLE • MELBOURNE • VANCOUVER • BOSTON

ALL THAT SMOLDERS

A Mystery

© 2025 James Sulzer

All rights reserved. No portion of this book may be reproduced, stored in a retrieval system, or transmitted in any form or by any means—electronic, mechanical, photocopy, recording, scanning, or other—except for brief quotations in critical reviews or articles, without the prior written permission of the publisher.

Published in New York, New York, by Morgan James Publishing. Morgan James is a trademark of Morgan James, LLC. www.MorganJamesPublishing.com

Proudly distributed by Publishers Group West®

Morgan James BOGO™

A **FREE** ebook edition is available for you or a friend with the purchase of this print book.

CLEARLY SIGN YOUR NAME ABOVE

Instructions to claim your free ebook edition:
1. Visit MorganJamesBOGO.com
2. Sign your name CLEARLY in the space above
3. Complete the form and submit a photo of this entire page
4. You or your friend can download the ebook to your preferred device

ISBN 9781636987576 paperback
ISBN 9781636987583 ebook
Library of Congress Control Number: 2025936889

Cover Design by:
Ale Urquide

Interior Design by:
Chris Treccani
www.3dogcreative.net

Morgan James is a proud partner of Habitat for Humanity Peninsula and Greater Williamsburg. Partners in building since 2006.

Get involved today! Visit: www.morgan-james-publishing.com/giving-back

In memory of my mother, Katharine

ACKNOWLEDGMENTS

Thank you to the readers who offered valuable feedback on my early drafts: Kathy Butterworth, Bill DePuy, Judy Belasch, Phil and Rochelle Highfill, Ben Green, and Steve and Natalie Sulzer. Thanks to Natalie, also, for polishing the book with her editing skills. And thank you to my wife, Barbara Elder, not only for her insightful reading, but for her kind support and encouragement through the challenging process of exploring a new genre.

Many thanks to the team at Morgan James for making the publishing process so seamless and enjoyable: David Hancock, Michael Harris, and Jill Nelson.

All writers of mystery owe a debt to the great Agatha Christie. In preparing to write this novel, I read a baker's dozen of her classics, including some of my favorites such as *Crooked House* and *Death on the Nile*. I came to them for enjoyment but also to gain insight into her methods and style—in particular the effortless way she could create several credible suspects, each with motive and opportunity. Her brilliance remains unmatched to this day.

It was illuminating to read Lucy Worsley's *Agatha Christie: An Elusive Woman* for her insights into some of the dramatic events in Agatha Christie's life.

The family relationship of my character Peter Christie to his "great-great aunt" Agatha Christie is purely fictitious. Agatha Christie did not, in fact, have a brother by the name of Harry, and Peter Christie's family bonds to the great writer exist only in the realm of mystery and fancy.

One important family connection, however, does inform this book. I undertook writing a mystery in memory of my mother, Katharine, who was a huge Agatha Christie fan. To this day my mother's voice lives within me, encouraging me to be my better self. I hope in some small way I have begun to repay the love and protection she gave to my brothers and me as we began our journeys through the mysteries of time.

Journal Entry
Fleeing

A crash. The wall shuddered like something under attack. Two sharp slaps. *Please. Stop. Oh. Please, darling.* Then another voice, a low growl, words inaudible. And her reply: *I won't do that again I promise. I will never spy on you again no matter what other women you—Oh!*

I was seven years old, I stood in the hallway outside their room, I had no name for what was happening within. But I knew fear and I could sense terror. What would a loving child not do for their mother in a moment of crisis? I reached for the doorknob and took it firmly in both hands.

It was locked.

For a short eternity, I was frozen in place as the wall shook a second time and the cries grew louder. Then something broke and I ran. Out the side door and into the woods. Dodged trees and broken limbs. Found shelter beneath a canopy of honeysuckle draped between some pines. A sticky sweat on my skin. Grabbed handfuls of needles off the ground and brought them to my face, the tart pure scent. Inside me, something was moving and changing. I sat in silence and plucked honeysuckle flowers off the vines and placed the slender tendrils on the ground. Yellow flowers and white flowers, arranged in a gentle oval. An order that nothing could disturb.

But an image and a question stayed with me.

The image of what was happening behind the locked door.

The question, Was it really locked?

CHAPTER ONE

Later, in the blur of early adulthood, I was still in various stages of fleeing.

Much was lost in the process. Friendships, relationships, a sense of comfort. My marriage, which dissolved in the final years of the 70s about the same time as the death of disco.

But as 1980 boogied onto the scene, a handful of talents did not desert me.

At the age of ten I'd learned to listen to my instincts about people—those who were trustworthy and those who weren't. An inner voice, quiet and assured, was there to prompt me. I had no idea where this voice came from, but it had grown stronger and more reliable over the years.

And I was able to foresee the outcome of certain events both near and far.

Distant events like the breakup of a celebrity couple. Gritty crime trials dominating the news. The slope of a shoulder, the way someone averted their eyes during an interview, a certain tone of voice—and I could sense guilt or innocence.

Closer to my own sphere, I could sense when a friend was cheating on his or her spouse. That knowledge, I learned over time, was best kept to myself.

Sometimes my skills came up short, for reasons I never understood.

Take, for instance, the deadly night on the remote island where my wanderings had taken me—a crime that involved massive wealth and the destruction of a family. Though the mystery threatened to tear the community apart, though I had a compelling personal reason of my own to solve it, the answer still eluded me.

The best I could do was to conjure up a moving picture of the crime scene, as fuzzy and grainy as an old home movie from the 1950s.

A flood of moonlight tumbled through the trees and onto the shoulders of a man wearing a Boston Red Sox hat. Fully absorbed in his task, he was bent low to the ground, sweeping a metal contraption along the grass. The disk at the end of the pole was flat as a dinner plate and emitted a series of small beeps. A minute later they merged into a single sustained tone, wavered, then began to rise and fall like the whine of a puppy. The man stopped and leaned forward.

Beside a line of ink-black holes, some mounds of dirt littered the shadows. Thick clumps of sod lay nearby. A wooden-handled shovel was jammed into the earth beside one of the holes, and three bulging burlap bags huddled nearby.

The hat was pulled low over the man's head, and his face lay in darkness.

Behind him rose a magnificent home, its lofty gables catching the glare of the half-moon. Beyond the house glimmered the harbor, a sheet of wrinkled silver.

A second figure took shape in the darkness and crept up. It raised something with its right arm and brought it down on the top of the Red Sox hat. A muffled *thunk*; the man shriveled to the ground. The figure leaned over, tested the top of the man's head a few times with something—as if checking for signs of life—and dropped an object that landed with a hollow clang. The figure bent again and fiddled with the pants pocket of the victim. Then it gathered up two of the bundles and slipped off into the darkness.

On an island this tiny, news has always traveled quickly.

Betsy Cranmore's watch read 5:30 as she began her morning walk on the back roads near the harbor with Bugsy, her golden retriever. She was making her way past a gravel driveway when a sound startled Bugsy and he whimpered and strained at the leash. Someone loading the back of a pickup truck. "Quiet, boy," Betsy comforted him. She could see that the bed of the truck was filled with the bushel-sized plastic boxes that commercial scallopers used for their catch. Fishermen were always up early, getting their gear ready, strapping the weights onto the dredges or checking their lines. Nothing out of the ordinary.

But a few minutes later, at the luxurious Douglas property, she came upon a strange sight. Sprawled out on the lawn was something that looked suspiciously like—could that be a body? Bugsy also noticed it, and again he strained at the leash, this time with enough force to pull Betsy forward several yards. The dog was already nosing the body when she dug in her heels and yanked him back.

"No boy, get back!" she exclaimed.

She retreated a few steps, stumbled, and almost lost her footing entirely. She saw that she'd tripped over a baseball bat lying there on the grass, and she ordered herself not to pick it up. Her eyes rested on a manhole cover, not far away, that Bugsy was investigating. Why a manhole cover in the flawless lawn? she wondered.

Then she willed herself into action and hurried back to her house to dial that new emergency number, 911. She had a breathless call with an operator and returned to the Douglas estate.

Minutes later, red and green lights flickered onto the few remaining leaves on the stately elm in the yard, and a cruiser pulled to a stop. Gesturing toward the lawn, Betsy gave a breathless report to the officers and hurried back home. She made herself a fresh pot of coffee and called a few friends, each of whom called more friends.

Within minutes, the shocking news had streaked across the island. Quentin Douglas was dead. The wealthy old recluse—dressed always in baggy pants and a Red Sox hat—had made his fortune in the world of finance, largely in commodities trading, for which he'd developed some algorithms that were years ahead of the other traders. Over time he'd grown more and more eccentric and eventually withdrew almost completely from public view. It was said that he'd developed a fierce distrust of the banks and government—a view that had recently gone mainstream in Ronald Reagan's rise to the presidency. But Douglas had taken this distrust to extremes. It was rumored that he'd buried much of his massive fortune in his side yard in the form of bags of gold and silver. Two Rottweilers, Buy and Sell, lay outside the house all night, no matter the season or the weather, protecting the treasure.

That same morning, Buy and Sell were found around the side of the house, splayed out side by side, with swollen bellies and grossly distorted faces.

Once it digested the news of the murder, the island came to a quick consensus. In the act of digging up a bag or two of his fortune, no doubt intending to gloat over it, Quentin Douglas had been dispatched to a better (or worse) world. The irony was impossible to miss. For several hours after the murder, Douglas had lain motionless on his lawn, mere inches from his precious metals . . . but now a lifetime removed. *You can't take it with you* was a common refrain.

At his age, there was some surprise that he'd been hardy enough to go outside in the middle of the night and dig his lawn. But greed is a powerful motivator, it was said, able to breathe strength into the frailest among us. And despite being in his early 90s, Douglas was known to work out daily with his aide and personal trainer. As for his choice of the middle of the night, his passion for privacy and secrecy offered a sufficient explanation.

There was endless speculation about suspects. Was there anyone on the island who didn't bristle at the treatment they'd received at the hands of this coldhearted miser? Any number of people could have been biding their time, waiting for the right moment to exact the ultimate revenge.

Not the least of these were his estranged family members: his two children and his three former wives.

There was also frequent mention of his housekeeper/trainer, some tradesmen who had worked for him, and the younger women Douglas was said to entertain in his house from time to time.

With all this material to sift through, the town could be certain of just one, rock-solid fact: Quentin Douglas was dead.

But there they were wrong.

Arriving at the scene, Officer Johnson and Officer Ramirez got right to work. They pulled on their gloves, checked the body for a pulse, and bent closer for a look at the face.

"Hey, José, do you know what old man Douglas looks like?" Johnson asked.

"What the heck, you think I hang around with rich dudes like him?" Ramirez answered.

"I dunno, there's something strange here." As Johnson returned to his vehicle and called headquarters, a brown woman in a plush bathrobe pulled open the front door and looked on through the glass storm door, balancing a nail file in her left hand. An old man in a walker appeared next to her and gazed upon the scene: the flashing lights, the cruisers and fire truck, the officers. He shook his head and turned away.

I've always been fastidious. In high school the baseball team kidded me about the way I'd scrape my cleats clean with a stick on the bench between innings. As an adult I passed on owning a cat because of the idea of a litter box. I avoided those soft, mushy muffins that leave bits of dough on your hands and the sticky feeling on your fingers that never quite left, even hours later.

I guess I went into journalism to clean up the world, root out messy ethics violations, tuck the world's shirt back into its pants. Where it belonged.

When I moved to the island, I still wore old-fashioned, classic clothes—khakis, crisp button-down shirts—but when it came to being fastidious about other people's personal ethics, I had to admit I'd lost the right.

That's what happens when you've been expelled from your paradise.

This island was supposed to be a post-paradise refuge, quiet and restorative. A place where no one knew me. A second chance.

Most of the families on this island had been here for generations, sharing friendships and feuds and lovers and offspring. The Coffins, the Douglases, the Patersons. I was an outsider, doubly removed. For one thing, I'd only moved there recently—a washashore, as we were called. For another, I was now a reporter for the *Island Forum*, the weekly local newspaper, a job that required a certain level of detachment.

I came there looking for a new start after a pair of bad endings. To my five-year-old marriage. To my six-year-old job at the *Boston Globe* as a business reporter. One bad decision—and poof! both were gone.

I was still young enough, twenty-nine. If not redemption, I thought at least I might find a species of steadiness in this isolated place where my past couldn't tip the scales against me. I charted out a careful plan. Show discretion. Avoid entanglements and relationships. But on that, life had other ideas. I'd only been there a month when I met her. A young woman with a weightless, otherworldly poise and a curious, perpetually surprised light in her eyes. Haddie.

There was no mistaking how special she was.

Only a few years out of college, she worked as a nature scout for the conservation commission. The job took her around and about the island, immersing her in the nature she held so dear, the shorebirds, the vegetation, the rhythms of wind and waves. I told myself we shared something important: an air of the old-fashioned. Looking back now, however, I see a difference. My attachment to the past came from a reliance on old-fashioned dictates like precision and timeliness, while hers was simply an expression of her gentle spirit, which drew about her the kinder mists of bygone ways and times.

For all her kindly ways, she sometimes surprised me with her candor.

Tell me something, she said to me early on, resting her grey eyes on me. What ended your marriage?

An affair, I confessed.

Yours—or your wife's?

My gaze shifted to a feisty freckle on her right cheek. It was my wife, I replied.

A change in her eyes.

At times my actions seemed like those of a stranger. They took place off in the distance, like something seen through a frosted glass.

She could tell.

What brought Haddie and me together in the first place was her desire to write about her experiences in nature.

She'd learned I was a writer and asked me for some feedback, which of course I gave with pleasure. Because she knew writing has deep roots in my family, she probably showed me more deference than I deserved. My great-great aunt was the most famous mystery writer in the world; it's been said that her books have sold more than any other books in history except Shakespeare and the Bible. At times I've wondered if that ancestral connection has given me a more than usual fascination with the seamier side of life—murders and affairs and contested wills.

"What was she like?" Haddie asked in one of our first get-togethers.

"I never met her."

"You never met her? Why not?"

I explained that there was a complicated family history. As Haddie watched me with a quizzical smile, I added that even though I'd never met Agatha Christie in person, I felt a kinship. I liked to think of my great-great aunt's spirit as riding sidecar alongside me in a frumpy tea dress and maybe sporting a crazy fascinator.

And though I kept this to myself, I wondered if the inner voice that counseled me was a distillation of my aunt's savvy wisdom.

Speaking of relatives, on this small island they played a greater than usual role. Everybody was some kind of cousin to everyone else. Take Haddie, for instance. She was a great-great-niece of Quentin Douglas, which made her a second cousin of Dorothy, Douglas's granddaughter. Haddie once confided to me that she had heard she might even be mentioned in the will.

Relatives were everywhere, and the connections could reveal themselves at the most unfortunate moments.

On the day of the murder, Haddie paid me a surprise visit.

It was lunchtime, and the newsroom was buzzing with the newest update. A completely new victim. And probably, an updated set of suspects.

I was bent over my typewriter, cradling a cup of coffee, preparing to compose a new lede for the story. I had just craned my neck to the side—a nervous mannerism I've never been able to shake—and was tapping on a few keys.

In the middle of this, Haddie slipped in through the front door, tripped up to my desk all grace and prettiness, and placed a paper bag in my hands. It was early October, already a bit chill, but she wore her conservation commission dark blue shorts. All the guys in the room had turned to watch her.

I looked up from the keyboard. "Hey," I said.

"I stopped by the Bake Shop on the way in from the Reserve. I figured you'll be working late today with the paper coming out tomorrow," she replied. "I hope you find them to your liking, they're blueberry." She gave a few confused glances around, taking in the frenzied scene.

"Muffins. That's so nice of you." They were the squishy kind.

"Is something wrong?" she asked.

"Not at all. You are so kind." A stab of pleasure at seeing the light in her eyes. "I guess you've heard the latest news?"

She had not. She'd been out at Minnipe Point since early this morning, setting up tape. Restricted areas. The first snowy owl had returned for the winter. "What happened?"

"An old man was murdered."

Her eyes widened. "Here, on the island?"

I nodded. "At Quentin Douglas's house. But—"

She took a step back. "Quentin Douglas? Oh my goodness, Quentin was murdered? That's Dorothy's grandfather. I need to go to her. She must be devastated."

I placed a hand on her arm. "It wasn't Quentin Douglas. Everyone thought it was—at first. But it was someone else. Someone else dressed just like Douglas, in baggy pants and a Red Sox hat."

The light in her eyes turned up its voltage. "Who was it?"

"It was a lawyer. Someone by the name of Chester Danville."

She recoiled as if she'd been struck by a blow to the face. She turned and slumped over.

From behind her horn-rimmed glasses, Stefanie, the editor of the *Forum*, gave me a look with her big brown eyes. I went over to Haddie and placed a hand on her shoulder. She collapsed against me.

It was the first time I'd seen her in tears.

"That's my grandfather," she sobbed. "He was my grandfather. I loved him so much."

"Your grandfather?" I stood there stiffly. I knew I should hold her, I knew some soothing words of comfort should come on my lips, but they were trapped as if on the other side of a wall.

She separated herself from me and dream-walked her way outside. Peering over her glasses, Stefanie tossed her head in the direction of Haddie. *Go after her, you fool.*

I followed Haddie's footsteps through the door, stopping a few feet short of her. The October sunlight was dazzling, even the pebbles cast shadows on the pavement.

"What do you wish from me, Peter?" A taste of something bitter in her voice.

"I wish I knew the right thing to say," I told her. "What can I say?"

"You expect me to tell you that? Now?"

"I . . . I don't know."

She held up her hand toward me like someone shielding her eyes from a stabbing light. She climbed into her battered old pickup and drove away, scattering the gravel behind her.

CHAPTER TWO

A Shocking Murder Stuns the Island
Treasure unearthed, clues still buried
BY PETER CHRISTIE

October 9 In the past two days the peaceful rhythm of life on the island has been torn apart by a shocking murder at the waterfront property owned by Quentin Douglas, said to be the wealthiest resident of Massachusetts.

The murder victim, at first thought to be Douglas, was later identified as Douglas's cousin Chester Danville, a lawyer and deacon of the First Congregational Church who has been described as a pillar of the community.

Multiple mysteries surround the murder, including the fact that the victim seemed to be engaged in the task of unearthing bags of gold and silver that were concealed in the side yard of the luxurious . . .

It was quite late by the time I got home. A hint of winter in the licks of wind. My apartment was over a garage in a section of the island that had a vaguely suburban air—modest frame houses with small yards, scraggly fruit trees and shaggy bushes. A few mature oaks. This neighborhood was several steps down the economic ladder from the downtown, with its ancient brick mansions built on the blood of whales and whalers, and from the waterfront, with its tasteful old summer homes and its new-wealth temples to unbridled vanity. Most of the wooden homes on the island were covered with cedar shingles that turned light gray over time from the salt in the air.

The apartment had no heat but the wood-burning stove that I kept stoked with pieces of timber I could gather up alongside the road. When first lit, a small wreath of smoke peeled up from the top of the stove and evaporated into the air.

It was a good stove, a Morso, built in Denmark. For a little stove, it seemed quite serious about fighting off the cold, broadcasting nice waves of heat even with a modest fire inside. As an added feature, it had a glass front that let you watch the wood burning. The romantic aura of those flickering flames didn't hurt in those first few weeks as Haddie and I discussed her writing

Once winter arrived with its cold blasts of air off the Atlantic, I'd need to purchase real firewood, and lots of it. I'd been told that the temperatures on the island, constrained by the warming effect of the ocean, didn't get quite as cold as other parts of New England. But the winter wind, sharpened by freezing spray, was ruthless and could cut through several layers of clothing.

The creaky old phone in my apartment tinkled like a child's bicycle as I waited for her to answer.

Hi, I said. Just got home.
   You worked late.
   How are you?
   A sigh. A quiet voice: I've been better.
   I . . . I had no idea he was your grandfather.
   I thought I told you about him.
   Can I see you?
   Not tonight.

I'm sorry. I mean, you never know on this island who's related to who.

I guess that's one way of putting it.

A short delay, and she added: Peter, I think I should tell you this now. We need to take a pause.

Uh, wow, really? I mean—

We can talk about it, Peter. Not tonight.

Okay—uh—I wish I could make it better.

Thank you. Sleep well.

She hung up. Silence. No, not really silence. The whoosh of a vacuum.

Journal entry
An impossible person 1

As dinner came to an end, I was still talking. Something had happened at work, a colleague said something insulting. As I continued to vent, I grew hotter and I was dimly aware that my wife's face had changed. She waved a hand in my direction.

I paused. "Are you telling me to shut up?!?"

She said no, that wasn't it, she was flapping her hand at what my coworker had said.

No you weren't, I came back. You were telling me to shut up.

I slammed my plate down in the sink.

Detective McGuane stood in his office, a large, comfortable man with a rectangular head and dark brown eyes that trended sleepy.

"You Peter Christie? *Forum*?"

"Yes sir. Hoping there's some info you might be able to share."

"Uh-hu. Bit early in the day to do much sharing, isn't it?"

My first thought was he's tough, tougher than he looks, and it's clear he doesn't think much of me. But the inner voice gave another opinion, advised me to take my time, we might find a way to work together.

McGuane welcomed me into his office and gestured to me to take a seat in a wooden chair by his desk. He explained he would only be talking in general terms. No scoops, no secret suspects, no murder weapons.

I got settled and opened my notepad on my lap.

"Something wrong with your neck?" He craned his neck in imitation.

"No, nothing, it's just one of my many annoying habits," I replied.

"We all have 'em," he conceded, with a shrug of his eyebrows. "Is it true you're related to that writer? Agatha?"

I admitted that I was.

"My wife loves her books," he said. "She's read every one of 'em. You grow up reading 'em?"

I said I did—but truth be told, I'd spent a good deal of my childhood reading books of just about every style and description.

"A literary guy, huh?" he asked.

I learned forward. "I wondered if you could tell me about the baseball bat."

"What baseball bat?" His eyes took on a bit more tinge of sleepiness.

"The bat that Betsy Cranmore told her friends about right after she discovered the body. It's public knowledge."

He shrugged. "Betsy Cranmore, nice lady, plays bridge with my wife, doesn't know squat about a murder weapon. Didn't even have the right victim. Confused the whole island for several hours."

I reminded him she said she'd tripped over a baseball bat. And if the murder was the result of a blow to the head . . .

A wry smile. "The coroner is still at work."

"Fair enough. The dogs were poisoned, though, weren't they?"

He didn't fall for it. "Dogs? Who said anything about dogs?"

"Someone—Bruce Gormley I think—told someone in the office about finding the dogs."

He snorted. "Any questions I might actually answer?" he asked, with a ripple of his fingers. "And no, I'm not talking about parties—Red Sox or any others. Ridiculous for anyone to think those losers will ever win another World Series."

"Parties?" I asked.

He wrinkled his brow. "Any more questions?"

I pulled my hands apart admitting defeat. "No more for now," I began—but at that moment something caught my eye, a bulging canvas bag hunkered down by his desk.

"Is that bag related to the case?" I asked. I leaned closer, expecting to see a glimmer of silver coin or gold bullion. But instead there was a sparkle, lots of tiny glimmers, as of quartz or some other rock.

McGuane rose to his feet, blocking my view. "How about I call you if I have anything pressing for you? Something I need to confess so I can sleep better?"

"I have a feeling I might give you a call first."

He allowed himself a small smile, which I took to be a hopeful sign.

Then I saw something else in the corner. A handle jutting out over the top of a side table. I knew that bat right away. It was a popular softball bat, the Easton Howard's aluminum Superbat.

"You've got my favorite bat!" I pointed at it.

"No kidding. You play slow-pitch softball?" he asked.

"Yeah."

A raised eyebrow. "Little too young for slow pitch, aren't you?"

"I'm mature for my years."

He allowed himself another small smile.

"Did that bat come from the murder scene?"

The smile disappeared. He waved his arm at me. Get out. Now.

And I did. While the inner voice chided me, *Don't push it with him.*

I won't, Agatha, I replied.

Slow-pitch softball, it turned out, was one of the true pleasures of small-town life. By now I'd been playing for several weeks, and in October the league entered the playoffs, raising the level of competition a notch from friendly-and-who-cares, to friendly-and-we-sort-of-care.

The league was open to men and women—in fact, the rules required five each on a team, and the batting order had to alternate female-male. The main point seemed to be to get a little exercise and have some fun. There were lots of laughs and teasing back and forth. There was also plenty of awkward running and catching and some wildly inaccurate throwing, interspersed with the occasional brilliant play or two that happened as often as not by chance—a diving catch in the outfield, a perfect scoop of a grounder behind second base, leading to that rarest-of-all softball league events: a double play, short to second to first.

Haddie and I were on the Dolphins, one of eight teams. Our roster was made up mostly of island natives, people who had known each other for a long time. At 24, Haddie was the youngest, while the plumber Bob Brown was the oldest—somewhere in his mid-fifties. He was Haddie's nemesis, one of the few people I'd seen who could make her uncomfortable. A too-pointed, too-long look, a lewd comment delivered to the sky. Sometimes too lewd to be tolerated.

The day after the murder, Haddie was still keeping to herself, so I went alone to our game against the Seadogs. Brown was in rare form. When I sat down near him on the bench in the top of the first inning, he gestured to me to slide over closer.

"I see your girlfriend's not here. Whatsa matter, you get tossed out?"

Did news travel that fast, or had he just made a good guess? "Yeah, something like that," I admitted.

"No loss," he said.

"That's not how I look at it."

"Women. Can't live with 'em, can't live without 'em." He patted me on the arm and made a comment about women, so offensive that I jumped to my feet and gave him a shove.

"What's the matter with you, Christie? I thought you needed some cheering up." He waggled himself away from the bench and strode over to the on-deck circle.

"Bobby." The shake of a head. "Hasn't changed one iota since high school." Rozzie, the accountant, had been close enough to hear his joke. She made her way over to him now and chewed him out, as he listened with a dull, distant expression on his face.

The odd thing, I thought, was that she considered him worth talking to. Rozzie was the team captain and could cut him from the team if she wished. Was there something likable about Brown? Some redeeming quality?

Most of the talk on the bench isn't lewd; in fact, it can be quite informative. From time to time the casual conversation leads to a scoop for the *Island Forum*. A not-yet-public plan to raise ferry rates. A scandal in the administrative office in the high school. A backdoor land deal for the former Youth Hostel.

Plonk! As Brown swung the bat, the conversations on the bench began to bubble up.

"It was Star, the son."

"No way, it had to be the caretaker."

"They found a baseball bat on the lawn. Star was an all-state shortstop."

"Hey people, baseball bats are more common than you realize. Look around, you might even find some here."

"I think it was the granddaughter. There's something about that girl that isn't right."

"Dorothy? She's only twelve."

"What if Danville was the target all along? And the murderer knew it was him?"

"That would change things."

"Star hated Danville. Danville wrote him out of the will."

"Maybe the old man got up to answer a call of nature, saw Danville trying to poach his gold, and took care of it himself."

"You gotta be kidding. That old turkey can't even get out of bed himself. He has to ask his caretaker lady for help."

Bob Brown favored us with that insight and added a few more colorful details as he took a seat on the bench. He'd just lined out to third, and he was still cradling his bat.

It was common knowledge that Brown had had some run-ins with Quentin Douglas over the years. A string of arguments over non-payment for work done. Not so long ago, there'd been a case in small claims court. Despite his massive wealth, Douglas was known for his aversion to paying bills.

"Go ahead, somebody ask me," Brown growled.

"Ask you what?" someone replied.

"Ask me if I killed the rich old turkey."

"Who, Douglas?"

"Yeah," Brown mumbled, smiling in his stubble.

"Did you kill him?"

He turned and gave a big shrug. "How could I? He's still alive, ain't he?"

"Well then, here's a follow-up," I said, adjusting my neck. "Did you kill Chester Danville?" There were some nervous chuckles.

Brown turned toward me, his broad face reddening. "Hey, pencil neck, tell your girlfriend now that she's had enough of you, she should try out a real man for a change. Someone man enough to—"

"Shut up, Bobby," snapped Rozzie.

Brown took a loud drink. The muscles on his neck wobbled, and I was reminded of a snake swallowing a rat.

My hand twitched on the bat I held. I banged my shoes together and knocked off the loose dirt.

Brown let out a long ahhh. "How many homers have you hit this season, Christie? Zero, right?" He mumbled something about me probably being a Democrat and a supporter of that all-time World's Worst Zero, Jimmy Carter.

Then he cracked his large knuckles. "As for that little twit Danville, I never liked his skinny butt, but I had no reason to put an end to him." He glared out at the field and growled again. "Argh, three outs already." He set down his bat, an Easton Howard's Superbat.

He rose, rummaged beneath him to retrieve his glove, and lumbered out toward first base.

I trotted out to third. When Brown threw me a warm-up grounder, he deliberately placed it down toward home plate, making me run for it. I zipped a low throw back to him that skipped past his glove and smacked him on the shins. He raised his head, like a bull buffalo preparing to charge.

The umpire pointed to the pitcher, and the next inning began.

CHAPTER THREE

The next morning Haddie called and asked me to meet her for coffee.

I dressed quickly and drove downtown. We met outside the little shop in a brief, awkward hug. She'd lost weight and looked exhausted. I had an image of what she'd look like in a few decades—face drawn and severe, but still beautiful.

We ordered our food and coffees and sat down. She took a bite of her muffin. "A biscuit? Very virtuous."

I tried to smile and mumbled something about being a neatnik.

Those grey eyes took me in. "So, how have you been?"

"I think I should be the one asking you that. I wish I could have been there with you."

She took a deep breath. I'd probably just given her the opening she'd been waiting for. "We're not at that stage, Peter. That's what I've come to realize."

"I had no idea he was your grandfather." I took a bite of my biscuit, cupping my hand under it to catch any crumbs. My inner voice said something that I couldn't quite hear.

She shook her head. "I'm talking about a level of trust. A level of connection that I thought we had. But we're not there yet." Her eyes searched mine.

The same wall that had held me silent at the office, did so again.

She set down her muffin. A flush of emotion filled her face. "You had to have known what he meant to me."

"For some of us . . . it's hard to know what to say—at a time like that."

"Why is it hard?"

"I don't know." Actually, I did know—well, sort of. Fleeing into the pine forest. Something inside me was moving and changing.

The start of many more days.

My wooden coffee stirrer clattered to the floor. She was watching me, and I had to force myself not to lean over right away and put it back in its proper place.

"If you truly care for someone, it isn't hard," she was saying.

She's right, you know, the inner voice said.

Haddie said she knew I'd just come out of a dysfunctional marriage. I was probably still in pain. I must be living with a truckload of unfinished business and regrets.

I slid the coffee stirrer with my foot, getting it into an easier position to pick it up.

I took a breath and asked if there was something I could do to make things better now.

She didn't miss a beat. "I need time, Peter. Time and space. We both need that."

"There must be something I can do," I continued. I bent over and picked up the stirrer and placed it in front of me. There.

Her gaze went past me. She was weary, but some other emotion was pressing through the weariness. "I don't think so," she said. But I sensed an opening.

"Nothing?" I asked. "You sure there's not something I can do?"

"Well okay then." Her eyes flashed. "Find out who killed my ever-lovin' grandfather."

I met her gaze and promised I would.

On my way to the office, I thought about one of our early writing tutorials. She liked to make fun of the formal tone I assumed at the start of each session. "What are some good options for effective endings?" I began the session.

A lifted eyebrow. "I can't say for sure, but I'm guessing you're about to tell me, professor."

For the next several minutes I pontificated about three types of endings that can work well.

An image chosen to linger in the reader's mind and suggest new and intriguing connections. Or a return to the lead sentence, but with a change in wording that reflected the insight revealed in the piece of writing. Or best of all, a mic drop: a phrase that hammered it all home.

"Find out who killed my ever-lovin' grandfather."

Mic drops? She had that down.

Quentin Douglas's house was situated on the shore of the harbor, half a mile from the center of town. It was best to approach the place from the beach, hidden as much as possible in late-afternoon fog. I could make my way onto the lawn without being seen and maybe observe for myself the aftereffects of the digging.

I'd bought my rusty old 1965 Jeep from a guy who lived far out on the west end of the island, in one of the century-old fishing shacks that were being revived as primo summer vacation spots. The vehicle was basically a rumbly engine, four rickety wheels, and a thin metal frame, but it would do—at least until the holes in the floor grew large enough to fall through. It did offer one big advantage: the four-wheel drive still worked, which meant I could travel over the soft sand roads that covered much of the island.

I parked the Jeep on a rutted lane not far from the Douglas estate and crunched along a trail to the beach. The weather had cooperated. It was a warm day, and the harbor, calm and glassy, was swathed in a thick bank of fog. Visibility was no more than twenty or thirty yards.

The shoreline was littered with old shells, rocks, and a few upturned empty husks of horseshoe crabs. A tangled mass of distressed seaweed and eel grass marked the high-tide mark.

I passed a dilapidated house with a red pickup truck parked in the drive. Definitely not the Douglas estate.

A few minutes later I knew I'd found it. Casting off the fog like a boxing champion throwing off his robe, a massive home loomed above the shoreline: white clapboard walls, huge leaded windows, three massive gables, a steep and exalted roofline.

A modest shell-strewn path led from the water up toward the Douglas lawn. Pretty good cover for an unexpected visitor.

But before starting down it, I stopped for a quick look at the grounds.

And it was well that I had. A pale figure stood on the lawn, staring toward me. Through the fog it looked to be female, perhaps twelve or thirteen years old, swaddled in a thick blanket. Motionless and silent. Glaring at me. I raised a hand and waved. No response. Was it a statue? Against the fog it looked flat and two-dimensional.

Not far from the figure, closer to the house, a manhole cover cut a circle of metal in the lush lawn. This, I knew, must mark the place where a gas tank was buried. Because the island was thirty miles from Cape Cod—too far for natural-gas lines to run—the heating fuel used in most houses was propane stored in tanks on site and refilled each month by trucks.

A massive elm tree dominated the yard, and near it, several yards to one side, stood a wooden platform about six feet off the ground, to which was tied a thick rope that hung from a branch overhead. This was soon in play as the statue came to life. Like a ghostly circus performer, the figure pranced over to the platform, climbed up on top, and let its blanket crumple to the ground. It grabbed ahold of the rope, leaned forward, and launched itself into the air, swinging up and out and back again. All in perfect silence.

I turned and made my way back to the car.

Stefanie was a large woman with dark skin and dreadlocks and an equally large presence. What was most arresting about her were her deep brown eyes, which roved about restlessly with an expression in them that seemed to say, *Uh-hu, I thought so.*

When I got back to the office, she greeted me in a way that let me know she'd been waiting. "Can that old Jeep of yours handle soft sand, Christie?" she asked.

I said it could.

"Good." She handed me a map. "The Haul-over. End of the harbor. There's a dead seal on the beach."

"A dead seal?" I asked. "There's something newsworthy about a dead seal?"

"It is when someone has shot it." She explained that for the past ten years or so, at least since 1972, seals had been a federally protected species. "I guess you didn't know that," she added.

"I didn't," I admitted. I'd learned there was no use trying to put on airs around her, she saw through them all.

"I want photos and a description. And I'm warning you ahead of time, because I know you're finicky—it's going to stink to high heaven."

The island was of medium size, fourteen miles long and six miles across. It had begun life as a large sand bar deposited by a glacier some thirty miles off the spit of land that later came to be known as Cape Cod. A walk through the moors that stretched across the center of the island revealed one of the more unusual legacies of the glacier: sizable boulders known as "erratics" that had been shoved out to sea along with the sand.

Over the years the island's grainy soil had grown enriched by farming and grazing and, more recently, by summer residents who fertilized their lawns. The nitrogen runoff from the fertilizer had already begun to choke the harbor with excessive plant growth, and the conservation group that Haddie worked for was trying to put through regulations to limit its use.

Once you left the town, many of the roads turned into gravel and then sand, as I quickly relearned today. The farther I drove on my quest to find the dead seal, the sandier and softer and narrower grew the roadways. They finally guttered out to nothing on the far shore of the harbor in a place known as the Haul-over, where a sand spit of less than a hundred yards divided the harbor from the Atlantic.

There was no mistaking that the seal was nearby. Fishy and fatty and fleshy and rotting—the stench was overwhelming.

Continuing on foot, it was impossible to miss the giant blob sprawled out on the waterline at low tide. It looked like a huge sausage, mottled grey with large dark spots

I came closer and saw that its face was surprisingly cute. Silky-smooth and doglike, tender whiskers, large eye sockets. No apparent ears.

When alive, the animal must have been lovely in its way, and for all its size it was surely graceful in the water, a performer of underwater ballet.

Holding my nose and venturing within a few feet, I observed the three red dots on its chest. They looked about the size of the bullets in the 22-caliber rifle that I shot as a boy in summer camp—back in those days in the early 60s when kids were still allowed to shoot guns in public.

But who would shoot such a defenseless animal?

I took pictures from a few angles, then headed back to the Jeep.

For a fraction of a second, I wondered if a bug-zapper was in one of the trees. A zing, a zip, a pulverized body.

My body understood before my mind did and sent me hurtling to the ground.

A zing somewhere in the dwarf oaks to my right. A zip closer to the ground on my left. A shattered branch directly over my head.

Then all was silence.

I waited a minute, two minutes. Still nothing.

That odd ability I had to foresee what was about to be? It was nowhere to be found. There was a void without me and maybe one within as well.

After a delay of an uncertain amount of time, my mind stumbled back to life. I thought about crawling over to the Jeep on my belly, like a seal dragging its massive bulk across the sand. But what was the point? I realized. Lying, crawling, standing . . . I'd be seen no matter what.

What difference did it make? I climbed back to my feet. If it was my feet. Was it my feet? I pointed myself toward the Jeep—if it was myself—and engaged the legs that had been lent me. The world was breathless and still. A void. Not a cry of a bird, not a breath of wind. No noise but the suck of somebody's shoes through the sand. At any moment I would not have been astonished to hear a zip, a crack, a tang of scorched air. Would it sting like fire, like hot oil, like the crack of a whip? Or like nothing?

It was nothing. Nothing happened. Nothing at all. In a daze, I climbed back into the Jeep and shuddered back to town.

Back in the office, I collapsed into a chair. Stefanie came over, concern in her eyes, and I managed to get out the basics of what had happened. She checked me over to make sure I was all right. She pointed out I'd need to report the incident to the police.

"Speaking of which, your friend McGuane called for you when you were out," she told me. "No rush on that."

She said once I felt better, she'd like a first-person account of what had happened on the Haul-over. This was above-the-fold material.

For a good while I sat there, doing nothing. I noticed colors around me, deeper than usual, the green desk blotter, the grey pencil sharpener. And sounds. The pencil sharpener sounded like someone sharpening knives.

Eventually the colors faded, and the sounds flowed back into their normal contours.

I picked up my phone.

"McGuane."

I identified myself and he said he'd being trying to call me.

"I know. Were you calling about the seal? I was just there. And you won't believe this, but—"

"I'm calling about something else. Can you come by the station?"

I told him I'd be right there.

Detective McGuane had no choice but to listen. Before he could say anything, I established a beachhead in the doorway to his office and recounted the whole bizarre affair.

He listened carefully, but took care to look unimpressed. He suggested it could have been random shots fired from somewhere else on the Haul-over. Maybe a couple of teenagers having some fun with an old guy, an over-the-hill guy who plays slow-pitch softball. The ghost of a smile loomed on his face. I suspected he was trying to settle me down.

"You don't think the shots were connected to the seal?" I argued. "A warning to stay away?"

He admitted that was possible but cautioned that there was no need to get ahead of ourselves—more often than not, these things turn out to be coincidences. He said he'd called me here for another reason. "If you feel ready to turn the page." He eyed me skeptically.

I said I was, and he gestured to me to take a seat, while he eased into his perch behind his desk. By the light of a single desk lamp, I could see that the bulging bag and the softball bat had both disappeared.

He clasped his hands on his stomach. "Okay. Whatever we discuss now is off the record. Agreed?"

I agreed.

He opened a drawer and pulled out a piece of paper. "This is a copy of what was found in the victim's pocket."

"You think it's from the murderer?" I asked.

He shrugged. "No idea."

"Is it okay if I hold it?"

He gave me a look. Know-nothing rookie. "Like I said, it's a copy. Original is in the lab."

I leaned forward. "What do you want from me?"

He adjusted himself in his seat and reminded me that I had a famous grandmother who wrote a book or two. As a literary guy, maybe I knew something about books and quotes and that sort of thing.

I said I'd be glad to help if I could.

"Tell me where this is from." He handed me the paper.

> *All that smolders isn't seen*
> *It often lurks betwixt, between,*
> *In smoky darkness hides its heat,*
> *Playing dead, in mock defeat.*
>
> *Delay will only make it strong.*
> *The reward is waiting all along*
> *For a pathway to its deep desire—*
> *Where fate ignites its glorious fire.*

He watched me carefully. "Any idea?" he asked.

I shook my head. "No. Except . . . it reminds me of something."

"Of what?"

"I don't know." I read it over again. "This is all about revenge. It's strong stuff." I gave him a blank look. "But I can't place it."

"Is it a literary—what's the word?"

"A literary allusion?"

"Yeah. Is that what it is?"

"Possibly. But it could also be a parody," I said.

"A parody?" His eyes narrowed. I was getting too cute for his taste.

"A parody of an old expression. You know, 'All that glitters isn't gold.'"

"Where's that from?" he asked. "The Bible?"

"It might be. It's gotta be as old as the hills."

"As old as the hills." He gazed out the window.

That night I thought more about "All that glitters isn't gold." How could I trace it down?

How else but in my copy of Bartlett's Familiar Quotations, left to me by a great aunt? The bulky red book sat in the midst of scores of books on the bookcase I'd built in the apartment out of cement blocks and pine boards.

I opened up the tome and turned to the thickest section of the book—William Shakespeare. And got lucky. There were hundreds of quotes from Shakespeare, and one of them did sound a bit like the poem—though he used the word of his day, glister.

> *All that glisters is not gold*
> *Often have you heard that told*
> *Many a man his life hath sold*
> *But my outside to behold.*
> *Gilded tombs do worms enfold*

Had you been as wise as bold,
Young in limbs, in judgment old,
Your answer had not been inscrolled
Fare you well. Your suit is cold—
—William Shakespeare, Merchant of Venice

I read it over a few more times and decided it wasn't really all that helpful.

Journal entry
An impossible person 2

I was a business reporter at the *Globe*. Assigned an intern. She followed along with me on several assignments. A friendly, bubbly air. Stories about college life. Laughing at me when I cleaned the dashboard of my wife's Saab (which I often drove to work) with a Clorox wipe at the slightest hint of dust. The way the intern looked at me, such youthful pure gratitude, when I praised a lede to a story she was writing. Innocence and gratitude, delicate as a butterfly wing. I knew full well what praise meant to her.

The next day, I finished my first-person account of visiting the seal, then worked on a follow-up story about the murder. Interviews with friends and family of the victim. An account of his generosity to the town. A request from his widow to make donations in his name to the Boys Club. No mention of the written passage found in his pocket, no mention of the bag of stones that found its way into the detective's office. Or the softball bat.

And so far, little to no progress on my promise to Haddie.

She and I hadn't known each other that long, so you would think the loss of the relationship shouldn't seem all that important. But if anything, the opposite was true. Was it because I'd recently gone through the loss of my wife? I often found myself thinking of Haddie and her special, quirky interests. On a shelf in her window, she'd carefully arranged her crystal collection of marine animals—dolphins, walruses, whales, sea lions. And, of course, a seal. She loved the way the little glass objects transfixed the streaming sunlight into shimmering rainbows that leapt onto the walls. Those little things delighted her no end, and at the memory my heart leapt up and crashed back down.

The voice was low and authoritative. "Peter Christie?"

I turned around and saw someone who seemed familiar, though I couldn't place her: an athletic-looking woman, late 40s, muscular arms. Slicked-back blond hair. A Nordic goddess. She stood behind me in the checkout line at the Stop and Shop, holding her basket of stuff.

"I'm Luna Douglas," she said. "We've seen each other on the softball field. I play on the Sea Lions." I remembered her now, a baseball hat smushing down her hair.

A girl of twelve or thirteen hovered around her.

"Nice to meet you, Luna," I said. "Haddie has told me about you." Luna, I recalled, was the estranged daughter of Quentin Douglas and therefore some sort of cousin to Haddie.

She gave a little nod. "So you're the one."

I searched her eyes (blue as ice) for clues about where she planned to go with this. Something about the set of her face looked hard and fixed. Alcohol? Trauma? Facial work?

"You and Haddie have been going out for a few months now. Sweet kid, isn't she?"

"Very sweet."

"She doesn't deserve to have a stranger swoop in and break her heart."

"That's not happening," I said quickly.

"I hope not." Her eyes didn't relent.

Her daughter rolled her eyes. "Mom, this is really embarrassing."

"Peter, this is my daughter, Dorothy." She said it as if introducing a foreign dignitary.

"Hi, Dorothy," I said. "It's a pleasure to meet you." The expression on Dorothy's face, like her mother's, was fixed and serious. She shifted her feet. There was something unusual about the way she moved, coltlike, a bit wild. She seemed present yet somehow far away.

"Haddie and Dorothy are like this." Luna held up two crossed fingers. "Dorothy tells Haddie all her secrets. All the ones she won't tell me."

"Mom!" Dorothy exclaimed. She folded her arms and turned away, her lower lip trembling, the sort of behavior you might expect from a three-year-old.

She struck a pose, silent and still, and I recognized her. The girl in the fog.

"Haddie comes over at bedtime and reads aloud to Dorothy. They recently finished the *Narnia* books. And now they're about to start—" She turned to her daughter. "What book is Haddie reading you next?"

"*The Hobbit*," Dorothy replied in a strained voice.

Luna moved closer to me. "I'm sure you know how upset Haddie is about the death of her grandfather. He was our relative too, but of course not as close a relation. Take care of her for us, won't you?"

I said I would. An inner voice said I could trust this woman.

The girl stared at me for a few moments, then turned away with a disgusted expression on her face.

Later that afternoon I took a deep breath and dialed a familiar number.

Hey—I know we're taking a break, but—

Oh hi, I heard you met Luna and Dorothy.

Yes, I did.

Peter, I did say we need to take a break, and I still believe that. But that doesn't mean we can never be around each other. Would you be interested in going scalloping with Dorothy and me tomorrow morning? Early?

Haddie went on to explain that I'd need a pair of waders and a scallop rake, which I could buy at the marine store. She said she'd see me at 6:30 a.m. at Shawnee Point, and she explained which back roads to take to get there.

I purchased the waders and the rake and brought them back to my apartment. Looping a strap of the waders over a hook so they stood upright, I set the rake beside it and left them there for the night, a mini-statuary to the gods of shellfish that ruled this island. Or maybe to the gods of love, which I definitely did not understand in the slightest.

CHAPTER FOUR

Eating into the darkness, headlights swept over the rutted roads and low vegetation. We pulled separately but almost at the same time into the sandy parking lot, Haddie and Dorothy in her truck and me in my Jeep. The handle of my scallop rake jutted out of my passenger-side window like a jousting lance.

A cathedral-like hush hung in the air. A hint of a glow rose in the East above the foreground of scrub oak and viburnum branches, supple and spare like a charcoal sketch.

An erratic rose out of the bushes, bulky and gnarled. In the faint light the fractured rockface gave off a silvery sheen.

"Dorothy, I think you already met my friend Peter." Haddie scraped and pulled a basket out of the back of her pickup.

Dorothy gave me the same look I'd seen in the store: boldly direct yet somehow shy and elusive. "Hi, Peter," she said, in a flat voice that seemed to hold a grudge of some sort. Then it came out. "You were married."

Haddie turned, as if about to reply. But I chose to answer her myself.

"That's right," I said. "I was married once before. Is that okay?"

"Not really." Dorothy shook her head. "How can we trust you to be any better the second time around?"

"Dorothy, Peter is my friend, not my husband." Haddie set a scallop rake on the ground.

"Well then keep it that way." Dorothy spun away and gazed out over the water. Little rivulets of waves caught patches of the pale orange light from the East.

All That Smolders

Most people who go family scalloping wear waders like the ones I'd just bought. I thought of them as big boots with overalls attached to them, made out of rubber or some other waterproof material. Putting them on—sliding your foot down into the leg and getting it to line up the right way in the boot—is an adventure in itself. You squiggle in your feet and toes and then hoist the rest of the waders up and around your body and wrangle the straps up and over your shoulders.

On land it's awkward, like walking in a spacesuit. But once you step into the water, it feels easier. There's one odd thing: the waders contract around your legs with a sensation like a blood pressure cuff. It's a bit startling but you stay happily dry.

We were there so early because of the timing of the first low tide that day. As we entered the water, the sun was still not up, but a cumulus bank not far above us burned fiery pink at the edges. With slow and patient care, the color painted itself across our cloud roof like a pale glaze. As the wind picked up, the cloud scudded off, carrying the color across the sky.

On the island they call this family scalloping to distinguish it from commercial scalloping, which is done from boats. As a family scalloper, you walk through the water, pushing the scallop rake in front of you. This is a long pole with a metal rectangular frame on the end, and a net lashed onto the frame.

We took a hundred or so steps and stopped, and I pulled up my rake, wondering what I'd find there. A nest of seaweed, which clung to my hand and felt yucky. A crab or two. Some rocks. A broken conch shell.

And scallops, four of them. Brownish orange and fat, with strong ribbing and nice neat edges.

Haddie looked over. "Good work. Into the basket with them." Still at a neutral distance.

I carefully placed the scallops into the basket and emptied the debris from the net.

The sky was changing even as we worked. New bulky clouds, ivory-toned. A focal point of light exploded near the top of one cloud, and the sun pulled free of the horizon, red and wobbly, a squashed pumpkin.

"Nice sunrise this morning," I commented.

"It's always nice here," Dorothy said.

By now there were about thirty scallopers out in the water near us. Some, farther off across the harbor in the channel, wore snorkel gear and were diving for the shellfish. Little buoys with red flags on top marked their location so boats would stay clear.

Closer by, a few scallopers held inverted wooden boxes with glass tops that smoothed out the waves and allowed them to peer into the water and scoop the scallops up with a light net that looked like a butterfly net. This form of scalloping seemed elegant and neat, but a bit slower. Most of the scallopers were pushing rakes like us.

There was a friendly, almost carnival air to the whole thing. Friends would cross paths and stop and chat. A lot of playful comparing of size of catch. Inquiries about relatives' health. Reminiscences of the old days. It felt like some ancient New England tradition, like cranberry harvesting or building stone walls, an activity that had woven together the social fabric for decades.

Some scallopers were out in deeper water, roughly fifty yards farther from shore. "Could there be more scallops out there?" I wondered.

"Don't stray too far out from shore," Haddie warned.

"Why not?" I asked. "They look like they're doing well out there."

"They have on wet suits. Not waders. They can survive in the deep water. You can't."

"Why? What would happen to me?"

"If you step off a ledge into water deeper than your chest, it'll flood your waders."

"So? I'll get cold."

"Not just that. The weight of the water will pull you under."

"I can swim," I protested.

"Only if you can get the waders off. And you won't be able to do that once you're trapped."

"So? What's the worst that will happen?"

"You'll drown."

A short distance away, Dorothy laughed.

It wasn't a kind laugh. If she hadn't made her feelings clear enough in the parking lot, this laughter cleared up any doubt.

The sun was climbing into the sky, having regained its perfect round shape, and the clouds subdued to coal-grey.

Side by side, the three of us trudged on through the waist-deep water. The water was murky, and it was difficult to make out the difference between bare sand and the spindly "eel grass" that provided a good habitat for the scallops. Every now and then we would stop, pick the scallops out of our rakes, and drop them into the basket that Haddie towed behind her, stuffed down into a floating inner tube.

"When you feel little bumps on the rake, little nudges from the harbor floor, that usually means you're in amongst them, you're getting scallops," Haddie told me.

She schooled me on the difference between the young "seed" scallops, flat and thin, which you have to throw back, and the adults, which are thicker and have a "growth ring" on their shell. Sort of like the growth ring on a tree. As incidental catch, we picked up small crabs, sometimes a tiny flounder, lots and lots of rocks, and a dark, sinewy seaweed that clung to the shells. And then something unusual.

"Look at this!" I exclaimed. "Hey, look, it's a starfish!" The creature was thin and curly, and it was a sickly-looking shade of yellowish grey, but with its five extended arms it could only be a starfish. I held it up for them to see. "I'll toss it back. Maybe it will grow up to be a big healthy starfish."

"Don't throw it back!" Dorothy shouted. The handful of other scallopers who were nearby stopped and looked over.

"Don't throw it back?" I shook a piece of seaweed off the back of my hand.

"Don't you know anything? Starfish eat scallops. They're pests."

"So you're an expert?" I challenged her.

"I never said I'm an expert," she replied in a frigid tone. "But at least I'm not a dummy."

Haddie cast a look her way. "Kindly watch your language, Dorothy."

"Aren't all of us here in the process of killing scallops? How are we any better than the starfish?" I pointed out.

Dorothy shook her head in disgust at my question. "We only take adult scallops. If we don't harvest them, they'll die this winter anyway. The seed scallops will live another whole year, and that's what the starfish prey on."

"I didn't know that," I admitted.

"That's no surprise. You can't even tell the difference between adults and seed." She walked over to the basket and picked up three scallops. "These are all seeds and I saw you put them in there. But I guess I'm not allowed to call you what you are." With a dismissive backhanded motion, she flicked them into the water.

"Dorothy, have you ever heard the expression about getting too far out over your skis?" Haddie inquired. This was one of her old-fashioned turns of phrase that always elicited a shiver of tenderness in me. She pulled Dorothy to the side and talked quietly, as Dorothy bent her head and listened. When they were done, the girl raised her head again and glared at me.

Like a fool, I still held the starfish. "What about this?" I asked.

"I'll take it," Haddie said. She sloshed over in my direction. "I'll keep it to the side in the basket, we can dispose of it later." She tipped closer and said quietly, "I would appreciate it if you don't bait her."

"Me? What about her?" I tried to keep my voice quiet.

"For goodness sake, be reasonable, Peter. She's twelve years old, she's always been different, and she's still very upset about the death of a relative." She took the creature from me.

You're not doing anything to help yourself here, commented a voice inside me, a voice I'd learned over the years to trust.

"Look . . . I'm sorry for the way I talked to you," I said in the direction of Dorothy. "I probably am a dummy. But hey, who knew starfish were such cold-blooded killers?" I detached another piece of seaweed from my hand.

"Why do you hate seaweed so much?" She stared at me, unblinking, and I didn't answer.

An hour or so later we were done and back on shore. It was a pretty good haul, over half a bushel. We carried them up and set the basket on the sand behind the truck. Heaped up in a mound, the scallops were cracking open and snapping their shells like a wild percussion section. Dorothy climbed with surly self-righteousness into the seat in Haddie's pickup. With a graceful, leggy motion, Haddie hoisted the basket up onto the bed of her truck and turned toward me.

"Well, there you are, Peter. Your introduction to a favorite island activity." Still distant and a bit formal.

It was worth a try. "Can I come with you—help shuck the scallops? Remember, you said you'd teach me sometime how to do it."

"Not today," she said.

I consoled myself with the thought that the insides of scallops were messy and yucky—not something that would be to my liking.

But there was something else that needed saying. "Um, by the way, I don't have any information for you yet."

"Information?"

I nodded. "I've found some clues, but nothing definitive. I've been looking—a lot. And I'm going to keep looking. I want you to know that."

She put a hand on my arm, just for a second, then turned and shut the tailgate.

"Thank you for your efforts." The voice floated back, almost indistinguishable, as she walked to the driver's side of the cab.

The truck rumbled off, leaving squishy marks in the sand.

Somewhere in the distance I caught a whiff of wild grapes, bittersweet and luscious.

Journal entry
An impossible person 3

Fog, memory. I was wiping down the counter. Hey Peter, I cleaned it already, you know. *It's still yucky. Look at all this!* I squeezed out the sponge in the sink and watched the dirt that sluiced out.

The house across the street from my garage apartment was large for the neighborhood—three stories, with a garden shed to one side and a neatly laid out rose garden on the other. For the past several days I'd seen a landscaping crew working there, mostly Latina I thought. A slender, middle-aged white woman was supervising the crew as well as doing some of the planting herself. When I came home from scalloping, she was loading a few tools into the back of her pickup, and she froze a moment, watching me get out of my Jeep.

I said hello.

She nodded. "Afternoon." She shoved a rake into the back of the truck. She had very short dirty-blond hair and brown eyebrows.

"Nice stretch of weather we've been having," I said. "Must be good for planting."

"You're the one who writes the stories in the paper," she said, while adjusting some of the tools in the truck. A bumper sticker read, *It used to be nice on the island.*

"I guess I am."

"I'm Beatrice Bond. Newest and most recent, but still-recovering wife—of Quentin Douglas, the murder victim who wasn't." She turned and gave a wry smile.

I strolled across the street and asked her if she might have a moment to talk sometime.

"Looking for leads, eh?" She smiled a slightly bitter smile.

"Always looking for leads."

She knelt down. "Look at this. Autumn clematis." She plucked something out of the ground and held it up, a thin clingy vine. "Ten years ago people were planting it for the flowers it produces in September. Now it's everywhere, another invasive species we have to deal with."

"The law of unintended consequences," I said.

"Yep." She gave a curt nod. "So okay. You like a good story, and I might have one or two for you. How about coffee tomorrow?" She named a place and a time, early afternoon the next day, then turned away and bent down trimly beside a lush, alluring smoke bush.

CHAPTER FIVE

"Nobody could stand him. Can stand him. Nobody except that granddaughter. They have a connection that no one else can understand."

"You did marry him?" I asked playfully. A dose of charm couldn't hurt as I tried to get all the information I could.

She gave me a look that said, Oh, I see how this is going to be. She took a sip of her cortado and remained silent.

She's deciding whether or not to trust you, the voice said.

I shifted to a more direct mode. "Tell me about him. How did the two of you meet?"

She brushed her eyes across me and started talking. She said he could be very insistent. The initial campaign was overwhelming. Gifts, invitations, trips to places you'd die to visit. St John. Bali. The Orkneys. He had his people research your secret desires.

"It's hard for a young woman to resist," she added. "Especially someone in a vulnerable state, someone who wasn't yet sure of her sexuality."

"Does he really have girlfriends visiting him still?"

"Oh sure. Young ones. Pretty. From off island. You can see them around town with their Diana Kim England earrings and their Louis Vuitton bags. They didn't get those working as landscapers."

"Were you aware of the gold and silver buried in the yard?"

A quick flush spread across her face. "He told me about it. I thought nothing of it. I thought he was trying to test my gullibility. Who actually buries gold and silver in their yard?"

"What do you know about Chester Danville?"

She frowned off into the distance. She said Danville was harmless as a titmouse. Loyal family member. Happy to serve on nonprofits. Cozily married to an upstanding member of the Congregational church.

"That's pretty much what I've heard."

She paused for a second, then hit the ground running. "That's what made it so surprising when he started the affair with Jenny Dyer. The librarian at the historical association. The bookish middle-aged woman with the big glasses. As dowdy as they come. Wore a tweed skirt to work. Preferred books to socializing. And yet there it was, they were secret lovers for several months before they were discovered. Deep in the stacks of the Historical Association, in the section on harpoons and trypots, if rumors are to be believed. She was said to be keening like a coyote. All right there in the stacks."

"My goodness. Was this public knowledge?"

She made a little face. "Not at first. A handful of relatives. Clara Danville, of course—Chester's wife, poor thing. She must have known for a while. I only found out a day or two before the murder."

I asked casually, "Do you suspect her?"

"Clara?" She shook her head. "She would never."

"She's not the type?"

Her brown eyebrows performed a slight maneuver. She said she wasn't sure there was a type. Any of us might be capable of anything, given the right circumstances.

Now I felt the color rising in my face.

She watched me closely. "Not Clara. But you never know about people, do you?"

As we were leaving, she swerved in closer and confided, "By the way, you know I'm with a woman now. Eileen. She's lots of fun. We like good company and good wine. No one leaves our flat complaining." She strode off in her boots and work shorts.

Voices rang out on the sidewalk, kids out of school. Across the street a solitary figure was drifting from store to store in the direction of a group of loud and lively girls. When the girls saw her coming, they swerved as one, like a flock of birds, and crossed to the far side of the street. "Hi," Dorothy called after them, but they ignored her and kept marching along to the beat of their social interactions. She stopped and watched them recede into the distance. When she started up again there was something both defeated and resolute in her gait. With a stab in my heart, I vowed to be nicer to her if I were given another chance.

Before our softball game against the Great Whites that afternoon, there was the typical pre-game scene. Teammates standing around, talking about the weather and trading batting tips. Across the way, one of the Great Whites was in an intense conversation with a large older guy. The big guy took a bat and cocked it behind his shoulder, demonstrating something. He handed it back to the player, who slipped the bat into a bag and got ready for the game.

For a whole inning there was no mention of the murder, but the topic was impossible to avoid for long.

In the second inning, Brown cracked open a beer and took a sip, then let out a pleased burp and said, "I got some news for you amateur detectives. You know the hat and the sweatshirt Danville was wearing?" He went on to explain that at one of the homes where he was doing a plumbing repair, he'd learned that a bunch of the older wealthier types on the island had a party the night of the murder.

"Not just any party," he added. "A Red Sox party. Grubby pants and Sox baseball hats. For watching the game." He belched. "I guess that explains Danville's get-up that night."

Party. A little bell went off in my head.

"It might," Rozzie commented from the on-deck circle. "But there's also a theory that Danville was trying to pass himself off as Douglas."

Brown shrugged. "All I can tell you is, Danville was at that party. Ten or twelve old rich white guys drinking their Macallan 15s, and all dressed the same."

"You're a white guy too," someone pointed out.

"Yeah, but I'm not a *rich* white guy."

"You're old though."

Brown gave a little smile. You got me.

Rozzie smacked a hard grounder to short, and the Great Whites shortstop rifled a throw to first. It was wild and to the right and caught Rozzie square on her left kneecap. She collapsed to the ground and lay there a few yards short of first base.

Our team hurried over to her. I was surprised to see who was there first, talking to her in a low voice, pressing on her knee, asking her where it hurt.

A minute or so later Rozzie raised her head. "I'm okay, BB. Thank you, I'm okay." She climbed to her feet.

The teammate providing the most comfort and help was none other than Bob Brown.

But when we returned to the bench, Brown was back on his usual track. He gave a loud belch and directed his attention to the

Great Whites' left fielder, Steph Sylvan, a wiry athletic-looking guy with a thick black beard. Brown gave voice to several choice insults, and Sylvan needled him right back.

Injuries seemed to come in clusters that night. A minute later, Sylvan ran hard after a fly ball in shallow center-left. He tried to call off the center fielder, who was also going for it, but the center fielder didn't hear him. They collided and fell with a thud that we could feel, as the ball fell harmlessly beside them.

The center fielder seemed okay, but Sylvan was limping when he got up. Our runner, seeing the injury, stopped politely on second base while the ball sat unattended out on the turf. There was a delay as the center fielder and shortstop helped the left fielder off the field, to be replaced by an eleven-year-old kid, someone's daughter.

Instead of remaining on his bench, the left fielder used a bat as a cane, worked his way over to our side, and stopped beside Bob Brown. It seemed they were buddies of sorts.

"How's that ankle?" Brown asked.

"Ok. Gonna swell up like a balloon tonight." Sylvan sat down with a groan.

"I hope you know, without you in the lineup, we're gonna run all over you. Even though our third baseman can't hit his way out of a paper bag."

"He's probably referring to me. I'm Peter Christie," I said, reaching across to shake hands with Sylvan.

"Nice to meet you," Sylvan said. His voice was flat and gruff. His eyes were hazel, and the dark beard blanketed the lower part of his face.

"You'd take back those words if you knew him. He thinks he's the world's greatest hero. Did you see his story about the dead seal—the one that tried to shoot him?"

"A dead seal tried to shoot him?" Sylvan asked skeptically. He nodded toward Brown. "I've heard you like to go out in the moors and shoot rats. Was it you?"

"Wasn't me," Brown replied. "I wouldn't 'a missed." He asked Sylvan how his night life had been recently.

Sylvan spent some time describing in full detail the physical delights of the girl who was the new bartender at the Clam Box. He said maybe Brown had seen her, she was an outfielder on the Sea Lions.

"Bet you haven't had the courage to even say hello," Brown told him.

"You are so wrong. I talk to her whenever she carries drinks out to the tables. She loves it."

"Yeah? Go ahead, tell us—let's hear what you say to her."

"I lower my voice deep down and say, 'I smell you and I feel your air.'" He kissed his fingers.

"And she likes that?"

"Oh yeah. She's feeling it big time. Can't wait to be tickled by this beard."

"Gentlemen, do we have to act like 15-year-old boys?" Rozzie stood up and moved down to the other end of the bench.

It was becoming clear to me that Sylvan and Brown were a matched set of loners.

Brown was a native, but Sylvan was a washashore. He'd arrived on the island five or six years earlier and had taken right away to commercial scalloping. He began work in the scalloping fleet on other people's boats as a culler and quickly built up his level of skill, establishing himself as one of the fastest scallop-shuckers on the island.

For the past four years, Sylvan had owned his own scallop boat. He was a relentless worker. Even outside of the commercial season (November through March), he could often be seen on the harbor, scouting out scallops, and he was known for his unerring sense about where to find them. His yearly scallop harvest, as recorded by the Marine and Fisheries Division, now rated in the top five on the island.

Like Brown, Sylvan had been known to have a run-in or two over the years with Quentin Douglas.

The problem was that he kept his boat at a mooring in front of the Douglas place. Some winter mornings at 6:30, Quentin Douglas was said to slide open the French door of his bedroom and yell at Sylvan to shut off his boat motor. Or Dayva Johnson, the housekeeper and trainer, would appear in her nightgown and yell at him. Sylvan would yell back at Douglas, but if it was the housekeeper, he would whistle a catcall. Which infuriated her and made her yell at him louder. Once or twice a threat of violence had slipped into his comments. That's what Douglas told the police the previous winter when he lodged a series of complaints against Sylvan. The imbroglio threatened to go to court, but at the last minute, Douglas' lawyer Chester Danville made a sudden motion to dismiss the case. There were rumors of a quiet exchange of money.

That should have ended the problem, but the aura of hostility lingered, like frozen salt mist hovering over the January waters.

With Sylvan next to him on the bench, Brown couldn't resist a mention of the murder.

"Get ready, Sylvan. The Great Reporter is probably getting up his courage to ask you if you killed Chester Danville." Brown dropped a smirk in my direction.

Well okay. I craned my neck and asked, "Hey Sylvan, your friend Bob Brown has been spreading a rumor that you were responsible for the death of Chester Danville. Would you care to comment?"

Sylvan scoffed, "Naturally that loser would accuse me. He's got to, to protect himself."

"To protect himself? Why is that?" Brown replied. He sat up straight, buttoned up his collar, and wiggled his head on his neck—apparently in imitation of me. "Mr. Sylvan, can you explain in more detail your thinking on this subject? Why would the good, gentle, and honest plumber Bob Brown desire the death of Chester Danville?"

"That's simple," Sylvan answered. He fingered his beard and explained that Danville had been the head of the Summer Rental committee. The new regulations the committee proposed would have hurt Brown big-time by limiting the number of times he could rent out his property. Brown couldn't allow that to happen. Danville had to go.

Brown unbuttoned his collar and let out a burp. He turned to me. "There you go, pencil neck. I'm your guy. Write me up on the front page of the *Forum*. Make yourself a hero. You know you're never gonna be a hero here." He nodded toward the field. "By the way, how's that ex-girlfriend of yours?"

Ignoring him, I made my way out to the on-deck circle. When I came up to bat, there were runners on second and third. Two outs, late innings, we were down by two. We needed a hit.

I was preparing to kick my shoes together to clean off the dirt, but the pitcher was already in the middle of her motion. I caught myself in time and turned my attention forward. I was still smarting from Brown's insults; and that seemed to put me in a state of hyper-focus.

The first pitch floated in as big as a watermelon, and I swung and blistered a line drive that skipped off the left fielder's glove, tipped up higher into the air, and landed on the far side of the fence in a clump of poison ivy. The trot around the bases was probably the first time in a year that I'd felt free of gravity.

As it turned out, someone else—someone with the authority to do so—was also requesting a new front-page article for the *Forum*. At the office the next morning, Stefanie peered over the top of her dusty old glasses and told me it was time I did some deeper digging on the Danville murder.

"What do you suggest?" I asked.

"I want you to interview Quentin Douglas."

That sounded like a daunting task. "I heard he doesn't do interviews."

"Be creative, Christie." She turned back to her typewriter. "You know I'm expecting you to make this worth my while."

Boom. She was playing her trump card, and we both knew it. When she hired me, she'd made it clear that she was taking a chance with me—someone who had messed up big time in a previous job. I took the job knowing I owed her. She didn't hold this over my head very often, but at any time she could bring it forth.

When it came to that, I wanted to please Stefanie for other reasons, too. She was smart and perceptive—a good and fair editor. She demanded accuracy and details that hit home, never mind the consequences. And she was something of a legend, one of the few Black editors in the small-newspaper business. She must have had stories of her own about rising through the ranks, though she kept them to herself.

How to give her the story that she wanted? I tried to dial up my devious inner-Agatha to full strength.

The interview would be high stakes. Besides pleasing Stefanie, it was possible that the information I uncovered might help with my promise to Haddie.

Of course, the easiest path to an interview would have been through Haddie, since Quentin Douglas was a relative. But I knew I had to do this on my own.

That afternoon, the custodian at the office, who doubled as a mail sorter, dropped a strange envelope on my desk. The address was written in pencil in large block letters. I opened it slowly, wondering what it might contain. Inside was a square piece of notepaper with a single sentence, also printed in block letters: THE DARK SIDE OF THE MOON HAS MORE SECRETS THAN MEETS THE EYE.

What? Who? Why?

In a way—I had to admit—the message was strangely germane. Secrets these days did seem to hide in dark, inaccessible places.

Who could have sent this? I had a few suspicions, but no one definite.

Anyway, there was no time to figure that out now. I needed to deliver for Stefanie and Haddie. Using my best reporter's voice, I placed a call and made my pitch for an interview.

In the past few weeks I'd done nothing but dig my hole deeper with Haddie. There was certainly no gold or silver to be had at the bottom of this hole, but there was something more precious: a second chance, a better life. Maybe a relationship that would last.

Journal entry
An impossible person 4

We sat side by side in my wife's Saab. For a man who's found real success in his career, you have some charming eccentricities, she said. It's really quite entertaining, the way you clean things constantly, all your mannerisms. I've never met anyone like you. *I've never met anyone like you*, I replied. Really, she asked. How? *You don't judge people. You just appreciate them.* What's the point of judging people? she asked. By now her face was right next to mine.

She was from a wealthy Texas family but seemed free of conceit or arrogance. There was a freshness to her that other people lacked, those who always judged.

She had the prettiest freckles, stars in a distant constellation.

I leaned toward her and she didn't pull away.

The inner voice said, *It's good that you remember, and you are right to feel shame.*

CHAPTER SIX

Dayva Johnson drew open the massive mahogany front door of the Douglas mansion in one smooth motion. She was in her workout clothes, a pair of short shorts and a loose tank top. Her shoulder and arm muscles shifted like a restless snake, and her skin, a beautiful walnut color, glowed with health.

"May I help you?" She sounded willing to do anything but that.

"I'm Peter Christie," I said. "The *Island Forum*. I'm writing the article on best workouts for older Americans."

"That's right," she recalled. "You called yesterday. You sweet-talked me with that baritone voice of yours."

"I hope this isn't a bad time." I looked around the large, beautifully furnished living room. Pale ochre walls, tasteful and delicate molding, cathedral ceiling with several generous skylights, dark Brazilian hardwood trim adorning the windows and doors.

"It's never a good time. Mr. Douglas is upset about some things this morning." She gave me a look that said, it's probably your fault.

"I would imagine your workouts help him in multiple ways," I said.

"How'd you know I do workouts for older people?"

"Word gets around." I mentioned someone in the newspaper office who had gone to the sessions she used to lead at the health club, before Quentin Douglas hired her away as a full-time live-in.

She said it was all about flexibility, strength, and balance, and offered to show me a few of her favorites.

She arched her neck and peered behind me. "I thought you'd bring a photographer with you."

I explained that the paper had cut the photographer position as a money-saving measure, and patted the camera I'd brought.

She was ready. She took a breath and gathered herself like someone about to enter an athletic contest.

For the next twenty minutes she ran through a selection of strength and flexibility exercises. Some were aerobic and others were more stationary, like the dead bug, squats, balancing on one leg, and so on. I kept snapping pictures.

She finished with some stretching exercises on the floor that resembled yoga poses. Finally she stopped and asked if I'd gotten the info I needed.

"I did. Thank you. This will make a very good article." I craned my neck. "And if I have any more questions?"

"I still do one class a week at the health club."

"Oh, I didn't know that. Maybe I'll see you there."

"Thank you for coming." Her tone of voice said you may leave now.

I cast a glance around the room. Time to start fishing. "Before I leave, are there any unusual exercises you're particularly fond of? Ones that might show up especially well in a photograph?"

She gave me a guarded look, assessing my sincerity, and said she did have one.

Sinuous branches spread in all directions from the trunk of the magnificent elm tree that towered over the Douglas lawn. From one of the larger branches, a good two feet in diameter, there hung a thick rope—the same rope I'd seen a few weeks earlier during my walk. Rather than dangling straight down, the rope was tied off to a platform about fifteen feet to the side of the branch and about six feet high. Dayva walked over to the platform, climbed up a short ladder, and reached up and unclipped the rope.

She held the rope between her hands and gestured to me to move off to the side. "Rope swinging," she said. "Good for strength, good for balance." She pointed out the knots on the rope that made it easier to grip.

Of course, I'd seen this rope in action a few days earlier but didn't mention that.

"Would you mind demonstrating it for me?" I asked.

She grasped the rope between her hands and feet, leaned forward, and propelled herself. As the rope swung it seemed to lengthen and almost touched the ground. Meanwhile, Dayva climbed up a few knots higher and leaned into the swing. The rope reached the far point of its oscillation and swung back, stopping just short of the platform where she had begun, but she kept it going, controlling the direction with shifts of her weight. Back and forth she went like a spider on a web, as I snapped photos of human, tree, sky.

She returned to the platform, looking completely unimpressed by herself. She tolerated my compliments and allowed me to walk back inside with her.

"Not to get too personal, but would you say that Mr. Douglas does most of these exercises?"

"Mr. Douglas is completely committed to his exercise regimen. If anything, I have to stop him from overdoing it. He wants to live to be a hundred, you know."

"A hundred! That's a worthy goal."

She gave a small laugh. "Don't bet against him. He works out like no other man his age."

"He keeps in top shape, then?"

"You could say that."

She said, unfortunately, that her boss was having a difficult time recently. People were always bothering him. Wealth attracted unsavory characters. For instance, a stranger had visited Douglas late in the summer; voices were raised; a door slammed as the stranger left. Douglas was visibly upset and had a slight wound on his arm that he refused to talk about.

"Since then I've been making sure he's had lots of good workouts. It helps him feel better."

"He probably still has any number of women who are interested in him."

A twitch on her cheek, her eyes narrowed the tiniest bit. No point pursuing that one. "What's his age now? Ninety-two?" I asked.

"Ninety-three," she corrected. "He had a birthday just last week. His son Star was here to celebrate it with him."

"Star was here? That's nice. I'd heard it'd been a few years." I tried to give my voice a friendly little lift.

She picked up a water bottle and took a long drink. "He seemed to be looking for . . . well, a new start I guess. To his credit, Mr. Douglas welcomed him. Despite everything."

"Was he here around the time of Mr. Danville's death?"

"I believe he was."

"It must have been good for the two of them to have each other at such a difficult time."

"I wouldn't know." She wasn't liking where this was going.

"Star isn't still here, is he?"

"No."

I guessed I was about to be ushered to the door, and I searched for a lifeline. "I never had a chance to reconnect with my father before he passed away." That, in fact, was true. All that remained to me of my father was his old toolbox, stashed away under my bed.

A hint of sympathy in her face. "Every family has its problems."

"After the way he treated my mother, I didn't want to see him again for years . . . and then, well—then it was too late." That was true also.

She watched me, waiting to see where this was going.

"Is it really possible to get a new start? Don't we have to atone in some way first for what we did?" I asked.

"I wouldn't know." *You're losing her*, the inner voice said.

"How did the Douglas reunion go? Were they able to reconnect?"

"That's none of your business." The voice came from a hallway on the far side of the room. A small, wizened figure lurched forward into the sunlight in his gleaming chrome walker, wearing a Red Sox sweatshirt and hat. Despite his obvious advanced age and frailty, his face radiated a powerful, cunning disdain, and the voice carried power.

"Oh, hello Mr. Douglas," Dayva said, setting down her water bottle and gliding across the room toward him. She fussed over his hair a bit, putting the thin white strands in place.

He pushed her hand away. "Who is this?" he demanded. He stood quite upright in his walker, wiry and wan.

"It's the reporter from the local paper. He's doing an article on fitness," she explained. "I was showing him some of the exercises."

"You didn't ask me." His eyes regarded her with the steadiness of a cat.

"I'm sorry, Mr. Douglas. I should have asked your permission before I invited him. I thought it was for a good cause."

I took a step forward. "And I apologize, sir," I said. "I didn't mean to intrude. But I'm honored to meet you."

"Oh, you're honored to meet me, are you?"

"Yes sir."

"That's baloney. You're here to nose around. You want to find out if I killed Chester Danville. Or if my son killed him. That's why you're here." He turned his eyes on me like a blast of low-angle winter sunlight. Glares seemed to be one of the family traits. Even the walker was glaring at me, caught in a blinding shaft of morning sunlight.

"But you didn't kill him, did you, sir?" I heard myself asking.

"You get out of here, you little rodent!" he snapped. His mouth was one of his most distinctive features, partially turned-down, like the snout of an armadillo.

"Is it true that Chester Danville was your cousin?" I continued.

"Of course, he was my cousin. And a heck of a good lawyer too."

"But he was digging up your gold and silver, wasn't he?"

He paused, just for a moment. "He was doing that for me. I asked him to do it. Now get out."

"Why'd you ask him to do it?" I pursued.

"What's your name?" he demanded.

"Peter Christie."

"Christie? Isn't that a girl's name?" Now his eyes played on me with the patient silkiness of a predator.

"Christie, like Agatha. The mystery writer."

He turned to Dayva. "Miss Johnson, get Agatha out of here. Now!"

I pulled out my camera, thinking an interesting photo might be in the offing. But events interposed.

Dayva lifted a finger, and a mountain of a man strode in through the front door and flashed an inquiring look toward Dayva. When she nodded, he placed a massive hand on my shoulder, gave a sudden yank, and before I knew it, I was flying outside into the fresh October air. I landed with a bump on my back on the newly mown grass and found myself gazing up at the blue blue sky.

"Get your butt out of here and don't come back," the man growled.

I sat up and brushed myself off. "Pardon me for asking, but by whom did I have the pleasure of being tossed out?"

"Bruce Gormley," he muttered. "If you need to know." He folded his arms and his biceps swelled up to the size of melons. The pale flesh of his face was loose and mottled, like meat that has been tenderized.

The massive front door shut behind him with a definitive click.

My camera was nowhere to be seen on the mahogany steps, nor in the grass below them. It must have fallen somewhere off to the side. I eased myself over the railing and down to the bare patch of ground between the steps and the arbor vitae. And there it was, face up, nothing broken.

It helped to have the camera back. No matter my ulterior motives, I did plan to write an article on exercise for the elderly, and a good photo or two never hurt.

As I walked over to my car, I sorted out what I'd learned. In my stumbling way, I'd managed to come up with a new lead, maybe two.

Quentin Douglas had ordered his cousin, Chester Danville, to dig up the gold and silver. Or at least he said he had.

And his son Star was visiting at the time. A long-estranged father and son.

Two facts worth noting.

Stefanie frowned and leaned back in her chair. The lenses of her ancient horn-rimmed glasses showed dirty swirls in the reflected light. "You okay?" she asked. "You look a little mussed up."

"I'm fine." I gave her a summary of what had happened.

She gave me a look of approval. "Dayva welcomed you in the house? And gave you some extra time? She's no pushover."

I nodded.

"You're a puzzle. For a by-the-book white guy, you show a surprising ability from time to time to sprinkle the charm."

I told her I just got lucky.

She frowned. "But let me get this part straight: Did you really walk right up to Quentin Douglas and ask him if he killed Chester Danville?"

"Pretty much." I shrugged.

"The direct approach. Didn't get you very far, though, did it?"

I told her it didn't, but maybe it helped open a few doors.

"Such as?"

I cracked my neck. "Well, for starters, he said he told Danville to dig up some of his gold and silver. Why?"

She said he probably wanted a sample or two to gloat over. Maybe he was planning to give some to one of his young girlfriends. And he was too feeble to dig it up himself. I agreed that was possible.

She asked why Danville was dressed up like his boss. I told her about the Red Sox party, but she didn't think that explained why he would still be wearing it out in the yard. Besides, everyone knew the Red Sox were never going to win another World Series.

She held up a hand and said, "So, okay. Douglas told you he ordered Danville to dig up the treasure. Can we believe him? What's your take on this?"

I told her I saw two possibilities. Douglas could be lying. He'd had no idea that his trusted relative and attorney was in the process of robbing him. So now, in an attempt to reclaim his dignity, he was pretending it had all been his idea.

Or maybe he really *did* order Danville to dig up the gold, and Danville took advantage of the opportunity to put some gold aside for his own use. But he was caught—by someone—in the act and given the ultimate punishment.

"You have a devious mind," she said.

"I came by it honestly," I replied.

"Your famous relative." She gave me a pained look.

In either scenario, I continued, Douglas could have ordered one of his flunkies to go after Danville. Maybe he told them just to knock Danville out, maybe they overdid it.

She asked why I thought Quentin Douglas might have a flunky, and I told her about Bruce Gormley tossing me out through the front door like an empty milk carton.

Her laugh was long and heartfelt. "I'd love to spend some time now picturing you flying through the air like an empty milk carton." She shook her head. "But business first. Tell me what you learned about Star."

I told her that was tough to understand. Why would Star come home now—after all those years?

She replied that his father was ninety years old. A son might see some value in having a reconciliation and getting himself back in the will.

"Especially if he's planning to do in the old man," I agreed.

She lifted an eyebrow. "Patricide. Where will your deviousness end?"

"Patricide is something any number of sons may have contemplated at one time or another."

She shook her head again. "Not likely. Star would have known it wasn't his father out there on the lawn."

I said there was another possibility. Star went outside for a walk and stumbled upon Danville digging up the treasure. His instincts told him to protect the family fortune.

She agreed that made a bit more sense, but added, "Danville was a straight arrow, wasn't he? Devoted family man, pillar of the church, all that?"

"Um, yes, that's what they say."

She watched me a moment in silence.

We discussed the murder of the dogs and tried out a few ideas but none of them added up to much.

Then she asked about Bob Brown and his rental properties. Could there be something to that?

I told her what I knew. Brown owned three small houses, all in mid-island, which he leased out in the summer as rentals for a few days or a week at a time. There had been a move on the island recently to regulate the number of summer rentals. They were being blamed for just about every ill on the island: lack of year-round housing, loud boorish tourists.

Danville had been placed in charge of a study group that was recommending new, stricter regulations of the rentals. One summer rental per owner. A limit of six rental contracts per summer.

At one of the public meetings, Brown had shown up reeking of alcohol and accused Danville of trying to close down his businesses.

Stefanie looked interested. "Has he calmed down now with Danville out of the picture?"

I shook my head. "They appointed a new leader of the workgroup who came out in favor of even stricter regulations. So back comes Brown to another meeting, and he swears at them all, shouting about how his God-given rights are being taken away. Word is, he tossed a table over on his way out of the meeting."

She smiled. "That's our island. The locals never fail to entertain."

I agreed and told her, "Well, that's about all I got."

Her mouth crinkled like a muppet. "No, it's not."

"It's not?"

"You're keeping something from me. Something about Danville. Out with it."

I made a gesture of surrender and told her what Beatrice Bond had revealed about Chester Danville's affair with Jenny Dyer. I said I had no idea if she was telling the truth.

She made a little clucking sound in her throat. "I hope you're not planning to break the news to your girlfriend about her grandfather's indiscretions."

"Not in a million years," I replied.

"Well, it will come out sooner or later. But I'm putting Lilly"—that was our other reporter—"on this lead. This one isn't for you."

I remembered something else that I'd been meaning to tell her about. I described my first morning in McGuane's office, that he had a bag of something in the corner.

She said it was probably gold or silver, nothing unexpected about that.

"But it wasn't gold and silver," I explained. "It was glittery, rocky, maybe quartz or something like it."

"You have a theory. Let's hear it."

"It's far-fetched." I adjusted my neck. "Maybe Danville was planning to take a few bags of gold and silver for his own use. And he didn't want anyone to know it was missing. So he planned to bury a few bags of quartz in its place."

"Wouldn't it be obvious that the lawn had been dug up?"

"From what I've heard, the sod had been cut extremely carefully and set it to the side. Ready to replace it as if nothing had happened."

"You have a wickedly devious mind, Mr. Christie." Her eyes glittered brown and intense through her horn-rimmed glasses. "And don't bother to say you came by it honestly."

To tell the truth, I hadn't come by it honestly—not in the usual meaning of the word. My family relationship with Agatha Christie is complicated. I'm a nonmarital, or out-of-wedlock descendant of Agatha's brother, Harold "Harry" Miller.

The whole thing is tied up in a complex linguistic knot. Agatha began life as Agatha Miller, the youngest of three children in the Miller family. She adopted the surname Christie at age twenty-four when she married her first husband, the charming war hero Archie Christie. Years later, after her divorce and remarriage and another name change, she held onto the pen name that had brought her fame: Agatha Christie.

My surname came via a different route.

My great-grandmother was a Christie by birth—in fact, a cousin of Archie Christie. Agatha's brother Harry Miller, then unmarried, learned somehow of my great-grandmother and heard that she hired out for housekeeping work, and by 1914 she was serving as his housekeeper (and more). The rest of the story is all too familiar for the times. My great-grandmother discovered she was pregnant, Harry disavowed all responsibility, and my grandfather Ernest was christened not by his father's name as a Miller, but by his mother's name, Christie. Though Ernest was Agatha's full-blood nephew and even bore the Christie name—as she herself still did at the time—I've been told that he received no recognition from his aunt, who was then consumed not only by her writing but also by a family crisis of her own. Ernest grew up in humble circumstances, worked his way across the Atlantic on a packet ship while still a teenager, married at the age of eighteen in New Jersey, and had a son Scott—my father—in 1932. Scott was betrothed to my poor mother in 1951 and less than six months later I came into this world—a Christie, for better or worse.

Back at my desk, I took a sip of coffee and opened another envelope that had arrived for me, printed in those same block letters. The note inside this one read: THE MARSH HAS AN EERIE SILENCE IN THE MOONLIGHT. BUT SILENT TOO ARE THE TADPOLES BEFORE THEIR MOMENT OF TRANSFORMATION.

I had no idea what this one meant. But I did know something about eerie silences. The pine forest. The oval of honeysuckle flowers. Escape. But only for a time.

CHAPTER SEVEN

New Clues Emerge in Murder Mystery
Was Danville following Douglas's orders?
BY PETER CHRISTIE

October 16. Though progress in solving the murder of local lawyer Chester Danville has been frustratingly slow, a few clues have surfaced in the past few days. Yesterday Quentin Douglas revealed to an Island Forum reporter that he had asked Danville, his first cousin, to dig up the bags of gold and silver that Danville was unearthing when he was murdered by an apparent blow to the head. And it was also learned that Douglas's long-estranged son Star was visiting Douglas at the time of the murder.

When asked for a reaction to this news, Detective Rick McGuane, who is leading the investigation, offered no comment.

Over the past week, a number of speculations have centered on . . .

The phone rang.
  Had you heard the rumors about my grandfather?
  Yes, I had.
  Why didn't you tell me?
  I didn't want to hurt you.
  Thank you but you should have told me.
  I'm sorry. I—I guess I wanted to protect you.
  She sighed. I don't know if I can forgive him for this. I love my grandmother. I thought he did too.

Give yourself time.
Well, there's plenty of that.
I hope you are starting to find some happiness again.
Thank you.
Can we get together?
Peter, I need more time.

The Dolphins' next game was against the Sea Lions in the tournament semi-finals: Win or go home.

Because of my newfound show of power in the last game, I was slotted into the cleanup spot, batting fourth, just ahead of Bob Brown. When I came up to bat, he made a few disparaging remarks about my batting stance. He said my feet were too close together and I held the bat too high. "You look like a freak from the old, old days—a harpooner waiting for a slow-movin' whale to swim by."

I turned toward him, waved a finger at him to shush, turned back for the pitch, and shot a line drive down the left-field line that landed me on second base.

"You swing the bat pretty good." Dorothy's mother, Luna, played second base on the Sea Lions. As always, her blue eyes were cool as ice. "Did you play in college?"

"I was planning to," I said. "But I got caught up in some journalism classes, couldn't make the scheduling work."

"That happened to me in college, too. I just dropped the classes. But lacrosse was my real sport." She gave her head a little toss. "I heard you went scalloping with Haddie and Dorothy."

I nodded. "It was fun. But I can't say I'm one of Dorothy's favorite people in the world."

"She's a tough one. Doesn't do well with most males. Except her grandfather, she just adores him. He's kind to her in a way he never was with his daughter. Me."

"Haddie and Dorothy seem close."

"How are you and Haddie doing?"

I explained that there were some difficulties, mainly of my doing, but I was hoping for the best.

"Keep trying. Haddie won't keep up a wall forever if she knows you're trying."

Bob Brown took a big swing that resulted in a grounder to second. I took off for third, thinking Luna would go to first for the safe out. But she took a chance on the lead runner, and her throw to third arrived a beat ahead of my slide. I was out.

Taking advantage of the throw to third, Brown crossed first base and lumbered down the base path toward second. The throw from third base had him beat him by a mile, and Luna stood in front of the bag, ball in glove, ready to place the tag on him. But instead of sliding, Brown remained upright, picked up steam, and plowed directly into her.

Luna took flight and hit the ground with a loud grunt as the ball came free. Looking over his shoulder and guffawing, Brown trotted on to third base, capering like a kid. He stopped there and perched on the bag with a smirk on his face.

Luna lay coiled up on the ground. Her teammates raced over and surrounded her in a knot.

The umpire strode down the third base line toward Brown and raised his right arm. "You're out."

"I'm not out, she dropped it," Brown argued.

"Runner interference."

"She was in the base path. Rules are the rules. Base path belongs to the runner."

The umpire stopped a few short of Brown and pointed a finger at him. "You're out of the game. Unnecessary roughness. Get your stuff and clear out." He turned and wrote something in a little book that he took out of his pocket.

"Try and make me," Brown snarled. He spat into the dirt.

By now Luna was sitting up and talking to her teammates. With their help she climbed to her feet, took a few steps, and nodded her head. She was okay.

The umpire spun around to face both benches. "Runner is out for interference. Runner is removed from the game." He raised a hand and twirled around his index finger. "Switch innings."

A few of us got up, preparing to go out into the field. But Brown crossed his arms and refused to abandon his perch on third base.

Sensing trouble, we lingered by the bench. After a few minutes, Roz approached him.

"Bobbie, you've been told to leave the game," she said in a quiet voice.

"I've been told a whole lotta things in my life, Rozzie. If I did 'em all, I wouldn't be who I am today."

"Cut it out, Bobbie. Get your stuff and clear out." Her voice was louder now.

"I was safe and you know it."

"C'mon, Bobbie. Don't make us all walk away."

"Walk away if you like, I don't care."

"You really don't care, do you?"

"Why is everyone against me all of a sudden? I didn't kill that skinny little lawyer." Now his voice was quiet, almost too still. He threw some hostile looks around the field. "It was most likely that psycho woman over there. Probably thought it was her father." He pointed across the diamond at Luna.

Rozzie turned to us all and shook her head.

We waited a few more minutes. There being no motion from Brown, the two teams looked at each other across the diamond, raised their arms in mutual surrender, and commenced packing up their stuff. Rozzie told the Sea Lions we were forfeiting. We were done for the season.

I caught up with Luna in the parking lot as she was placing a Superbat in the trunk of her compact car, a new model from Ford called an Escort. "Hey, I hope you're okay."

It takes a lot more than Bob Brown to keep me down for long."

"He's a big guy."

She nodded. "And a bigger jerk. With major anger issues."

"That's for sure."

"I had a feeling he was going to try to take me out. But I wasn't about to back off." Her right hand fluttered like a little bird and she pressed it against the chassis of the car to stop it. She paused a second. "Did you hear what he said to me?"

I said I didn't.

"When he knocked me down. He bent down right over and said something pretty weird." A look of revulsion rippled across her face.

"What was it?"

"'I smell you and I feel your breath.'"

"Oh," I said.

She gave me a look. "You know where that's from?"

"No. But I know a friend of his likes to say it." Except I was pretty sure Brown had changed one of the words.

"Brown has a friend?"

I explained it was Steph Sylvan.

"Another lost soul." She shook her head. "He got that quote somewhere nasty. Probably porn. It sounds like porn." She climbed into her Subaru and rolled down the window.

"If you find out, I'd be curious to know," I told her. "There's something familiar about it that I can't place."

"Don't tell me you're into porn too." A wicked half-glimmer of a smile.

"By the way, congratulations on making the finals."

"Thanks to Bobby. It's an ill wind that blows no one any good." She gritted her teeth and put her car in gear.

Later that night I thought about Brown's behavior, and one trait of his in particular.

Lack of impulse control.

A quality, I imagined, common to many murderers.

But also common to many others, such as myself.

McGuane called the next day and asked me to come back in.

Before we got down to business, he leaned back in his chair and said he'd seen me out family scalloping. He asked how I liked it, and I said I liked it a lot. I thought it showed the island at its best—friends out in the water, sharing stories and jokes and just being together.

He nodded. "Not that much fun trying to open the little blue-eyed devils, though, is it?" he asked.

"That's what I've heard. I haven't tried my hand at that yet."

"Smart. Let the ladies do it." He gave me a long look. "Where you from originally, Peter?"

I told him I grew up in Cheyney, Pennsylvania, a small town not far from Philly.

"Parents alive?"

I explained that they'd both perished in an automobile accident my last year in college.

"Sorry to hear that."

I thanked him for his sympathy.

"You like it here on the island, I take it?"

"I do," I said. "There's a sense of community. Not that I'm exactly a part of it yet," I added.

"Well, if you want to be a part of it, you might consider giving up your gonzo journalism."

I gave him a blank look. "You need me to explain?" he asked.

"Are you talking about the story on Quentin Douglas?"

"That's right."

I shrugged. "Look, it was pretty simple. I asked Quentin Douglas some questions and he answered them. And I reported what he said."

"Not exactly. You snuck in on someone and caught him unawares."

"He wasn't about to agree to an interview. I did what I had to."

"Come to me next time. I can give you a crumb here and there, as long as you keep the source anonymous."

"Oh. Okay. Thank you."

He raised a finger. "But when I say something is off the record, it better stay that way."

I nodded.

He hummed a stray tune and pulled open a drawer. "Okay. The real reason I called you in." He pulled out a note and set it on his desk. "All this is off the record."

He said the lab analysis had come back with two sets of fingerprints, both blurred beyond recognition.

I asked how I could help, and he said he wanted me to take another look at the piece of writing. Make use of my literary knowledge. Help them interpret what it might mean. What was this really about? Was it a code of some sort? A threat? A warning?

And so for the second time, I read it over, as he watched in silence.

> *All that smolders isn't seen*
> *It often lurks betwixt, between,*
> *In smoky darkness hides its heat,*
> *Playing dead, in mock defeat.*
> *Delay will only make it strong.*
> *The reward is waiting all along*
> *For a pathway to its deep desire–*
> *Where fate ignites its glorious fire.*

"Seeing any new connections?" he asked.

"Not really. I think it's about having a grudge. And—well—and waiting," I said.

"Waiting . . . for what?"

"To right a wrong." I pointed. "There's that word, 'reward.'"

"Isn't a reward something good?" he asked.

I thought a minute. "I think it's different here. Something stronger. Something a lot stronger."

"What?"

"*Revenge.*"

He wrung his hands. "Revenge." He stood up. "Maybe so. But who would want revenge?" He crossed his arms and frowned. Outside the window, a swarm of birds had descended on a tree laden with purplish-red berries and were feasting on the fruit.

"Confounded Wahoo tree," he muttered. "Confounded starlings."

It wasn't much of a stretch to think of someone who might have wanted revenge.

Back at the office, I asked Stefanie if she knew Jenny Dyer's husband, Anthony.

Her eyes narrowed behind the horn-rimmed glasses. "Didn't I tell you I'm putting Lilly on that?"

I told her I was just curious. Did she think Anthony Dyer knew about it?

"About his wife's affair? Of course," she said. "Everyone on the island knows."

"But did he know . . . beforehand? And for how long?"

"What's the matter, you running out of suspects?"

I shrugged and said I probably was.

She tried to warn me off. Anthony was a calm, sweet man. A consummate tradesperson. Quiet. Skilled with his hands. Liked to work on all things mechanical, from woodstoves to old cars.

Could fix anything on the island. Nice to his wife. Never said a mean word to anyone.

She rolled her shoulders. "The police can question him if they like. But for us he remains a private citizen, until and unless the official investigation brings him forward as a person of interest."

I understood the paper's policies. But I wasn't looking just on behalf of the *Island Forum*.

Anthony Dyer froze in the doorway of my apartment. He was a man of medium height and slender build and seemed to have the gentle air that Stefanie had led me to expect.

"Sorry to be late." He explained that he'd been playing a round of golf at Bender Point Golf Club, and he'd been delayed when one of his partners kept spraying balls into the rough and losing them. He asked if I played golf, and I said no, but I was hoping to pick it up later in life. He said, well in that case I should look him up, he was one of the commodores of the Club, he could get me some good tee times, and he also had access to some excellent equipment from the pro shop at a nice discount. He drew something out of his pocket and it sparkled.

It looked like a bottle opener. He brushed it off with his fingers and put it back in his pocket.

There's something about him that doesn't add up, said the inner voice.

Once he started talking, it seemed hard for him to stop. He said he was captain of a shooting club that met out in the moors and mentioned that they were always looking for new members.

After I thanked him again, he took a few steps forward and turned his attention to the wood stove.

"Morso. Nice piece of work, good Scandinavian craftmanship." He squatted down in front of it. "For such a small unit it generates a significant amount of heat. The long, narrow design allows the use of standard firewood." He spoke with the respect of one who appreciates good engineering.

I waggled my finger toward it. "It's been a great stove. But I think it might have a crack there in the top."

The thin crack at the top, of course, was what had given me a convenient excuse to call Dyer and request his help. He bent forward and placed a finger on it. Then he let himself down on one knee, pulled the door open, and pointed a flashlight into the innards of the stove, like a doctor looking down a patient's throat.

I kneeled down not far from him. Dyer pulled his head farther into the stove, looking this way and that. Then he sat back and let out a huff of breath. His mouth set grimly.

"Bad news?" I asked.

Head nod. "That's not just a surface crack. It runs all the way through the casing."

"Oh, man. Tell me, is it still safe to use?"

He said the stove was probably good for the rest of the season. The crack was still small enough for the metal to swell with the heat of the fire and close itself off. I might have noticed that the stove gave off some puffs of smoke for a few minutes when first lit, then stopped smoking.

I said that was exactly what'd been happening.

He raised a finger. "Long-term, it's a different story. That crack will grow bigger and will separate more and . . ." He let his voice trail off.

"And then?"

"Well, in the worst scenario, the whole stove could split apart."

"That sounds like a bad idea."

"A catastrophe is never a good idea."

The words came out of me quickly, as if on their own. "Well, we certainly don't need any more catastrophes on this island."

Immediately, I wished I could take it back.

"Say again?" he asked, a new chill in his tone.

"I mean, we're all feeling the effects," I sputtered. "The hard times around here that, uh, that we've all been experiencing."

A muscle twitched on the side of his jaw. Something flashed behind his eyes. Then the surface calm returned, like a pond a minute or two after a large rock has been tossed into it. He leveraged himself back onto his feet.

"Any more questions about the stove?" he asked.

"No," I said, standing up. "I really appreciate you coming over. What do I owe you?"

He stuffed his tools into his toolbox. "There's no charge," he said. He picked up the toolbox and left without looking at me again.

What was I expecting—that he would turn to me and say, "Yes, now that you mention it, I was responsible for one of those catastrophes. The murder. How in the world did you know?"

That, of course, was beyond ludicrous.

But I had discovered something surprising: the flash of anger behind his eyes. Then there was his strange pride about being a commodore at the golf club. It all seemed a bit off, somehow.

Was gentle, serene Anthony Dyer capable of a violent crime after all?

But to quote Beatrice, weren't we all?

You're trying too hard.

I knew that. I was struggling to make progress of any kind, something that would impress Haddie. But forcing it wouldn't get me anywhere.

The autumn days were still pleasant, as the abiding warmth of the ocean helped to prolong the blessings of September and early October. But the evenings were growing colder—upper forties outside, just fifty-eight in the apartment. With some sticks and pieces of wood I'd gathered that afternoon, I started up a fire in the stove. I grabbed a beer out of the fridge and sat down as a whiff of smoke from the stove wreathed into the air, drifted up toward the ceiling, and curled back on itself.

For a short time it curled back on itself in the prettiest little shapes—and then it was gone.

CHAPTER EIGHT

The voice was sudden and rough. "I'm looking for Christie, where is he?"

A female voice murmured back at him, there was an exchange or two, and then the female voice was louder. "Sir, you can't just—"

Too late. A big guy in loose-fitting pants and a brown peasant shirt towered over my desk. "You Christie?"

"I am. May I help you?" I asked, in my best professional tone. He moved in closer, casting a shadow across me. I thought I'd seen him somewhere before, but I wasn't sure where.

"*Help you?*" he repeated. "You think you can *help* me?"

He placed a hand like a slab of ham on the desk.

I stood up. I was almost as tall as him, but not nearly so massive. "Maybe. If you can tell me who you are and why you're here." My heart was pounding.

"I'm here to warn you to stay away from my father." He leaned toward me across the desk. "You understand?" His hair, blond and shot through with patches of grey, was held straight up like a mown wheat field. His eyes seemed to contain moving circles.

"I might. If I knew who your father was," I replied.

The eyes narrowed. "You know full well who my father is. You snuck into his house and tried to pull one of your 'gotcha' reporter tricks on him. You baited an old man into telling you things that were none of your business. That were private to our family. That were nobody else's business—you get it?"

His face was flushed, and a damp sheen of perspiration had formed on his wide forehead.

He's safer than you realize, the voice said.

"It's true that I had the pleasure of meeting Mr. Douglas recently, at the end of an interview I'd conducted with Dayva Johnson, for a feature we're running on exercise programs for our older citizens."

"That's hogwash," he shot back.

Maybe it was time to drop the pretense. I raised my hands in the air. "Okay," I said. "You got me. I'm guilty as charged. And I'm sorry. But I felt that it was important to get to the truth and—"

He let out a hiss of air. "Well, let me tell you something important: You set foot on those grounds again, and you won't know what hit you." He jabbed a finger like a hot dog at my face. "You got that, buddy?"

I returned his gaze and wondered what I could say to defuse his rage.

But there was no need.

"Star, is that you?!" Stefanie had edged around from her desk and now pushed up beside him. "It's been more than a few years." She lunged toward him—what was this going to be? An embrace? A pat on the back? A slap? And then, before my astonished eyes, in perfect unison, left foot forward, they executed some sort of complicated handshake. It involved several deft turns of the hands, some elbow bumps and a few waggles, and ended with a loud high five.

Seeing my surprise, Stefanie gave a little smile and said, "Class handshake. We've been told we were the most inventive class ever."

"Class of 55. The best there was," he told her, and then he turned in my direction and his face resumed its angry glare.

But here was good news. He and Stefanie were buddies. Perfectly at ease with each other. Old-school island life, black and white—none of the subtle tension between younger professionals of different colors that you saw in most places today.

I recalled something Haddie had told me once: For centuries there had been a Cape Verdean population on the island—a strong middle-class presence of people of color—and many of the longtime islanders saw little or no difference in skin color.

"So, Star, why are you here?" Stefanie asked, in a slightly sing-songy tone of voice.

He nodded toward me. "I'm here to tell you to call your trained dog off the trail of my family. Okay?"

Stefanie smiled indulgently. "Now Star, you know I can't do that. We have a job to do."

"A job that stinks like an outhouse," he said.

"Star, you know how the newspaper business works. You have to take the good with the bad. Can you remember who was the editor of the high school paper, the person who put your picture on the front of page one when you pitched that no-hitter? Huh?"

He shook his head. "Now you look here, Stefanie," he began. "That's different and you know it—"

"If I remember right, at the time you thought that front-page photo did some pretty nice things for your love life."

"We were kids, we didn't know nothing. This is different. This is my family and—"

She refused to back down. "This is your family, and a man was killed on your family's property, and everyone in the community is understandably worried and sad and scared and confused. And the island has a right to find out what happened. It's for the good of us all, Star."

For a moment he bowed his head like a chastened little boy. But only for a moment. He raised his head and pointed at me and said, "You keep that little rat-hound away from my father. Or you'll regret it."

"What will we regret, Star?"

"You'll regret being alive."

Her face transformed into an exaggerated look of shock. "Are you really threatening me, Star? After all we've been through together?"

That froze him for a second. But then he came back to life. He waved his hand at her and said, "You know I'm not threatening you, Stefanie. Just keep that rat-hound away from my father, okay?" He let out an exasperated sigh and turned to go.

Stefanie watched him shamble across the room. He was still in earshot when she called after him. "I'm glad you saw him again, Star. I hope you'll visit him often."

He strode out the door without answering.

Stefanie had the strangest hint of a smile when she turned to me. "'Rat-hound.' I like that for you," she told me. "I may use that myself." She pushed her horn-rimmed glasses up on her nose and marched back to her desk.

Another envelope with big block letters sat on my desk.
PEOPLE SAY, "I OWN THIS LAND." DON'T THEY REALIZE THE LAND BELONGS TO THE GHOSTS THAT WANDER THE BEACH AS THE FOG ROLLS IN?

I half-suspected these were from Dorothy. The quirkiness, the slanted directness seemed to fit her personality. But why would she be sending them?

And—assuming it was her—why would she be talking about ghosts?

Late that afternoon I ran into Beatrice Bonn in the grocery store. She gestured to me and said she had some information for me. She gave me the address of her apartment on Main Street and asked if I could stop by for a quick visit that evening.

After dinner I drove downtown. Main Street was a wide cobblestone street lined with pricey jewelry stores and realtors and one old-style pharmacy that hadn't been plowed under yet by the demands of the new tourism for nonstop luxury. This time of night, the street was deserted, and it was easy to find a parking spot near the apartment, which was up a long flight of stairs above a high-end clothing store.

Still in her landscaper's shorts and loose T-shirt, Beatrice opened the door, smiled, and invited me in. It was a surprisingly large apartment, richly furnished, renovated according to a new design idea: open concept. The kitchen countertops were of that fashionable material, Corian. They were sparkly in a refined urban way that clashed a bit, I thought, with the old-fashioned aura of Main Street.

Beatrice's partner, Eileen, appeared with a bottle of white Burgundy and some glasses. She was medium-height and thin with dark curly hair, very attractive, with an edgy, nervous energy. We made small talk, and Eileen passed out the glasses of wine as Beatrice and I talked.

Eileen watched carefully for a few minutes, then excused herself and danced across the room to the fridge.

Beatrice swung into high gear. She told me that Star had been spending more and more time with his father. He seemed to be staging a desperate attempt to get back into Douglas's will, several decades after he'd been written out of it following a well-known disagreement that had turned violent. In recent weeks, he was thought to have apologized and asked for a fresh start. No one knew if Quentin was warming up to his son or was playing him for a fool. He had to know he held the ultimate revenge card in his hand, which wouldn't be revealed until after his death. In Beatrice's opinion, Quentin had no intention of writing Star back in.

Star was already a ghost, she added. He'll never inherit anything.

She pointed out all the people Douglas had written out of his will over the years. His three former wives. His daughter, Star's half-sister Luna. The truth was, Douglas disliked and despised them all.

Then why was he letting Star visit him now? I asked.

Beatrice smiled wryly. "You can't underestimate how much he enjoys seeing his close relatives twist in the wind." She tossed back her head. "You aren't married to someone for five years without learning what floats their boat."

I said that was true. My ex-wife and I had been married about that long, and she probably had learned more about me than she ever wanted to know. Beatrice gave me the same sort of side-of-the-eye look that Stefanie sometimes used for effect.

There was a brief pause as Eileen returned with a tray of crackers and cheese. "How do you like the wine?" she asked, watching me with her dark eyes the color of cognac.

I told her it was delicious.

"It's that minerality. Those old chalky hills in Burgundy have been doing this for centuries. Saint-Aubin is my favorite." She spoke with precision, but the look of intense pleasure on her face spoke of a euphoric side of her personality. She disappeared again.

She's cute but she's not for you, the voice said.

Beatrice then revealed that she had some new information on the Dyers. Jenny Dyer had left the island and was staying with her sister near Hartford. Anthony was keeping mum about the whole thing. He probably had no one to talk to. Though he was generally respected, he had few if any close friends except for his cat, a grey-and-white tabby that had been a rescue animal. Some people blamed his isolation on his early childhood experience: he'd been adopted as a toddler after kicking around some horrid foster homes. His strange air of remoteness was thought to be a result of those early experiences.

She said, however, that the town was being surprisingly sympathetic toward Jenny Dyer. A few religious types condemned her, but most felt she'd been locked in a marriage with a man who was unable to meet her emotional needs. She was said to be devastated by both the loss of Chester Danville and by the public exposure of the affair.

"I know you're writing about the case and I thought this information might help in some way," she told me.

"Thank you. We're not mentioning anything about the Dyers, at least for the moment, but naturally I have some interest in them."

"I thought so. That's why you asked him over to check on your wood stove, isn't it?"

I recoiled slightly. "You know about that?"

"It's a small island, Peter. But no one was spying on you—this was by chance. I'd come back to the job site that evening to pick up a few tools that had been left behind, and I saw his truck outside your apartment. With the bumper sticker you see everywhere, *It used to be nice on the island.* It didn't take a genius to figure out what you were up to. And why. I know you want to help Haddie get past all this. And you probably figure, the truth will set you free." For some reason I couldn't fathom, there was a bitter edge to her tone.

"Do you think Dyer is a possible suspect?"

She said she was sure he already was. Who had a clearer motive? But she thought Star was a suspect as well. The word was, Star thought Chester Danville had been advising Quentin Douglas not to put him back in the will.

I asked why.

She said one line of thinking was that Chester Danville himself was now mentioned in the will in a significant way, to the tune of a million dollars or more. And there was a rumor about a trust, maybe two trusts, that would tie everything up for years.

"So you might say Star was killing two birds with one stone," she added with that wry smile again. "But was it really Star? I can't say. You can't overlook that caretaker/personal trainer."

"Dayva Johnson?" I asked. "Why her?"

"At one point it was said she was the one in line to get a million dollars. The word is, that's the money that got shifted over to Danville."

"A million dollars?" I repeated. "To a personal trainer?"

"Some guys will pay anything for a bit of pleasure." She smiled sardonically. "But once he lost the ability to enjoy it, why would he bother to pay anymore?"

I turned my wine glass in a circle. "Doesn't sound like you're feeling much love for your ex-husband."

She picked up her glass and took a sip of her Burgundy, a half-smile on her lips.

I asked her why she thought Chester Danville had been dressed like Quentin Douglas the night he was murdered.

"You solve that and you'll solve the case," she said.

I don't think so, I said to myself, and wondered how much faith, if any, I could put in Beatrice and her insights. The truth was, the whole family was bonkers.

But I couldn't ignore the new information. It seemed quite possible that two of the suspects hated the changes that Chester Danville had been making in the will.

Dayva might have lost a million dollars. Star may have lost out on his bid for much more than that. And all because of Chester Danville's involvement.

If there was even a glimmer of truth in Beatrice's gleeful disclosures, it was worth looking into.

Star had made it quite clear in the newspaper office that there was no way I could contact him directly and question him. I'd have to think of some other route to him. But with Dayva, there was a path for me to move forward on my own.

She still taught a weekly exercise class at the senior center, and according to the sign-up form on the website, it was open to people of all ages.

At 7:30 the next morning, I showed up at the senior center with an old yoga mat that once belonged to my ex. I did not own any exercise clothes, so I'd opted for a blue-and-red running suit.

Most of the other participants were already there: all women in their fifties and sixties and older, most in sweat suits, some with head bands, some with tights and knitted leg warmers. I rolled out my mat near the back of the room and did a few stretches. I was aware of a glance or two being sent my way.

The stragglers filed in, and Dayva took her place at the front of the room. She threw me one sharp look but otherwise ignored me.

For the next forty-five minutes we did squats, stretching exercises, modified push-ups, and a host of aerobic exercises. Dayva dominated the room with her sheer, sinewy strength and clear voice. She could keep talking right through all the aerobics and not show a puff of any effort. For myself, I was pretty thoroughly winded by the end—more so than the regulars.

As class ended, they nonchalantly rolled up their mats, chatted with each other, confirmed coffee dates, and strolled off. A few curious looks flitted over me in passing.

Before long it was just me and Dayva. She was bent over something on her desk, and I rolled up my mat and approached.

"You're not here just for the exercise, are you, Peter Christie?" she asked, without looking up.

"No, I'm not," I admitted. I found a purple beanbag near her and plopped myself down.

"You must have enjoyed flying through the air."

"I admit, it was a bit of a thrill," I told her. "But I'd rather avoid any more flights for now. Might confuse air traffic control."

A slight chuckle. "But you're headed in that direction."

"I'll keep this short then. I have a question or two for you about Chester Danville."

"Did Detective McGuane deputize you?"

"Not exactly. I'm working more or less on my own. For the *Forum* and for myself."

"And for that nice girl."

"Yes, for her too. By the way, speaking of nice girls, is it true that Quentin Douglas is still entertaining young women in his house?"

"What's it to you?"

"Always looking for suspects."

She gave me a look. "Everyone knows he still invites 'friends' into his house, and everybody also knows it ain't nobody's business what they do. Including yours."

"Fair enough. I'm sure you and Bruce Gormley protect him from any gold diggers. No pun intended."

She raised her head and looked directly at me. "You have one minute. Ask away."

Don't delay.

"What did you think of Chester Danville?"

"He was a nice man."

"On good terms with your boss?"

"As far as I could tell."

"Was he in the process of changing Douglas's will?"

"You really expect me to answer that?"

"I'm hoping you might."

She bent back over her desk. "You can take that question and put it somewhere where it ain't gonna see the light of day."

"Does that question threaten you?" I asked.

"It's insulting, is what it is."

"It's only insulting if it implicates you in some way."

"You little jerk, it don't implicate me in any way."

"Then you can answer it."

She looked up for the briefest second. "I have nothing to be ashamed of and nothing to hide. And also no reason to talk to you about his business. Or mine."

I pulled a card out of my pocket. "This is in case you change your mind."

She took it from me and tossed it into the trash. "Don't come back."

"I won't," I said. "And I have no hard feelings. I respect you, Dayva."

"Respect yourself and get outa here."

So I did. I left in a slow, measured walk. But it felt like running.

Journal entry
Fleeing 2

Home from college. I was nervously expansive at dinner, going on and on about an eccentric professor I had in a course. After a few minutes my father raised his hand and waved it in my direction. The signal he'd used throughout my childhood at the table. Shut up.

What's wrong? I asked.

Stop talking.

I think I can talk if I want to.

Not at my table.

It's my table too.

He stood up. If you don't like it here, you can leave.

I stood up opposite him, fingered my water glass, slowly carefully raised it, and splashed the water onto his face.

For a brief moment he was stunned to silence. Then he let out a sharp breath and lunged toward me, knocking me back against the wall. I regrouped, turned, and edged toward him.

We fought, at first carefully, then wildly, hitting punching slamming into each other. Knocking over the table, lunging into the living room, upsetting lamps and chairs. My mother was screaming at us to stop.

In the midst of it all, I turned toward her and tried to keep my voice calm: Mom, I'm fighting for you.

He saw I wasn't looking and landed a stunning blow on the side of my head.

I sank to the floor. I think she ran at him and pushed him away. *Stay away from him!* I fought my way back onto my feet and stumbled toward the door. Something warm and wet streamed down my face.

I paused in the doorway.

Peter, are you alright?

I turned and raised a finger. I was about to say something but I couldn't remember what it was. Then I ran away, just like I'd run away years earlier.

Just like I was doing now.

CHAPTER NINE

When I decided to come to this island, I knew I was running away. But only, I told myself, in a superficial sense. After all, my life had already come undone—I'd already lost my job and my wife. I'd even lost the apartment in the Back Bay, which we'd agreed should go to her. In a way, I was merely acknowledging the need for a new start in a new place.

Was I running away? Yes, in the sense that I was fleeing my big city life. Was I not running away? Also yes, in the sense that maybe—just maybe—I was starting to learn a few things. I knew by now that I couldn't go to a new place without dragging along all the same issues, the same strengths and weaknesses, the same problems. Maybe, just maybe, I could bring to them some new discernment or judgment. But those new skills, if they existed, would only make themselves known over time.

It turns out that running away is something of a family tradition. My famous relative Agatha also ran away from her life, and in a much more dramatic fashion. It was 1926, and she was thirty-six years old. She'd recently been devastated by the death of her mother, with whom she'd shared an unusually close bond. At the same time, her first marriage was falling apart. Her husband Archie had fallen in love with a much younger woman who played golf and had a charming girlish laugh and wasn't obsessed with her work the way Agatha was with her mystery stories. On the night of December 3, wearing her usual outfit of a knitted skirt and a cardigan and a small soft hat, Agatha got into her car and quietly drove off. She left behind her young daughter, Rosalind.

She simply disappeared.

Agatha was already a well-known author, and her disappearance created a sensation that lasted for several days. Had she been murdered? Had she had a nervous breakdown? Was it all a publicity stunt to increase book sales?

In truth, she was so worn down that she may have had no plan but to get into her rickety old Morris and start driving. It seems likely that she felt she had no options left to her, no prospects for happiness, nothing to look forward to. Even her hereditary family fortune, mismanaged by her ineffectual father Frederick Miller, had dwindled away almost to nothing.

For much of the night, Agatha followed the course of winding crooked English roads, mile after mindless mile, that led into the Surrey Hills region, an area of countryside she knew and loved. Finally, she settled on a definite course of action. She aimed her car in the direction of a cliff that fell off into a deep quarry. That cliff would have been the final chapter of her life. But she never got there. Her car snagged in some bushes, then shuddered to a stop against a tree only a few feet from the abyss, saving her life and saving too the career of one of our most accomplished writers.

What did the great Agatha Christie do next? She pulled herself out of the wreck of her car, stumbled off, and found her way somehow to a fancy department store some miles away, where she washed up the next morning and gave herself a new identity: Mrs. Teresa Neele from South Africa. She later claimed that she was suffering from memory loss and disassociation. That may or may not have been an excuse, cultivated as cover. It seems likely that she took on an assumed name to gain the freedom of time and space she needed to begin to recover from the trauma of knowing that her marriage had come to an ugly end.

Agatha then repaired—where else?—to a luxurious spa for a water cure. For several days, no one knew what had become of her. When her family finally tracked her down and joined her in the dining room of the spa, everyone acted as if nothing had happened. A three-course meal with fine wines and afterward, a glass of Port.

But once they got her home, it all fell apart again.

Over the next months, Agatha somehow found the strength to move forward in her life. She sought and received a divorce from Archie. She moved to a new home in Chelsea with her daughter and with Carlo, a much-trusted servant. And as Archie married the golf-playing Nellie, Agatha set out on a far-flung vacation that led her to Iraq, where she met a cadre of archaeologists who would become her good friends, including one, Max Mallowan, who would be her second husband. Her trips to the East would not only lift her spirits, they would give her the settings for some of her most popular novels. *Murder on the Orient Express. Death on the Nile*. And many others.

Will running away yield anything of value for her great-great-nephew?

In Agatha Christie novels, poison is often the murder weapon of choice. One famous example is *Crooked House*: a twelve-year-old girl poisons not only her grandfather but also her nanny. Poison makes an appearance in any number of other Christie novels, including *4:50 from Paddington* and *Five Little Pigs*. The option of poison allows any character, no matter how small or feeble, to commit murder or at least be a suspect.

Which brings us back to the island. Though the death of Chester Danville was the result of a blow to the head, probably delivered by someone of physical strength, there was also a poisoning of note: the grotesque deaths of Buy and Sell, Quentin Douglas's two guard dogs.

What relation did those deaths have to the murder of Chester Danville? Did they show—as Stefanie and I had discussed—that the murderer must have planned ahead of time to put the dogs away, in order to gain dog-free access to Danville? But for that to be true, wouldn't the murderer have needed to know ahead of time of Danville's plan to dig up the gold and silver? Which seemed unlikely.

I was sitting at my desk one afternoon, puzzling through all this, when another envelope was delivered. The single sentence on the square piece of notepaper read: NOTHING STAYS BURIED FOREVER.

True enough, I thought—whether it be treasure or the truth about a murder. It was time for me to press on with my digging.

I decided to pay another visit to my almost-friend, Detective McGuane.

He leaned back in his chair. His eyes maintained their lazy sleepiness. "Peter Christie. How can I be of help?"

I explained that a few more weeks had passed, and there had been almost no news about Chester Danville's murder. Was there anything of note I might be able to pass along to our readers?

"Nothing I can recall." He brushed something off his cheek.

"Some people in the town are saying they thought the case would be cracked open by now."

His sleepy eyes grew sleepier. "Anything else you wanted to share?"

I said I'd heard a rumor that Chester Danville had been in the middle of making some significant changes in Quentin Douglas's will. He looked unimpressed.

I had come to ask him about the dogs, of course, but with the way the conversation was going, I knew my chances of getting an answer were slim. I needed to do something that could bring him more on my side.

Trust yourself, the voice said.

Okay, I replied in my thoughts, and paused a moment.

"So yeah," I said finally. "I've been thinking about the poem that was found in Danville's pocket. I have an idea." Of course, I had no idea—nothing. I'd have to come up with something on demand.

Trusting in the voice. Maybe it was the legacy of my dear Aunt Agatha.

McGuane's eyes turned to me and focused for the first time. "Go on."

"'All that smolders isn't seen,'" I recited. I waited a beat. "It does remind me of something."

"Of what?" he asked, leaning forward.

And in the moment, something really did pop into my head.

"Yes, you see . . . so it's similar in a way to Shakespeare. Except it isn't Shakespeare. It's Shakespearean in influence. Heroic British, to be more exact. Like the history plays."

He sat back. "Heroic British?" Voice flat as a tidal pool.

"Heroic British, the legacy of William Shakespeare's history plays. You probably know the names of some of the authors who followed after old Will. Sir Walter Scott. Sir Edmund Spenser. Chivalrous knights and ladies and heroes and dragons."

His mouth made some motions. "You going to explain how this might actually help us?"

"Sure." I spread my hands apart. "It tells us something about the person who wrote the poem."

He half-nodded, half-shrugged. "Like what?"

"Well, to begin with, the author of the poem has an outsized sense of their own importance. They have delusions of grandeur. Of correcting past injustices. Of making the world right again." This actually was starting to make some sense.

"So you're telling me to look for a crazy Brit with a sword and armor?"

I gave a guarded laugh. "Think of the kinds of people who immerse themselves in fantasy stories and games. Like that new game craze—Dungeons and Dragons. Those people keep to themselves. They tend to be reclusive, they're ill at ease in social settings. If they work, they get a job that can be done alone, in solitude. They play life close to the vest, they nurse a secret grievance or two. For months. For years. Maybe for decades."

"Well, okay." He stared out the window, past the Wahoo tree, at a squirrel that was scurrying across the sidewalk. "I'll keep that in mind." He was unimpressed, but he was thinking about it.

I might have earned myself an opening.

"Now, may I ask you a question?"

He rearranged himself in his seat and nodded.

I told him I'd been thinking a lot about the poisoning of the dogs. I wondered, for instance, if the type of poison might offer a clue.

"Not likely," he said. "But this one I can tell you. It was rat poison—strychnine. Anyone can pick it up at the local hardware store."

"Rat poison," I said. "That makes sense. But what doesn't make sense is this: the murderer poisoned the dogs. That means he must have known that Danville was going to dig up the gold and silver. Otherwise, why get rid of the dogs first?"

McGuane replied that he'd given that some thought, too. It didn't really add up. What it did do, however, was to let some of the family members off the hook. Star, for instance. The dogs were on his side, they were there specifically to protect the family treasure. Star had no reason to go after them.

"Of course, he could have taken them out knowing that would give him cover," I suggested.

"You come of devious stock, Christie," he observed.

I left soon after. Rat poison—strychnine—something my great-great aunt sometimes wrote about. Pretty generic. But who knows, I thought, it might lead somewhere.

Or not.

The phone rang and I jumped. But a very nice voice was on the other end.

What are you doing tonight?

Nothing, starting a fire, eating hamburger and green beans. Maybe I'll have a beer.

Can I come over?

You know I'd really like that.

Be there soon.

Light footsteps on the outside stairs, a discreet knock on the door. "Hello?" she called and pushed open the door.

A graceful glide and she was beside me; a quick hug, not intimate but not unfriendly, which seemed promising. And there she was, seated on my saggy sofa, gazing at the flickering flames in the Morso stove.

"What's someone have to do around here to get a beer?" she wondered.

I hopped up, got one out of the fridge, and handed it to her. She had on a thick old smoky grey sweater that complemented her eyes. She looked prettier than ever, but I suspected she didn't really want to hear that from me.

"It's wonderful to see you." I took a seat across from her.

"I ran into Luna yesterday and she said to say hello."

"Luna has been nice to me."

"Is that thing smoking?" She nodded toward the stove, the thin wreath of vapor snaking toward the ceiling.

I explained that the stove had a small crack, but it would soon close up. I gestured toward it, a backhanded flop. "Like me, that stove has things it needs to work on."

She was silent for only a moment. "We all do, Peter."

"But maybe I've been more smoky than the average stove."

She patted me on the hand, paused a minute, then started talking. In the past few weeks, she'd been through some deep water, wave after wave of it. The grief over her grandfather's death. The revelation of the affair. And all the suspicion and worry about the identity of the murderer. The sense of betrayal by someone she'd probably known and trusted. Her eyes swept the floor in front of her.

"Had to be someone from the family or a friend of the family," she concluded.

I said I thought so too, and told her I'd made some progress recently. I asked if she'd like to hear anything about it.

She shook her head no, not until I had something definite.

"Okay." I took a sip of my beer and decided it was worth a try. "Is it too soon for us to start to see each other again?"

She gave me a pained look. "Too soon."

I sat back.

She went on to say that she did have a favor to ask of me. "Dorothy wants to cook a scallop dinner for my birthday next week, and according to Luna, she's determined to go out and harvest the scallops herself. Luna won't let her go unless an adult comes with her. She wondered if you might be available."

"Hmm. Luna does know how Dorothy feels about me, doesn't she?"

A half-smile. "She thinks Dorothy might be ready for a reassessment. She's slow to warm up to people, she takes her time, and sometimes she surprises us."

What was there to lose? And anyway, it might give me a chance to try something out on Dorothy. "I'd be honored to go out scalloping with her."

"Then I'll set it up." She gave some details, time and tide.

"But I'm probably not invited to the party," I added, and immediately wished I'd kept my mouth shut.

She shook her head. No, I wasn't.

And she was gone.

CHAPTER TEN

Were Key Provisions of the Douglas Inheritance Being Altered?
Where there's a will there's a way
BY PETER CHRISTIE

October 23 Rumors have surfaced in recent days about potential changes to Quentin Douglas's will that could have eliminated some beneficiaries and shifted the massive inheritance to others. It is thought, at the time of his murder, that local lawyer Chester Danville was in the process of drafting those amendments, some of which may have been designed to benefit him personally.

When asked about these rumors, Detective Rick McGuane offered no comment. But it is thought that the beneficiaries who were to be eliminated from the will may have had a motive for . . .

It wasn't awkward so much as strange. Dorothy did not converse as we drove, and she just watched in silence as I parked the Jeep, still chirping on about what a nice afternoon it was and how it was more convenient, wasn't it, when low tide happened to arrive during the afternoon? My talk sputtered into silence.

Her expression wasn't sullen, or disapproving, or hostile. Or even blank. She showed signs of attentiveness and observation, pure and simple. I noted in passing that she had even, attractive facial features like Haddie's though lacking Haddie's sensitive flights of expression.

I lifted up the glass part of the tailgate and slid the scallop rakes out the back. We opened the side-hinged metal gate. There was a slight incline to the parking lot, higher on the right side, and the metal tailgate kept trying to swing back closed. Dorothy saw what was happening and leaned against the gate to hold it open as she stepped into her waders and pulled them up around her. Before I had my second leg inside, she had hers snug and in place, straps fastened up over her shoulders.

She lifted out her basket/inner tube combo. We would share the basket, as I had only a rake.

Finally, I was geared up—waders on and strapped in place, waterproof gloves pulled onto my hands, hat on my head with the scallop-license medallion in full view in case the shellfish warden came by to check us—and we bulky-walked down the sandy path like two Lego figures.

The harbor at Shawnee Point was bumpy today, lots of whitecaps running before a cold and gusty offshore breeze. Even here in the relatively sheltered harbor, the waves broke with a discernible crash and retreated with an ominous hiss. Despite the turbulence, a few other family scallopers were already out in the water, bracing themselves against the waves and pushing their rakes before them. If you didn't know what they were doing, you might have thought they were trying to clean up the bottom of the harbor with push brooms.

On a rough day like this, the water was too cloudy to see much of anything, and the snorkelers must have known this because none of them were in sight.

"How far out do you think we should go?" I asked, and Dorothy chopped her hand midway up her thigh.

From where we stood on the point, the steel grey waters of the harbor spread around us almost 270 degrees, lined with whitecaps like teams of horses. Plump in the middle of the opposite shoreline stood the town's huddle of buildings, bordered at either end by a church tower, one a white wooden spire, the other a round gold-leafed dome. Dull brown marshlands drifted off to the margins, dotted here and there with patches of yellow and red, the final gasps of autumn's bloom.

The air was probably forty-five degrees, and I guessed that the water was about the same. The waders kept us dry for now.

We trudged through the water side by side for eighty or ninety steps, then stopped and lifted up our rakes to see what we had in the netting. The catch was disappointing—lots of little rocks, small green crabs, some tiny seed scallops, and only a few adult keepers.

"I thought we'd find more," I said.

"I did too." Those were practically her first words of the afternoon. She gazed down the shoreline and fixed her attention on something. "Up there. They're getting them there."

I peered toward the distant figures. "How can you tell?"

She stood at attention. "Watch their motions—the rhythm of their motions. Each time they stop, they're tossing ten or twelve scallops into the basket."

"What if they're just tossing junk back into the water?"

"It's two different rhythms. Watch! Do you see?"

I did see. There were two distinct motions, one for throwing back the unwanted stuff, the other for placing the scallops in the basket.

"That's cool," I said. "I wouldn't have seen it if you hadn't pointed it out."

"It's just a matter of paying attention," she explained.

I saw my chance to try out a quote or two on her.

"Until I knew what to look for, it was buried." I spoke deliberately. "But nothing stays buried forever."

"I guess not." She gave me a puzzled look and turned back to the task at hand.

There was no other sign of a reaction and I decided no more tests were needed.

We started off down the shoreline toward the other scallopers, stopping every hundred steps or so to check our catch. We still weren't coming up with much. As we approached the others—close enough to call out to them if we'd wanted—we had just a dozen and a half keepers in our basket.

"I want to try out deeper," I said. "There might be some good ones out there."

Her eyes swung toward me. It looked like she was considering making some sort of objection, but all she said was, "Okay. We'll meet up again opposite the cedar." She pointed to a tree some fifty yards farther along the shoreline, one of the few there that seemed able to survive the harsh conditions.

Be careful, the voice said.

I headed out, away from shore. Some thirty or forty steps later, my rake began to bump in a nice rhythm along the bottom. Haddie had said those bumps could be a sign of scallops, little nudges from the harbor floor. The deeper I got, the more frequent the little bumps.

I felt the pressure of the water reach my stomach, then inch up to my chest. A large wave sloshed up and dropped a frigid dash of water over the top of the waders. The cold crept down my shirt and across the front of my pants, but I kept going. The bumps were coming faster and faster. That meant scallops. It was important to get the scallops. They were for Haddie's birthday.

When I stopped and lifted up the rake, the shredding water sluiced away from the ribbed surfaces of many fine scallops caught in the net, brown and glistening and glorious. I brought the rake around and twisted the net closer. I leaned forward to take hold of the net just as a very strong wave rose up beside me and slurped over me.

An icy brace of water surged down my front and I lost my grip on the rake. It all came too quickly to know exactly what happened. I must have tripped or lost my footing. I found myself on my side, half floating like a disabled ship, and water was pouring into the waders. Then I was being carried down beneath the frigid waves.

I was under. Somehow I managed to get my head up to the surface for half a breath but was pulled down again. Water flowed into my nostrils and found its way into my throat.

The cold was a wall, a powerful wall. I'd slammed into a pitiless wall of cold. It was a wall but somehow it was also all around me, solid and hard but wet and flowing.

A hard cold wall and then something softer bumped into me, pliable and rubbery—floating and dreamlike—I grabbed onto it with one hand and tried to pull it to me, but it crumpled beneath the pressure and came loose. There was a commotion, somewhere in a world on the other side of the frigid wall, I thrashed about, found the rubber thing again, lost it again. I was in a grey swirling world. More commotion. Wall. Darkness.

The rubbery thing hadn't been real. Nothing was real but the cold frozen wall.

I was on my back and sinking. Water rushed down my throat, full-bore, alien at first, then oddly inert and inevitable. Time was ceasing to be. A weightless state and motionless. Silence.

It's not your time.

Sometime after that—a moment, half a minute?—I felt something strong take over. A force outside myself propelled me backward and upward. My head came to the dazed surface, light was around me, I coughed and coughed and gasped and gasped and passed back into darkness several times and retched and retched some more, salty horrid fluid. At some point I realized I was half awake and choking and being towed into shallow water.

"I shoulda let you die." Somewhere off in a dream Bob Brown in a wetsuit yanked me in toward shore by my shoulders and Dorothy splashed alongside, towing a sinking basket with our clattering scallops. On her shoulder she bore my rake, bulging with that night's dinner.

It was a hospital room like any other, a metal-encased bed and IV poles and wires and beeping machinery, and a plastic tray that swung around at bedside.

But not really like any other. Because Haddie was there.

When I woke up, she was seated in a chair a few feet away, leaning in toward me and watching my every move.

I grunted and tried to lean forward.

"Hey," she said.

I rested a few minutes and then forced myself to half sit up and murmur, "I found you some scallops for dinner."

"You did," she replied. "And almost got yourself drowned."

I sank back and rested my head on the pillow. For several more minutes we sat in silence. "A sight for sore eyes," I said finally. She had an odd look on her face, displeasure or maybe worry. "I mean you are," I added. "Nice old saying."

"Is it from Shakespeare?" she asked.

I shook my head. "Jonathan Swift."

"*Gulliver's Travels?*"

"Something like that," I mumbled.

"You must be exhausted, my boy." She leaned closer and rested a hand on my shoulder. She smoothed out my hair.

I nodded. For the next few minutes, neither of us spoke. Then, in a gravelly voice, I asked, "Was that really Bob Brown who pulled me out?"

"It was, and he's already told half the island about his heroic efforts."

I succumbed to a coughing fit. When I recovered, I asked, "Is Dorothy okay?"

"She is. She feels terrible. She says she should've stopped you from going out into the deep water."

"It wasn't her fault. I'd been warned."

"I don't know if you were aware of this, but she rushed over to you and pulled the inner tube off the basket and pushed it down toward you but you couldn't hold on."

The soft rubbery thing. Real after all.

I leaned back and closed my eyes. "I put her in danger. Not to mention that I messed up her birthday plans for you."

She placed a hand on mine. "You didn't mess up anything, Peter. Luna has been opening your scallops and she and Dorothy are cooking them up." She glanced at her watch. "Oh. I promised to join them right about now."

I patted her hand. "Well, what do you know, I got to be with you on your birthday after all."

Though her hand remained in mine, I felt something retreat like the slip of a shadow into the dusk. For goodness sake, Peter, did you have to go and ruin it? I asked myself.

In a careful voice she said, "I wanted to be sure you're okay. And to thank you for . . . well, for making all that effort."

"Tell Dorothy I'm sorry." My voice guttered out.

"She's fine. She'll be glad you're okay. You need to rest, Peter." She tapped my hand and was gone.

"Happy birthday," I whispered to the hallway.

Journal entry
An impossible person 5

A month after the affair began, it was over. A week after that, I was called into my editor's office, asked to verify what had happened, and was let go. Did I go home and do what any rational and mature adult would do: get down on my knees, apologize to my wife, and beg for her forgiveness?

I did not. I sulked around the house and waited for her to come home, and I sulked some more once she was there. Later that night her antennae went up when a friend from work called to ask how I was doing. I think he's okay, she said, a question in her voice. She brought the conversation to a close and hung up.

She stood in the door to the study. What happened?

I told her. The short version.

Her eyes blazed. Did you think this was all right? Were you not going to tell me?

I think I was going to tell you, I replied.

You *think* you were going to tell me?

I nodded.

Didn't you *think* I would find out anyway? And didn't you realize it would be better if you told me?

I straightened out a pile of paper clips.

I knew that.

Do you have anything else to say to me now?

I was silent. I couldn't speak. Trapped. Trapped by the pressure of the walls as they pushed closer.

On the other side of that wall, two twisted thoughts had always been chasing each other round and round. It took me a long time to realize that both thoughts had to do with my father and what he had visited upon us.

The first one came from knowing that my mother was a victim of his bad behavior, and so, in a less direct way, was I. Being a victim had affected me in a number of ways. For a number of years, I believed I'd done something wrong—all this was my fault somehow. And then, over time, around the annoying irritant of feeling I'd done something wrong—like an oyster spinning a pearl around a grain of sand—I built up a multilayered belief in the opposite: my own virtue. As the years passed, I began to take the belief in my own virtue a step further. Because I'd been violated, anything I did must be good. Against all sense of reality, I'd come to believe I could do no wrong.

That was the first thought. The second one was much simpler: my father never got in trouble for what he did. Never. He always got off free. My mother always forgave him and accepted him back. So in some selfish and wounded part of myself, I assumed that I too should get off free.

Two misshapen thoughts. I could do no wrong. I should get off free. Maybe they weren't even thoughts, they were unspoken assumptions. But whatever they were, they had me trapped.

And so with my wife on that crucial day, I had nothing more to offer.

You have nothing to say? she asked.

I stared at my feet.

I'm sorry, Peter, I'm going to ask for a divorce.

On that evening in the hospital bed, I lay there and contemplated walls. Somewhere inside me, the walls were probably still there. But something had changed. When I was trapped underwater, a wall of cold blasted onto me and pulled me down and almost killed me. I escaped from it, and the escape left me altered in some way. Maybe at that moment I got a sense that even the worst wall can be surmounted, undermined, dismantled and left behind.

When Haddie sat beside me at the hospital bed, I made an effort, however misguided, to reach past the wall. My approach to her was awkward and my timing was bad. The presence in her hand slipped away like a shadow. She still sensed the wall and didn't trust that I was free of it.

Maybe over time I could prove otherwise.

One more thing. Getting free of the wall would mean something entirely different from my father's getting off free.

And anyway, my father didn't really get off free. He lost the love of his son and, in all the ways that counted, the love of his wife. In the end he was pathetic, a bully, angry and self-obsessed, worthy of nothing but scorn.

It seemed likely that I'd been headed down something of a parallel path. Was it too late to change course?

Things work in strange ways on this island. The next day when I slipped into the pharmacy to pick up some cold medicine, who stood directly in front of me in the checkout line but Bob Brown. His red flannel shirt bulged out of his blue jeans. A tall bearded guy stood beside him, leaning on a crutch.

Brown paid, turned to leave, and saw me and froze. "It's you. You're alive. You're walking."

"And it's you," I replied. "My personal savior."

He lifted his hands and raised up his round face toward the heavens. "Am I magnificent or what?"

"Thank you, Bob Brown. Thank you from the depths of my waterlogged soul."

"It seemed a shame to lose a half-decent third baseman," he said with one of his trademark half sneers.

"At least you finally admitted I'm half decent."

He flapped a hand at me. "You were lucky I was right there. The girl wasn't strong enough to pull you up, in fact she was about to go under herself."

"I know." I felt the other guy watching me carefully.

"Why'd you do it?" Brown asked. "Why'd you go out so deep?"

"Because I'm an idiot."

He shook a finger at me. "Not an idiot. A fool. A fool for love. You just had to get her those birthday scallops, didn't cha?"

News sure traveled fast on this island. "Yeah, you got me."

"You pathetic loser," he said. The bearded guy gave a grunt of agreement. Now I recognized him; it was Steph Sylvan.

"That's me," I said with a shrug.

"No woman is worth it."

It was the way he said it. Something about Bob Brown suddenly became clear to me.

"You don't really believe that," I told him. "Because behind all your tough talk, you're really a softie, aren't you?"

A look I couldn't recognize flashed into his eyes. "Gotta run," he said.

"Well, thank you again, Bob Brown."

He flapped a hand again and marched off toward the door.

Sylvan limped past me on his single crutch but stopped and turned back. "Don't kid yourself, Brown's no softie." Above his beard, his face was all planes and angles, like a sculpture; his eyes regarded me with a neutral glare, hard and unblinking.

"You sure of that?" I replied.

"You get a beer into him, he might seem to soften up a little. Two or three, and he's the most selfish guy you'll ever meet."

"Huh. Aren't you his friend?"

"What's that got to do with it? Don't I know him better than you?"

I spread my hands apart. "All I know is, he's my savior."

"The heart inside your savior is a cave where sun has never shone."

Listen carefully, the voice said.

"I'll bring a flashlight next time."

He snorted and limped off.

More strange island ways. I was out in the parking lot, climbing into my Jeep, when what should pull up next to me but a Ford Escort.

"Well look at you," Luna commented in her husky voice as she climbed out. "You okay?"

"I'm fine," I assured her. "How's Dorothy?"

She waved her hand. "Her? She's fine."

"I want to apologize to her next time I see her. I put her at risk too. I feel bad about that."

"Don't lose any sleep over it, we all help out each other here. Oh, speaking of which, could I ask a favor?"

It turned out that the finals of the softball tourney had been delayed a few weeks by weather and the game was finally scheduled for that night. Luna said she couldn't find her bat—in fact, she hadn't seen it in weeks—and she wondered if she could borrow mine. As it happened, I had mine stashed still in the Jeep and I rummaged around under the seat and handed it to her.

As I prepared to leave, she said, "Thank you. And thank you again for agreeing to go out scalloping with Dorothy."

I gave a little wave and drove off.

At the time I had no idea of the importance of that missing bat.

By midmorning the town was abuzz with some breaking news. In the middle of the night there'd been a disturbance at the Danville house. Clara Danville, Chester's widow, had been awakened in the middle of the night by her house alarms screaming at full pitch. Within minutes, three police cruisers and a fire truck were on the property, lights blazing and sirens blaring.

It was the talk of the town, but no one knew exactly what had happened or why.

It was said that an object had been hurled into the living room, but there had been no fire and no intruder. Apparently all that remained of the disturbance was one single object, and no one seemed to know what it was.

From the newsroom I called around to everyone who might conceivably have some information. I talked to Luna—nothing. Beatrice—also nothing. Stefanie also wasn't able to get much from her contacts. She tried to contact Star, but he was out of reach. I left a message for Detective McGuane to call me back. I talked to everyone I could think of except Haddie. I knew this wasn't the right time or the right reason to contact her again.

I was stuck.

As I waited for something—anything—the mail guy dropped another envelope onto my desk.

I READ THIS SOMEWHERE: ANIMALS DECEIVE ONE ANOTHER BUT THEY NEVER LIE. HUMANS LIE BUT IN THE END THEY NEVER DECEIVE ONE ANOTHER. WHAT IF BOTH ARE AS FALSE AS DECLARATIONS OF ETERNAL LOVE?

Well, that was pretty bitter. And hopeless in a weird way. It seemed like we were all stuck.

I was wondering if that would ever change, when Detective McGuane called and invited me down to the station.

McGuane was still the same big, comfortable man: the oversized rectangular head, the wide brow, the dark eyes. But today, instead of trending sleepy, those eyes looked agitated.

"Take a seat, Christie. How you doing? Heard we almost lost you the other day."

Echoing Mark Twain, I said rumors of my death had been greatly exaggerated.

Speaking of rumors, he wanted to know why I had been reporting rumors on the front page of the *Island Forum*. "You have no proof that the Douglas will was being altered," he pointed out. "Zero."

I said it was a judgment call: Stefanie and I had decided that the rumors had risen to the level where they had to be taken seriously and put on the record.

He shook his head. He didn't buy it. In any case, he said, I'd better remember that everything today was off the record. More than off the record. I was not to share this with anyone. I knew that meant I was still stuck in one sense—in what I could use as a reporter—but it seemed possible there could be a way to use it for my own investigations on Haddie's behalf.

I asked how I could help.

"Seems like we have another literary illusion on our hands."

Allusion, I said to myself. "Sure, what is it?"

He slipped on a pair of latex gloves, reached down beside his desk, and lifted up a long cardboard box. "It's this." Out of the box he pulled a wooden baseball bat.

"An Easton Howard's aluminum Superbat," I pointed out.

He nodded.

The same type I used. The same type Luna used.

But also the same type almost every team on the island used.

"Someone tossed this into the Danville house last night through a window."

"That's odd."

"Even odder when you see what's written on it." He pushed it closer and gestured to me: look as close as you want but don't touch.

In tiny letters, a spidery scrawl down the side of the bat read:

> The reward is waiting all along
> A precious treasure to unearth
> A simple tap keeps the lineage strong
> The flawless bloodlines set by birth.

"Holy smoke!" I murmured.

"Haven't heard that expression in a while." McGuane fixed his eyes on me. It actually took me a little by surprise when I said it, though I knew full well it was one of Haddie's many endearing expressions. "Well, what do you make of it?" he continued.

"It's more of the same. Strong stuff," I remarked.

"How strong?"

"Someone is gloating about the murder. '*A simple tap.*' Has to be a reference to the death of Chester Danville."

He shrugged. "Might be. Or it might not. What else do you see?"

"Well . . . a threat of revenge. And maybe a warning."

"A warning about what?"

"About messing with the family lines of succession." I took a long moment to phrase the next sentence. "Which seems to suggest that maybe Chester Danville *was* in the process of altering Douglas's will."

The sleepiness returned to McGuane's eyes. "No idea what you're talking about."

"'*The flawless bloodlines set by birth.*' Someone—probably someone who stands to inherit a gleaming treasure—is worried that the family legacy is being disturbed."

"The chowline, if you will."

"Right."

McGuane shrugged. "There's no proof."

"Could I ask you to indulge me for a minute of idle speculation?"

He nodded to me to proceed.

"Let's assume that Chester Danville had been hired to change the will," I said. "For instance, to cut out a relative who previously was a part of it."

"That's assuming any relatives were a part of it previously."

"Fair enough. But if they were, and if those relatives then got word that they were being taken out of it, well—"

"You're saying you detect a motive."

I nodded.

Little shakes of his head, back and forth, fast. "Maybe. Maybe not."

"Is there anything else you'd like from me?" I asked.

His sleepy eyes shook themselves awake. "What about the literary stuff in the poem? What can you tell me about that?"

"It's more dyed-in-the-wool British heroic," I replied.

"Any clues about the person who wrote it?"

"Not much. Probably someone with a big ego. An inflated sense of themself."

He bit his lip. "Maybe someone who thinks they've been mistreated?"

"Yes."

I saw that McGuane was more insightful than I'd given him credit for.

"Why the bat?" he continued. "Anything literary there? Casey at the bat—that sort of thing?"

"I doubt it." I paused. "On the face of it, the murderer is flaunting his weapon of choice. But what murderer would be dumb enough to toss his own murder weapon through the widow's window?"

"That's easy. They're trying to frame someone. Someone who was known to play ball."

"Yeah. That makes sense."

A cunning light played in the sleepy eyes. "Unless the murderer is playing with us somehow."

"How?"

"Hard to say." His lips and cheeks set ponderously.

"Has the bat been analyzed?" I asked.

"It will be. Looks like there's some blood on it, maybe some prints, and the lab's gonna run some tests."

We talked a few more minutes. McGuane was disappointed that I couldn't nail down anything more definite on the literary side. He still had a hunch that the answer to the crime could be found, like a diamond buried deep in a cave, in what he called "literary illusion."

Which I now doubted.

But one conclusion was clear. There were a few definite possibilities.

Star. Or someone trying to frame Star.

And also Luna—based on the mysteriously missing bat.

After leaving McGuane, I wished I could take all this directly to Stefanie and talk it out—all the details and possible implications. But I couldn't, the conversation with McGuane was off the record, there were hard and fast limits to what I could share. Still, there was a way to share just enough to get Stefanie to do what I was about to ask of her.

CHAPTER ELEVEN

Luna and Star. First, Star.

The horn-rimmed glasses, newly cleaned, offered a clearer window than usual onto the skeptical brown eyes that peered out at me.

"You want me to do what?"

"I want you to question Star about the break-in at Clara Danville's."

"For what purpose?"

"To find out if he shows any knowledge of it. Any hints that he's hiding something."

"You're saying you think Star is the one?"

"I'm saying it's not impossible." I waited a beat and added the one thing that really mattered. "And if you can bring him back here, I'd appreciate it. I'd like another chance to talk with him."

"You probably think the moon is made of green cheese too."

"Scientists have already settled that. It's Mozzarella."

"The moon is made of Mozzarella and Star Douglas not only committed a murder but was stupid enough to go and harass poor Clara Danville." She let out a dismissive tsck.

I agreed that it probably wasn't Star who did either thing, but we had to check it out. And I wondered if there might be some tricky double-thinking behind the break-in. It was so blatantly intended to look like an attempt to frame someone—Star being the most likely target of the framing—that it made me wonder. What better way for Star to clear himself in the eyes of the public than by creating a clearly staged and patently false piece of incrimination?

She gave me a withering look. "You forget that I know Star. He has his good points, but being clever is not one of them."

I said it was also possible that the break-in was an aberration—a moment of temporary insanity or drunken acting-out. Did that sound more like the Star she knew?

She said maybe but added, "Let me ask you something. Have you learned anything about the object that was thrown into the home?"

"No."

She held my eyes. "You're hiding something from me, Christie."

"Yes, I am." I owed her that much.

She looked me up and down. "You have your reasons, I take it?"

I nodded.

"They better be good."

I told her there were things I couldn't talk about right then.

She sighed. "I'm concerned for you, Christie. I sense that you're getting desperate to solve this."

"Aren't we all?" I replied.

Another sigh, longer. "Well, okay. I'll talk to Star. But I'm going to approach the subject from the side—indirectly. I won't insult him in the ways you're suggesting."

"I'm not suggesting anything of the sort. But can you try to get him back here?"

She gave a humph and signaled that she wouldn't be upset if I were to return to my desk.

"You and your great aunt," she mumbled—or did I just imagine that?

Journal entry
Fleeing 3

It was tempting to believe that my great-great aunt would have figured out by now the identity of the murderer—assuming of course that she was alive and among us all on this intriguing little island. With her super-subtle mind, she might have been able to assemble a network of clues, no matter how seemingly minor and unrelated, and suss out the murderer. She wouldn't have been grasping at straws, as I was.

It was also tempting to assume that Agatha foresaw and planned out every clue in each of her murder mysteries, laying them out ahead of time in perfect succession. Certain novelists report that they're able to outline the plan for each and every chapter even before they begin to write. Wouldn't Agatha have done that?

Not according to the evidence. It turns out that Agatha Christie was as surprised as the rest of us about the twists and turns of her stories. In some of her books, in fact—including the famous *Crooked House*—she wasn't even sure of the *identity* of the murderer until she was more than halfway through her first draft. She later pronounced that novel to be one of her favorites and admitted in a foreword that she didn't know what put the Leonides family into her head. She added that she felt she was only their scribe.

Only their scribe. That quote was a tipping point for me; it carried me from distant adulation to a genuine love for Agatha.

Despite her super-subtlety and cleverness, what truly mattered to her was not the shallow meaning of the word *mystery*—who committed a murder or why. What she actually cared about was the deeper sense of *mystery*: the mystery of life, the strange otherness of our experiences on this always-slightly-foreign planet of ours.

Even when writing a seamless murder mystery—the most diligently plotted genre in existence—she was "only their scribe."

I knew I lacked my famous relative's shrewdness. But I wondered if I might be able to solve this murder through other means, maybe by developing some other strengths. Maybe by embracing the odd truths about myself and my life, the buried bits of coal and ashes that I was finally stirring into the light. My understanding of myself had always been sporadic and limited—the mistakes I'd made, the hurt I'd caused to others. Any little gleams of self-knowledge that surfaced now could only help in figuring out the reasons behind the behavior of others.

I wasn't a murderer and didn't think I ever would be, but the processes inside me probably weren't all that different.

Running away.

Agatha Christie and I both ran away from home, but there was a difference in how it played out. Agatha steeled herself to come back to her life and did the painful work of starting all over. She quietly created a whole new version of her life, still with her daughter but without her first husband. She was able to move forward, having integrated some of the lessons of her past losses and probably, too, her past misconceptions.

And me? After running away from my childhood home, did I move forward with my life? At the time I probably thought I did.

I found an intelligent and sensitive partner who was openhearted and trusting enough to accept me in marriage. I found a good and challenging job at the *Globe*. By all appearances my life was sailing along just fine, but some unexpected shoals lay ahead—the visible incarnation of my own weaknesses and blind spots. And so it was, after five years of marriage, I committed my own version of my father's faithless approach to family. Not through violence and bullying like him, but like him in infidelity—and to make it worse, with a younger woman who had been entrusted to my professional care.

Running away had saved me from the unbearable family situation of being around my father, but it hadn't saved me from my own impulses. Like a splinter erupting in a swollen blister, the truth eventually made itself known. Having been a victim didn't, in and of itself, imbue me with virtue. It only gave me a false shield of self-pity.

If there was a way to create virtue in myself, it was probably time honored and simple, or at least simple to say. Be true to the people you love. Treat them with care and respect. Consider their welfare more than your own passing needs or desires.

In various ways over the years, my mother had shown me this, though I realized now that I'd mostly taken them for granted. When I was nine I was sitting next to her in the front seat of the car when another car ran a red light and crashed into us. As we crunched to a stop, she instinctively reached her arm out in front of me to keep me from slamming into the dashboard.

She'd also tried to shelter me from my father's rage in various ways that I was only beginning to understand. A word here and there, a suggestion that I go outside and enjoy the sunny day, an invitation she'd worked up for me to go play at a friend's house.

I'd had it better than many victims. And calling myself a victim had led, ironically, to nothing but a re-creation of my father's behavior in new and diverse forms.

But—connecting all this back to the present situation—could any of these thoughts help shed light on the identity of the person who had killed Chester Danville?

There did seem to be some parallels to my life. It was likely that the murderer was wallowing in a deep conviction of victimhood—and believed they could do no wrong as a result. Along with that had come an inflated sense of worth and a conviction that no one else was granting them their true value.

That inflated self-worth had come to full flower in the "heroic British" quality of the poems. It was enhanced by an apparent belief that revenge was more than acceptable, it was justified.

The inner dynamics of the murderer weren't all that different from my own. The differences were probably in degree, not in kind.

A cruel father. A sense of victimhood.

You're on the right track.

Star? Luna? Both of them?

Stefanie delivered. She brought Star back to the office, still chatting pleasantly, and somehow deposited him by my desk. And there he stood, towering over me in his loose-fitting slacks and a grey-green peasant shirt.

"Nice to see you again, Star," I said, getting up and putting out my hand, which he took like a bear shaking hands with a raccoon.

"I'm only here to please an old friend," he told me, utterly serious, not a glimmer of humor or irony. And for the record, little visible evidence of affection for the old friend.

"I get that." I gestured to a narrow wooden chair, and he frowned but backed himself into it like a moose lowering itself onto a gopher hole.

"I only have a minute or two."

"Okay. You know Star, I want to apologize if I was rude to you last time you were here." He looked on impassively as I continued. "I've thought about it, and I understand your feelings. I can see why you might have thought I was inviting myself into your family home in a way that was less than forthcoming."

"'Less than forthcoming'? You were a freaking liar. You baited my father into revealing some family stuff that was none of your business."

"I apologize for that. I guess I thought the reward was waiting all along—"

I paused. Had he registered anything?

The only thing he registered was frustration. The color of his face deepened a shade. "What reward was waiting all along? What the heck are you talking about?"

"I'm talking about the glowing story I was hoping to write on your family and its, well, its flawless bloodlines."

"What do you mean *flawless bloodlines*?"

"Well, certainly to those of us on the outside, your family is special. There's something flawless in all that Douglas family history. Something precious."

"Flawless? You mean, like having no flaws?"

"Yes, that."

"Do you have any idea how many marriages my father had?"

"Well, I—"

"You think those bloodlines are *flawless*? My half-sister Luna? Don't take my word for it—ask anyone who knows her. She's got all the warmth of a block of ice."

"Are you suggesting she might be the murderer?"

"I'm not suggesting anything. You're the one who does that. All I'm saying is, there's no flawless bloodlines. Especially when you include all the others."

"All the others?"

He nodded. His face was reddening more. "Outside of marriage."

"There were other relationships? And other children?"

"It's not for me to say how many unclaimed Douglases are wandering the Earth, looking for a payoff when my dad kicks the bucket." He tapped his fingers on the desk.

"Not for me to say either," I admitted. I nodded toward his fingers. "One of life's small pleasures. A simple tap," I murmured.

He pulled his hands away, glared at them, clenched his fists, then leaned forward to glare at me. By now his neck and face had flushed bright red and his face had swollen up a size or two.

"You are uttering some of the dumbest phrases I've ever heard on this Earth," he snarled.

"I apologize for that," I said with a shrug. "But at least I hope you still don't think I'm—"

"You're still a rat-hound," he pronounced, and he leaned forward and hoisted himself to his feet, bringing the chair halfway into the air with him. It clattered to the floor and tumbled over onto its side. He kicked it away and lurched off toward the exit.

From across the way, Stefanie gave me an eyebrow wave. *Not sure what you did or why you did it*, she seemed to be saying, *but I hope it was worth it.*

Maybe it was. One thing was clear: Star'd had nothing to do with the language of the poem or the inscription on the bat. And I knew now what he thought of Luna. He seemed to consider his half-sister capable of anything, including murder.

More importantly, I knew now what was upsetting Star so much.

His father had other offspring. Maybe they were identified, maybe they were unknown. Far away, or possibly right here on the island. Whoever they were, wherever they were, they troubled him immensely.

On to Luna.

That afternoon I called and asked if it would be okay to come by her place and thank Dorothy for her role in saving me. Of course, Luna replied, and gave me directions to their house.

It was a small, weather-beaten cottage on the west end of the island, perched at the far end of a narrow, rutted road. I parked on the dirt driveway next to the Ford Escort, got out, and peered across the patchy lawn. The cottage hunkered down no more than thirty yards from Crooked Creek, the tidal creek that ran into West End Harbor. A small shed was nestled behind the cottage.

In contrast to the dilapidated old cottage, with its shredded shingles and rotting sills and sagging roof, the creek looked vibrant and fresh even in the late October chill. The incoming tide surged forward, bearing a flotilla of ducks of various types: buffleheads with their big squarish white heads, mergansers with their high hooded foreheads and exotic yellow eyes, and the more familiar mallards with their iridescent green heads and goose-like bodies.

"Pretty, isn't it?" Luna said. She had stepped outside to greet me and wandered over near me. "I guess it makes it all worth it."

"I should think it would."

"The cottage isn't much to look at. But the rent is good, there's enough room for my loom, and Dorothy likes being by the water."

"It's a beautiful place for a child to grow up. Have you ever thought of purchasing this cottage?"

"Oh no, I don't have the resources for that." She waved a hand. "My father thinks his children need to make their own way in the world, and he's never offered me a penny."

"But possibly at some point in the future, some assets might be coming your way?"

She took a step back and searched my eyes with hers. Blue as ice, unwavering.

"Are you trying to pry information out of me, Peter Christie?"

"Well, it's my job."

"And you promised Haddie you'd figure the crime out, didn't you?"

"Well yes, that too."

She expelled her breath in a quick laugh. "Do me a favor and keep me out of this."

"As you wish."

"Anyway, for the record, I don't think I was ever included in the will, and I don't expect I ever will be. And unlike my big brother, I have no interest in trying to crawl back into our father's life at this stage."

"Do you think Chester Danville was in the process of making some changes to the will?"

"Didn't you promise, like two seconds ago, to leave me out of this?"

"I guess I can't help myself."

"But just so you know, I have no idea about any of that, and not much interest in Danville, one way or the other. I've written that man out of my life—I'm talking about my father now—and though I'm surprised and pleased that Dorothy has managed to build a relationship with him, I'm perfectly content to keep my distance."

As she said all this, her face showed no change—it maintained that frozen expression which had made me wonder on first meeting her if she'd had plastic surgery or perhaps substance issues. Now it seemed to me more likely that it was simply a projection of her personality: all facts and items, little or no emotional nuance.

I knew I'd already broken my promise once. But there was still one question I had to ask.

"Did your bat ever show up?"

She put her hands on her hips. "No, now you mention it, it never did. I think someone took it! But why?" She shook her head. "And that reminds me, I have your bat." She opened the back door of the Escort and pulled out the Superbat.

"How'd the championship game go?" I asked.

"Argh, we lost by a run. We were down four, almost came back in the last inning. Bases loaded, two outs, I was up. I hit a scorching liner and the third baseman made a great leaping catch. Game over."

"Oh, geez, sorry." I placed the bat on the floor of my Jeep behind the front seats.

"Hey, that's sports. Let's go inside and find her majesty."

Dorothy was lying on her stomach on the dining room table, reading a book.

"Dorothy Douglas! How many times have I told you not to lie there?!"

She raised her head sleepily. "I like reading this way." She went on to say she was reading a history of the island and she had learned that the island plunged into a deep recession in 1859 after the discovery in Pennsylvania of petroleum. People didn't need whale oil anymore, and so the island lost the main source of its wealth. Many homes and businesses went vacant for decades. Prosperity didn't return until the early twentieth century, when wealthy tourists began to spend the summer season on the island and—

Her mother told her to climb off the table and say hello to a visitor.

"Oh, hi," she said. She unfolded herself from the table, hopped down, and walked up to me, gazing past me with that indefinable expression of hers that seemed both very near and very far away. "Are you recovered?"

"I'm recovered. And I came to tell you I'm sorry. I'm sorry I did something stupid and ended up putting you in danger too."

"I wasn't in danger," she replied. "I thought I could save you but you were too far under."

"Well, thank you for trying. And thank you for calling for help."

She shook her head, her face still showing no discernible expression. "I didn't call for help."

"You didn't? But then how did help come so fast?"

"Bob Brown just showed up on his own. I guess he was watching us."

"Another mystery," I commented.

She looked at me and decided there was no need to say anything else.

"Hey, if you ever need someone to scallop with, just have your mother give me a call," I told her.

"Okay," she agreed. Her eyes wandered away, and I thought it was time for me to go. But as I turned to leave, something in a side room caught my attention, and I froze.

"Oh wow!" I exclaimed. "That's beautiful."

In a loom, mostly finished, rested the sumptuous threads of a tapestry. Somehow, through the artful arrangement of dyed wool, the tapestry recorded the scene outside the cottage. The wide, vigorous tidal creek, deep blue. The humble brown bushes fringing the edges. The layered earth tones of the marshes. The grey outline of a cottage or two. And some brilliant white and green dots that were clearly buffleheads and mallards.

"It's nothing," Luna replied. "It's something I'm working on." She gave a quick wave of her hand and turned away.

She is very proud of this, as she should be.

I approached the loom for a closer look at the woven wool, so subtle and sensitive in shading and shaping and design.

So this was where Luna made her contact with the intricacies of her world. "You're a true artist," I said.

"I tell my mom that, too," Dorothy added. "But she doesn't want to hear it."

Luna shook her head. In her world, there was no need for praise or condemnation. "I just do what I do."

"Well, you keep telling your mom until she finally believes it," I told Dorothy, and I said my goodbyes and let myself out the door into the dusky world of marsh and duck and, somewhere above us, falling stardust or—wait, no—it was the Milky Way, warm and silky and silent, spread across the island sky.

CHAPTER TWELVE

An Island Still Troubled by a Horrid Crime
A murder casts a long shadow
BY PETER CHRISTIE

October 30 The cherished serenity of autumn on the island stands in stark contrast to the troubling uncertainty that still surrounds the murder of long-time lawyer and community leader, Chester Danville.

While no new incidents of violence have been reported except for the inexplicable shooting of a seal, the mood among islanders is said to be weary and apprehensive. In the three weeks since the murder, some parents have not allowed their children to play outside after school. A number of after-school programs have also been canceled. And last week a trivia contest at the First Baptist Church was rescheduled to daylight hours.

In a recent interview, Reverend Brenda Gonzalez of the First Congregational Church revealed that many of her church members report difficult sleeping and feel constantly "on edge." She said that additional mental health resources have been asked to come to the island to . . .

The next day I spent several hours in a stinky section of the southern end of the island, researching a report on the threat to the island sewer beds from the erosion brought on by recent storms. The bed closest to the water had already been filled in with gravel and retired, and the others were expected to face problems within the coming decades.

Some environmentalists pointed out that these developments and others like them were the early signs of global warming or climate change, a science still in its infancy.

The days had grown shorter, and it was almost dark by the time I left. My route home led me through town and across Main Street, where I was surprised to find that the intersection was blocked. Something big was going on. Groups of figures carrying lights were wandering up and down the cobblestoned street. But these weren't your everyday islanders. They were ogres, giants, fairies, princesses, and vampires.

Of course—today was October 31.

It turns out the island has a long tradition of a Halloween Parade. At 6:00 p.m., parents and children congregate for a full-scale invasion of Main Street. Everyone is in full costume—many of the adults as well as all the children—and the whole assembly proceeds in cheery organized chaos up Main Street, passes the various stores, and slows down at the marble steps of the bank, where volunteers hand out small bags of candy. From there the families disperse, some to the side streets in town where a handful of summer people still linger in their homes, and others back to their station wagons and pickup trucks to rumble off to the less pricey neighborhoods that are occupied year-round.

The festivities looked like too much fun to miss, and besides there might be a story to report, so I found a parking spot and made my way onto Main Street. I had another secret wish: I might run into Haddie.

The formal part of the parade was about to start. The Town Crier was clanging his hand bell and summoning all the spirits and goblins of the night to make themselves known and join the fray. And so the tidal surge began, similar in a way to what I'd witnessed the previous evening at West End Creek; but instead of buffleheads and mergansers, the tide bore along the bedazzling, scary, ethereal creatures of the night. They flowed up the wide cobblestone street, past the jewelry stores, the pharmacy, the realtor shops, and the clothing boutiques.

For ten or fifteen minutes I walked alongside the groups, interviewing parents and also, with the parents' permission, the kids. Like the family scalloping that I'd taken part in earlier that month, there was a joyous and buoyant feel to the gathering. Not to mention some humorous incidents. One tiny princess, dressed in bright red taffeta, lifted her magic wand into the air and declared that every night from now on should be Halloween.

"That's stupid," retorted a larger child next to her, most likely her brother. "You can't make every day Halloween."

The princess turned and aimed her wand at him. "FROG!" she commanded.

I didn't wait to see if the spell had worked. Several groups ahead of me, I thought I'd recognized the gait of a pair of trick-or-treaters. The smaller, slighter one had a disjointed, not-of-this-world way of walking, while the adult beside her stepped with the perfectly measured tread of an accomplished athlete.

Dorothy and Luna.

I picked up my pace to catch up to them and say hello. Closing in on them, I saw that Dorothy was dressed in rags and baggy old pants and was carrying a stick with a kerchief tied onto the end. A hobo. Luna was all in black, with white paint on her neck and the side of her face. Probably a vampire.

I was only a few steps behind them when, from the left, a lean wolflike creature darted out of the night shadows, paused, and then sprinted directly toward Luna. A step or two more and it was beside her. Its arm was raised above her as if to strike, and something in its hand glittered in the light from the street lamps.

"Mother!" Dorothy cried.

"Hey!" I cried at the same moment, and instinctively I lunged forward, threw my elbows in front of me, and gave a hard bump to the creature, knocking it off to the side. Dorothy screamed. Something clattered out of the creature's hand onto the cobblestones, and as the wolflike head turned toward me, its dark eyes locked onto mine for the briefest second. Then the creature bolted away, scurried up the curb onto the brick sidewalk, and disappeared down a side alley.

Dorothy bent over and picked up the object that had fallen, and the three of us, like some six-legged beast, stumbled over to a bench, where we plopped down and tried to recover our breaths. Dorothy was perched between her mother and me.

"What happened back there?" Luna asked. In the orange glow of the street lamp, her painted face looked strained and wild.

"A creature tried to attack you! Look what he had in his hand!" Dorothy held up the fallen object. It was a hypodermic needle.

"What creature?" Luna asked.

"I don't know. A wolf. A werewolf. A wolverine."

"A what? What are you talking about?" Luna blurted out in a strange rush of sound.

"Mother, that creature was trying to inject you with something! Maybe poison!"

I reached out and asked Dorothy for the needle. "I know a detective who will want to see this," I said.

"Peter Christie—how in the world did you get here?" Luna asked.

Before I could reply, Dorothy cried, "Peter saved your life! He shoved the creature away! That's the reason it dropped the needle!"

When Dorothy finished, I explained that I'd been interviewing families for a story about the parade when I saw the two of them. I was coming over to say hello when that creature flew out of nowhere.

"I don't understand," Luna said. I said I didn't either.

But you will.

As the parade flowed off into the distance, Dorothy's breath started to catch and she began to cry in deep, stricken sobs.

Before taking the needle to the police station the next morning, there was a work assignment I had to fulfill. November 1 marked the beginning of commercial scalloping on the island, an event that Stefanie said was begging for a story. She'd arranged for me to go out on a boat with Bill Barnes, an old friend of hers who'd been working the water for close to thirty years. At 6:30 a.m. I met him at his slip on the docks.

Barnes looked as if a photograph from *Yankee Magazine* had come to life. He had the weather-beaten skin, the stubble, the merry eyes, and the easy manner of an old-time fisherman.

His boat, a Sea Ox, was also weathered, showing signs of fiberglass repairs and a newly painted deck. It was fitted out for the scalloping season with a culling board that stretched from one side to the other of the boat, midway back in the cockpit. This was a wooden structure with a broad plywood surface for dumping out the scallops and then "culling" them—separating the adult keepers from the immature seed that would be thrown back into the water along with seaweed, crabs, and other detritus. The process of culling was not all that different from what we did in family scalloping when we plucked the adults out of the net and slid the rest of the stuff back into the water—but here the scale was larger and the process much faster. When Bill worked, his hands kept up a blur of motion.

In family scalloping we used rakes to pick up the scallops, but out on the water, the commercial scallopers towed dredges behind their boats, three on a side. These were squarish metal frames, about two feet wide, with a chain-mesh net lashed to the bottom of the frame.

Affixed to the front of each frame was a thick metal weight, in the shape of a long bar with rounded ends. Its purpose was to keep the dredge bumping along the bottom as the boat dragged it forward. Barnes explained that most of these weights were actually retired window weights. The windows in the old houses on the island had been constructed with a narrow vertical channel on either side. In each channel there hung a weight that descended when the sash was lifted, counterbalancing the sash and holding it up. The channel was covered by a piece of trim, hiding it from view.

Over the years, the old windows had been replaced with new-style windows with pressure tracks. In the waste-not, want-not ethos of the island, the weights were repurposed for the scallop industry, keeping the dredges scraping along the bottom of the harbor.

Around 10:00 a.m. we stopped early and ate the lunches we'd brought. Mine was a salad with cucumbers and canned tuna; his was a ham and cheese sandwich. With the fresh air from the harbor to whet the appetite, no lunch I could remember had ever tasted better. As we drifted with the wind and waves, I realized that we were not far off Shawnee Point. Marshland and shores spread around us in shades of grey and brown, subtler than the bright blue water and sky.

Someone else was working the water not far away from us, a wiry bearded guy, intently setting his lines, pulling them in, and culling. Rinse and repeat. "That's one hard-working fisherman," I commented.

"Yeah, he's a go-getter. Steph Sylvan," Barnes replied. "He knows what's he's doing out here."

By 11:30 we were back at the dock. Bill Barnes had been a gracious host, and the morning had been a welcome break. It would be a pleasure to write up this story for the paper.

But first, there was some unfinished business.

Detective McGuane turned his sleepy eyes on the hypodermic needle that I'd placed on his desk.

"Luna Douglas gave me a heads-up," he said. "Sounds like a tough night with the spooks."

I described how the creature came sprinting out of the shadows, and I had just enough time to shove it to the side.

"Sometimes you have good timing, Christie."

"It was luck."

He nodded at the needle. "What do you bet?"

"Rat poison?"

He nodded.

"Dissolved in water?"

He shook his head. "Strychnine doesn't dissolve in water, but it does in alcohol. This is probably an alcohol-based tincture. We'll have the lab take a look at it."

"Can you let me know what they find?"

He said okay but warned me that the results would be off the record. He added, "And if I were you, I wouldn't write a story about any of this."

"But I was there. It's like what happened with the seal. This one can't be off the record," I protested.

He said he knew that, but a public report might have some very bad consequences for some of the people involved. It could goad the assailant, whoever it was, to try again, and soon. Leaving the incident shrouded in silence might make him think he still had room to maneuver and buy more time for everyone.

McGuane asked if anyone else had seen the attack. I doubted it, there was so much going on at the time: kids scaring each other, parents chatting about this or that, strange creatures appearing and disappearing in the half-darkness.

"You okay with keeping this to yourself?" he pressed me.

I said okay. But in return, I had a favor to ask.

Something in his eyes flashed. "Ask away."

He's finally beginning to trust you.

"The softball bat that was tossed in through Clara Danville's window. Has the lab work come back?"

A slight yes motion of his head.

"Is there anything you can tell me about it?"

"Off the record, I can."

I agreed, and in a calm, matter-of-fact tone he said the blood sample on the bat was a match with the DNA of Chester Danville.

"So is the bat the murder weapon?" I wondered.

"Sure seems like it. And I'll tell you something else, also OTR." I agreed.

"Fingerprints on the bat. You'll never guess who they belonged to."

"Who?"

He paused a moment before he spoke. "Star Douglas."

"Holy smoke."

A muscle contracted on the right side of his face. "Yep. Puts Star right in the middle of the conversation."

"I guess so," I acknowledged. "But for what it's worth, whoever was in the wolf costume last night, it definitely wasn't Star. He wasn't nearly big enough."

"Was he tall?"

"Not sure. It happened so fast, it was hard to tell. It could just as easily have been someone of medium height. But they were on the thin side—I'm sure of that. Which is definitely not Star."

He harumphed and peered down at his desk. This new information wasn't fitting his latest theory. He gestured toward the hypodermic needle. "By the way, am I to assume that all three of you held this at different times?"

I said I was sorry, we were rattled and we didn't even think about disturbing the fingerprints. Dorothy and I had both held it.

He said not to worry, if the creature's costume came with gloves, there were probably no prints anyway.

He leaned back in his chair. "Must be awkward for you as a reporter, Christie, being in the middle of all this and having to keep quiet."

"Sure," I agreed. "But look, I just want the murderer to be caught."

"Don't we all." He stared at the needle. "You sure the creature was thin?"

"Very sure."

"It was nighttime, there were a lot of people around, everything was in motion, it was chaos. You certain that you saw it right?"

"I'm certain."

"Well, I don't know." He shook his head.

Could I have seen it wrong? Had the darkness, the suddenness of the attack, clouded my perceptions? At this point, it was my subjective impression against some compelling physical evidence—the blood and the prints on the bat.

Could there be some other explanation? The person in the wolf costume didn't have to be the murderer, did it? It might have been an accomplice—or maybe someone entirely different, with a different agenda and their own set of motivations.

But how many would-be murderers could live on one little island?

Things looked bad for Star Douglas, and that didn't sit right with me. Sure, he had a temper, but he struck me as a goofy, moody giant—someone who would stalk off in a fit of pique when he got upset, but not someone who would plan out and execute a murder.

Of course, those thoughts were based on two relatively short encounters.

Some things about the evidence weren't adding up. Logically, only one baseball bat should have been involved in the murder.

Why were there two? Betsy Cranmore had stumbled upon the first one at the murder site; it was probably the same bat I'd seen propped in the corner of McGuane's office a day or two later. That was the bat that should have had traces of blood and maybe fingerprints. But it was the second bat, the one that was tossed through Clara Danville's window, that carried the incriminating evidence.

What did we know about the first bat? It occurred to me that I'd never asked about the lab work on it.

By now I figured I knew McGuane well enough to give him a call. And as luck had it, he picked up the phone on the first ring. I asked him if he could tolerate another question, also off the record.

He sighed. "You and your questions, Christie. But go ahead." It wasn't a good sign when he used my last name.

I explained my doubts about the bats and asked if the first bat also had blood and prints on it.

"Clean as a whistle," he came back.

"Clean as a whistle? How could that be?"

"Beats me. Maybe it was an extra weapon that wasn't needed. Or a decoy of some sort, but why, I can't say."

I told him I might have an answer. He groaned and replied, "Okay Christie, out with it. Don't keep me in the dark."

I said I agreed that the first bat was a decoy. But believe it or not, so was the second. Because the real murder weapon wasn't a bat at all, it was something completely different.

He snorted. "Oh, that's very informative, thank you very much, Christie. But just for the record, can you remind me what the real murder weapon was? Because I think it slipped my mind."

"I'm working on it."

"*You're* working on it? As opposed to the rest of us?"

I told him I was here to help any way I could.

"Any way you can." He grunted. "I don't know, Christie, I guess you think you're a whole lot smarter than the rest of us. Where I come from, the victim's blood and a suspect's prints are pretty darn good evidence."

"I know it looks airtight. But something's not right, it's too . . . too easy," I protested. The first bat had been left at the murder scene on purpose, I was sure of it. Maybe to give everyone the idea that a bat had been the murder weapon.

"Christie, chill out, you're overthinking this. Sometimes the real solution is the simplest one. The one staring you in the face," the voice on the phone was saying.

"Think about it, detective, something doesn't add up. The second bat—the one with the blood and the prints on it—why wasn't it found at the scene of the murder?"

"Who knows? Maybe the murderer held onto it? Why he would do that, I don't know," he admitted. "And I'm guessing you don't, either."

I said I didn't, but I was doing my best to figure it out.

"Doing your best. Uh-hu. That's what we're all trying to do, in't it. So here's what, Christie, I'm gonna make a suggestion. I'll handle the physical evidence, and you put your mind to work on the literary illusions. I'm still of the opinion there's something there that can help us, and I am also of the opinion that you've been missing it so far."

I said I would search my books and my memory banks for something, anything, that could help.

We hung up without saying goodbye.

CHAPTER THIRTEEN

By the time I got home that evening, I was exhausted and almost missed the note that was pinned to the right of the door.

"Hey, stranger, long time no see. How about coming by after dinner tonight for a glass of wine? I might have something for you. -Beatrice."

I got the stove going with some scraps of wood that had been donated to me by Stefanie's brother, a carpenter. Then I heated up a bowl of soup in the microwave and settled back in my chair by the fire to eat. It would have been easy to fall asleep then and there. I didn't really want to go out again, but if Beatrice had something important to share, I couldn't ignore it.

The window dummies in the clothing store below Beatrice's apartment sported stylish new winter coats, and a festive string of scallop lights, artfully hung from the window frame above them, shed twinkling colors over them. Scallop lights? I bent closer and saw that someone had glued pairs of shells around a line of diminutive holiday lights.

Almost no one was around on this autumn evening to witness the cozy display. Main Street was close to deserted.

Beatrice pulled open the door and gave a nod. She gestured me over to the sparkly white countertop, where Eileen was opening a bottle of wine. She poured a glass and watched carefully as I took a sip.

"What is it?" I asked.

"It's another white Burgundy. A Meursault. You like?"

"It's delicious," I said.

"As good as the last one?"

"Even better." Something about the scrutiny in her cognac-colored eyes made me shiver.

Why such a shiver?

Her smile was one of polite disagreement. "Meursaults are said to favor honey or melon, while the Saint-Aubin is earthier, more minerality," she explained in a precise and measured cadence. "I prefer Saint-Aubin."

"I'm sure you can't go wrong either way," I replied.

"There is no contentment like a good glass of Burgundy." She gave her fingertips a quick kiss and strolled off.

"Isn't she something?" Beatrice asked.

"She sure is," I agreed.

"And so pretty."

"Yes she is."

Beatrice smiled and gave a little finger wave. Not for you. Her brows furrowed again as they had when she greeted me at the door. We took a seat at the counter.

"The broken window. I might have some information on that." She said a friend of hers who lived near the Danvilles hadn't been able to sleep that night. About 2:00 a.m. she got up to take some Nyquil, and while she waited for the medication to start to take hold, she stood in her front room, looking out at the night. And at that late hour, in that peaceful neighborhood where no one went anywhere after midnight, she saw to her surprise that a car drove by their house. A classic car, a Land Rover—the boxy old version of a Land Rover, a vintage model perfect down to every detail, including the spare tire (whitewashed, no less) on the front hood.

"Do you know anyone who owns one?" I asked.

She rolled her eyes. "My ex-husband Quentin, for one."

"He doesn't drive anymore, does he?"

"One would hope not. But he has live-ins. That body builder Dayva. That big lug Gormley. And, for that matter—though I'd hate to implicate him in any way—my stepson Star has been back and forth to the island in recent days."

We talked about the various possibilities and what they might mean. Why the people around Quentin Douglas would have an interest in throwing something through Clara Danville's window.

She believed Dayva wouldn't get involved in something like that. Dayva was too protective of herself to take a chance like that, and anyway she only put up with the old man for financial reasons. Gormley was a big lug who liked to knock people around, but he had a history of arrests already and was trying to keep clean.

Beatrice said that left just one person. Her stepson.

She folded her arms in front of her. "Star has struggled most of his adult life. He's been in and out of treatment centers, in and out of debt, in and mostly out of jobs. But what would he be doing, picking on a poor defenseless widow like that?"

I said I didn't know.

She sighed and said it was all a mystery.

Eileen showed up, poured another glass of the Meursault for each of us, and then retreated as usual to somewhere in the back of the apartment. Having been up quite early that morning to go out scalloping, and having jousted in-person and on the phone with McGuane, I was just about spent, and the excellent wine was threatening to send me floating off down a river of contented drowsiness.

It also engendered a different kind of river, and I asked Beatrice if I might visit their bathroom. She told me where it was and, once I was up and moving down the hall, she called out to Eileen to warn her that I was coming in her direction.

As I made my way past a back bedroom and then the laundry room, I came upon an Eileen I hadn't seen before. For once, the expression on her face lacked the peaceful contentment of a fine glass of Burgundy; she looked stressed and rushed. But why? She was simply stuffing something into a laundry basket. It was the *way* she was doing it that caught my attention: hastily, frantically, like . . .

Like someone with something to hide.

Had I imagined it, or was there something shaggy about the piece of clothing? At the very least, a messy fringe on the side? True, it could be a bathroom rug. But if so, why the haste?

"Sorry to intrude," I called out as I let myself into the bathroom and pulled the door shut behind me.

Whoosh. If there was a reply, I didn't hear it.

When I arrived at work the next morning, another envelope sat on my desk. By now I received them with a shrug of weariness.

THEY ARE LIKE IMAGES ON A SCREEN, TWO DIMENSIONS. THEY ARE PAINTED IN PLACE, THEY CANNOT ESCAPE TIME. TIME HAS PRESSED THEM IN PLACE, DRIED FLOWERS IN A BOOK. IN THE END WE ARE NOTHING BUT X-RAYS OF DEATH. AS YOU WILL BE IF YOU ARE NOT CAREFUL.

Right, thank you, I said. I folded it up and placed it back in its envelope. I was thinking about Eileen's behavior in the laundry room. And then I froze.

It suddenly occurred to me why I'd shivered when Eileen trained her dark eyes on me the night before, as she observed me sipping the Meursault.

The baseball bat and its inscription were off-limits even to share with a coworker, much less write an article about it. And the attack at the parade was off-limits for the paper.

But since the attack had been my experience, there was no rule against sharing it with a coworker.

Stefanie didn't even look up. "You done hiding things from me?"

"Not entirely. But there's something new I need to talk about with you."

She gestured to me to sit down.

As I told her about the assault on Luna at the Halloween parade, she set her mouth and shook her head. "Why isn't this at the top of page one this week?" she interrupted, and I explained McGuane's warnings about Luna's and Dorothy's safety. She sighed and said okay. I then told her about going over to see Beatrice, who had informed me about the sighting by a neighbor of the vintage Land Rover on the night of the break-in.

"Quentin Douglas has one of those. More than one. Ugly as sin in my book. White power and privilege incarnate."

"Quentin Douglas doesn't drive anymore. But Star does."

"Was he on-island the night of the assault?"

I said I didn't know.

She looked pained. "It all keeps adding up to Star, doesn't it?"

I agreed but pointed out that the wolf at the parade was on the slender side.

"That's not the Star I know," she grunted. "So is that it? A whole lot of yes and a little bit of no?"

I said there was something else.

Just before the wolf retreated from Main Street, I told her, it locked eyes with me for the briefest time, a second or less. They were dark eyes, eyes I felt I'd seen before.

And last night, when Beatrice's partner Eileen poured me a glass of Meursault, she watched me carefully as I tasted it, and as she did so, well, I shivered.

"You men. Doesn't matter to you what a woman's sexual preference might be."

I said the shiver was caused by something else: the dark eyes.

They might have been the same eyes.

I described walking past the laundry room and seeing Eileen stuffing something into a basket, something that might have been hairy . . . like a wolf costume.

Stefanie sat back and seemed to sink into herself. Finally she spoke.

"You're saying you think it was Beatrice's partner in that wolf suit?"

"It might have been," I replied. "She's the right body type."

"Is she tall enough?"

"It was dark, the wolf was bent over, but yes I think so."

"So, what do you want from me?"

I told her I was hoping she'd talk it through with me. What motivation would Beatrice and Eileen have?

She didn't even pause. "That's simple enough. If Beatrice is in the will, then eliminating a rival—her stepdaughter Luna—would leave a higher percentage for her."

"For that matter, so would framing her stepson," I added. "By dropping on us the story of the Land Rover."

"Maybe a Land Rover really was spotted that night—but driven by Beatrice, framing her stepson."

I placed the palms of my hands together and bowed to her. "You are slyer than I am. But I doubt Beatrice has a Land Rover."

"There's others on the island," she came back. For instance, a good friend of Beatrice's, a wealthy philanthropist named Cynthia Gamble, was known to have a collection of vintage Land Rovers that rivaled Quentin Douglas's.

"So what do I do now?" I asked.

Her eyes didn't even blink. "You go back to Beatrice's apartment tonight and find out."

"And how will I do that?"

She rearranged a few pieces of paper on her desk. "I can tell you how you won't do it. You won't take the direct approach. You won't go up to her and ask, 'Hey, Beatrice, did you and Eileen have fun at the Halloween parade? And do you still have the awesome wolf costume?' Because simple and direct won't work any better than it did when you presented yourself to Quentin Douglas. And got yourself some bonus flight miles for your pains."

She gave a muted laugh that sounded like a bent nail being yanked out of a piece of oak.

"I suppose if you ask a murderer, 'Did you do it?' they might choose not to reply with perfect honesty," I reflected.

"You may be onto something," she allowed.

"I'm rather proud that I figured this out all on my own." I gave a Sunday School smile.

She pointed a finger at me. "You'll be a real reporter one day, Christie. And maybe even a passable murder mystery writer, like your great-great-great-aunt-whoever."

The scallop lights shed their colors on the well-clad dummies, but the light didn't strike me tonight as festive. More like garish and eerie.

In my hands I held a bottle of Puligny-Montrachet—a village (I'd been told) that was famous for producing the very best white Burgundy. Stefanie had helped me track it down through a friend of hers who owned a wine store, and it cost well over a hundred dollars. "Make sure you get a few sips for yourself," she counseled.

Beyond the wine, I had no idea what I was planning to do. No brilliant plans had taken shape in my mind. I'd have to trust in my ability to improvise.

As Beatrice opened the large oak door, her face registered surprise. "Peter! What are you doing here?"

I told her I'd happened upon this wine, and after the two wonderful bottles they'd shared with me, I just had to return the favor.

She saw the label and nodded. "We won't turn you away." She called Eileen over and held up the bottle for her to see.

"A Puligny-Montrachet! A premier cru," Eileen whispered. She turned to me. "How'd you come into this? You tramp! Did you sleep with—" She mentioned the name of the woman who owned the wine shop.

I said, on the contrary, that I'd taken possession of the wine in the old-fashioned way—by paying for it.

"Then you have money," she replied.

"Or used to," I came back. "But I'm curious. I'm wondering how this one compares to the Saint-Aubin and the Meursault."

"Let us not delay the quest for truth." Eileen brought out three glasses and placed them on the smooth countertop. She popped the cork and poured out three glasses of the golden liquid. We clicked glasses and raised them to our lips.

Placing her glass back on the counter, Eileen tipped her head back and sighed deeply.

"We may describe her reaction as orgasmic," Beatrice told me, with a slight wrinkle of her eyebrows.

Eileen let out a languorous breath. "It's exquisite," she murmured. She turned her dark-cognac eyes on me, which brought another shiver from me. "But what do you think, Peter? How would you describe this wine?"

I pursed my lips. Come up with something good, Peter. "The Saint-Aubin was mineral, the Meursault was honey, but this is the best of both—the crispness of mineral, the soft seductiveness of honey. In short, a beverage for the gods."

"You are a born lover of wine," Eileen congratulated me. She leaned back and drained her glass.

As we made our way over to the sofa, Eileen brought along the bottle, and she soon filled our glasses again, emptying the bottle.

Beatrice settled back, crossed her legs beneath her, and asked, "How are you liking our little island, Peter?"

I said I appreciated the strong sense of community. That was something you couldn't find just anywhere.

Eileen replied that it was a good place for couples, but singles sometimes found it hard to meet someone on the island. It was nice that Haddie and I had found each other so quickly. She took a sip from her glass and added, "Though I understand from Beatrice that you're a bit on the outs?"

"More than a bit," I replied, and realized that there might be a way to turn this to advantage. I allowed my voice to take on a speculative tinge. "Haddie decided she needed some time and space. It's been a while since I've seen her. In fact, the other night at the Halloween parade, I was hoping I might run into her. Do you know if she was at the parade—that is, if you happened to be there?"

Eileen said they were there, and were passing out bags of candy to kids by the steps to the bank.

"I felt like I was one of the only adults who wasn't in costume," I said. "Did you find some good ones?"

Their costumes were okay, they were aliens of sorts, Beatrice explained, as Eileen excused herself for a moment and disappeared in the direction of the bathroom.

"Aliens are fun," I replied. We talked about the various versions of aliens that appear in popular culture: insect-like, squid-like, wolf-like, pudding-like. All with strangely elongated eyes and willowy limbs and creepy voices—

The conversation stopped. Because there in the hallway stood one of the hairiest aliens known to the universe.

Chewbacca let out one of its patented yowls or growls, took a step forward, and pulled off its head, revealing a human creature with short dark hair and beautiful cognac-colored eyes.

"This was me on Halloween," Eileen announced. "And Beatrice was my twin."

"Awesome," I replied.

"But there was an accident," Beatrice put in.

"Yes, an accident. A little boy got too excited when he saw me, or maybe it was the candy, but anyway he peed. And I mean peed. All over me."

"So Peter, when you came over the next night and had the Meursault—"

"We had the costume still hanging by the shower to dry off—"

"But then you went back to use the bathroom—"

"And I grabbed it, took it down, and was stuffing it away in the dirty laundry when you came by—"

"Because it still smelled—"

"And we had yet to wash it—"

"Which we did today."

"And now I am taking this horrid thing off because I'm too hot, and I'm going to open another bottle of Saint-Aubin," Beatrice concluded.

And that was that.

After a few sips of the new wine, I said goodbye and took myself home.

I lit a fire in the stove and laid out on my desk the odd messages I'd received over the past several weeks:

THE DARK SIDE OF THE MOON HAS MORE SECRETS THAN MEETS THE EYE.

THE MARSH HAS A STRANGE SILENCE IN THE MOONLIGHT. BUT SILENT TOO ARE THE TADPOLES BEFORE THEIR MOMENT OF TRANSFORMATION.

PEOPLE SAY, "I OWN THIS LAND." DON'T THEY REALIZE THE LAND BELONGS TO THE GHOSTS THAT WANDER THE BEACH AS THE FOG ROLLS IN?

NOTHING STAYS BURIED FOREVER.

I READ THIS SOMEWHERE: ANIMALS DECEIVE ONE ANOTHER BUT THEY NEVER LIE. HUMANS LIE BUT IN THE END THEY NEVER DECEIVE ONE ANOTHER. WHAT IF BOTH ARE AS FALSE AS DECLARATIONS OF ETERNAL LOVE?

THEY ARE LIKE IMAGES ON A SCREEN, TWO DIMENSIONS. THEY ARE PAINTED IN PLACE, THEY CANNOT ESCAPE TIME. TIME HAS PRESSED THEM IN PLACE, DRIED FLOWERS IN A BOOK. IN THE END WE ARE NOTHING BUT X-RAYS OF DEATH. AS YOU WILL BE IF YOU ARE NOT CAREFUL.

Early on, I'd thought they might be whimsical little messages from Dorothy, random flowerings of the weirdness of early adolescence. With someone who was "different," as she was said to be, those flowerings seemed likely to take unusual forms.

But knowing Dorothy better now, I no longer believed she could have written them. And over time, the messages had grown less whimsical and more pointed and hostile—almost certainly the products of an older, more disturbed person. The welter of themes was troubling: darkness, silence, deceit, threats, and death in two dimensions, no less.

Do you see who wrote them? the voice asked. *And why?*

And suddenly—yes, I did.

The assertions of a grandiose ego were too glaring to ignore. These messages could only be coming from one person: the author of the poems.

I'd probably missed the parallels because the messages weren't written in the British heroic mode. They were closer to the ancient veiled idiom of seers and prophet. But they showed roughly the same level of literary skill as the poems.

And of self-importance.

But why had they been sent to me?

Maybe the killer knew that I—a lowly local reporter—was nevertheless staging an investigation of the murder for reasons both professional and personal. Maybe, somehow, they knew I wasn't about to stop. And so, with an odd flourish of venom and virtuosity, tailoring their messages to my penchant for mystery and literary forms, they were telling me in no uncertain terms to cease and desist.

But that wasn't about to happen. There would be no more running away.

CHAPTER FOURTEEN

One by one, the suspects had fallen by the wayside.

Luna looked like a fearsome Nordic goddess, but at heart she was a gentle artist, a weaver of surprising sensitivity, and her love for Dorothy helped to soften any rough edges (though I suspected she could be a mama bear when necessary). Her reaction to the attack by the wolflike creature had been to go into some form of shock. She wasn't one to attack someone else. Like her daughter, she told her own truth and lived by her own lights.

Beatrice and Eileen were too into their playful ways and their white Burgundy to be killers. The fluffy dirty laundry had turned out to be a complete red herring—twin Chewbaccas, not a lone rampaging wolf. And anyway, out of all the possible suspects, they were the only ones who seemed genuinely happy with their lives as they were.

Steph Sylvan had no real motivation. Behind that beard he did strike me as a bitter guy, but whatever hostility he projected, it seemed focused not on Douglas or Danville, but on just about everyone he met—including his friend Bob Brown. The early-morning dustups with Quentin Douglas about his scallop boat hadn't flared up recently.

Dayva Johnson projected steadiness and integrity. Furthermore, she was too scrupulous of her image, too careful in her words and actions, to be so rash as to commit a crime—even if she wanted to, which I doubted. She had a brand to protect, and she wasn't about to damage it. And besides, she may have been confident of her place in the will.

Bruce Gormley was just a big lug. He was good at initiating wingless human flight, but didn't have the motivation or the brains to plan out a murder.

Bob Brown was something of a conundrum. He was selfish and self-righteous. He was truly despicable in the way he talked to women, and he had a track record of getting violent when drunk. Not only when drunk—he wasn't drunk when he plowed into Luna on the basepath. But he did have other sides that spoke better of him—for instance, the way he showed genuine solicitude for his classmate Rozzie when she was injured on the softball field. Not to mention the fact that he had saved my life and seemed almost embarrassed about it afterward. He was smarter than he liked to let on—which, of course, could cut in either direction. And it was worth remembering that he had showed simmering anger toward Chester Danville for his role on the summer rental committee and its potential impact on Brown's income. Given all of this, I had to conclude that Brown was still a suspect, though not the main suspect.

Because there was Star.

I knew Stefanie would hold to her belief that her friend Star was no murderer. She felt sorry for him: he was a creature of the moment, unable to hold on to a decent life, prone to substance abuse and erratic swings of behavior. She thought his combination of qualities let him off the hook. But couldn't those same qualities have led him to commit a murder of passion? Star must have known that Chester Danville was poised to make changes to the will that would benefit himself and cut out Star.

Star would have recognized Chester Danville in the yard that night. (No way he would have thought it was his father.) He would have been able to guess Danville's intent—to secure an extra bag or two of gold as a way to jump-start a new life with his lover, Jenny Dyer.

But why would Star have poisoned the dogs, when they surely knew him and wouldn't bark at him? I resurrected an earlier theory: maybe he poisoned the dogs to shift the attention to someone outside the family.

The rest of the evidence was even more incriminating. The sighting of the Land Rover near Clara Danville's house could implicate Star—assuming he was on the island at the time, which I couldn't corroborate but which seemed likely. More telling was the baseball bat tossed through Clara's window, and that puzzling line, *The flawless bloodlines set by birth.* The only people with "flawless bloodlines" were Star, Luna, and Dorothy.

Finally, the blood sample on the tip of the bat matched the victim's DNA. And let's not forget whose fingerprints were found on it.

It all added up to Star.

I knew Stefanie would try to talk me down to her reality. I had to work through this on my own.

But how? I had no plan for contacting Star. No plan but to take a walk on the beach early the next morning and hope to shake out some evidence.

Just a few weeks had passed since I'd last parked the Jeep at the end of the rutted sandy road, but it seemed like months. The air was much colder. There was a slight crunch of ice in the bracken that littered the cinder trail to the beach.

The water of the harbor was a color I hadn't seen before, a pale, almost transparent shade of green. I'd heard that the plunging temperatures killed much of the microscopic life that gave the water its deep blue of summer.

The shoreline was littered with more shells than before, mostly empty scallop and hermit crab shells. The sand above the water looked darker and grainier as winter approached.

Some fifty yards down the beach, I came to the Douglas estate. The clapboard-covered home loomed massive and unassailable in the lambent late-fall light—the steeply pitched roof with its widow's walk on top, the three large gables dominating the harbor, the dark mahogany deck.

By contrast, the path that led from the beach toward the house was simple and modest, a sandy path winding between the scrub oaks and viburnum bushes, brown and bare.

I took a breath, buried my hands in my pockets as if to declare the absence of any ulterior motives, and followed the gentle curves toward the Douglas lawn.

Had I imagined it, or did something blink in one of the upstairs rooms? Quick as a shuttle—the motion of someone by a window?

Any reaction was good. The point of my plan was to be seen. To lure Star out of hiding, one way or another.

I came to the still-lush lawn and made my way across it to a midpoint, where I imagined the digging had taken place the morning of the murder. And sure enough, though it was barely discernible, I could make out the outline of some replanted chunks of sod. It had been cut with care, in nice rectangles about two feet by three feet, and then replaced with equal care. Any evidence of disruption would surely disappear by next spring once the grass rerooted and reestablished itself.

The digging had taken place over an area of about four feet by twelve feet. The rest of the lawn looked undisturbed.

Several yards closer to the house, a manhole cover glimmered in the sunlight, keeping watch over an underground propane tank. I recalled being told in the newsroom that in the past year on the island there had been two separate explosions of propane tanks, and each explosion had leveled two or three nearby houses. At least this tank was protected and safe.

A few feet from me, something shiny caught my eye, and I bent down and picked up a small metal tool. It was about three inches long, round on top, with two projecting legs at the bottom. It looked for all the world like a poorly designed bottle opener.

I was about to place it in my pocket when I realized that a small precious stone was embedded in the round bulge at the top. I tilted it in the sunlight and saw that it glimmered with the clear, true light of a diamond.

"How curious," I said to myself.

"You like it?" a voice from behind me inquired.

"Very much," I replied, not turning around. Best to show no sense of alarm.

"Do you know what it is?"

"It's a bottle opener that never grew up," I said. "A case of arrested development, I'd guess."

"Speaking of arrested, I could have you arrested if I wanted." A massive person sauntered around in front of me and planted himself a few feet away.

"Hi, Star," I said. "Fancy meeting like this."

He looked me up and down. A grim smirk lurked on his face. "Digging for treasure, or for a story?" he asked.

"Well, I wouldn't mind either—but to be truthful, I'm here for the story."

He held out his hand. "I knew I'd dropped that somewhere."

I placed the piece of metal in his hand.

"You don't know what it is, do you?" He explained that it was a golfing tool, used to repair the divots or dents that a ball made when it landed on a green. "You've never played?" he asked.

I told him no, that softball was the extent of my sporting life. As I spoke, I tried to reconstruct how he'd been able to sneak up on me. He must have been out for a walk, I figured. I also wondered what storm of accusations or violence awaited me once he cracked through his thin shell of civility and entered the next phase of his behavior.

"Stefanie asked me to come over and chat with you to help clear up some rumors," I told him.

"Hogwash. Stefanie told you to stay away. And she knows there are no rumors."

"What about the Land Rover that was seen driving by Clara Danville's house the night the bat was tossed through her front window?" I countered.

He frowned. "Bat? What bat? I didn't hear about any bat."

Too late I realized my mistake. "Maybe it wasn't a bat. I just figured, if you threw something, it must have been a bat. Weren't you a star baseball player—um, no pun intended, okay?"

The use of humor as a bonding agent clearly wouldn't work with him. His eyes were narrowing, and he seemed about to enter the enraged state.

"Whatever you're babbling about, I had nothing to do with it. Zero. And for the record, I haven't driven one of my father's Land

Rovers for over thirty years—and I haven't played ball for longer than that. Not with these shoulders." He rubbed one of his shoulders. "Frozen. For years," he added.

I hoped another question might delay the rage. "You were aware, weren't you, that Chester Danville was about to amend the will? And cut you out of it entirely?" There was no point in not going for the whole thing in one fell swoop, I figured.

"What the heck are you talking about, Christie? What do you know about my father's will?"

"I know that Danville needed money for his new lifestyle. I know that he was planning to make changes that would benefit him personally. I know—everybody knows—that you caught him in the act of trying to dig up some gold and silver for his own purposes."

"You don't know the first thing."

"And I know that you have a temper, Star. One that might lead you to commit an assault, possibly a fatal assault if it went too far, on someone who was stealing family property." I stood there, looking him in the eyes, telling myself to be ready for what was coming.

But instead of punching me or taking me down, he bent over and started laughing. It was a good laugh, an easy laugh, a long laugh. It was at least half a minute before he stood up again and brandished a finger in my direction.

"You really don't know, do you?!" he exclaimed. "You really don't know what was going on, and why. Why the will was being changed. Why our father lived in fear for all those months. Why he told Danville to dress up like him and go outside and dig up some of the bags of gold."

"No, I don't," I admitted.

"Oh what the heck, I'll tell you," he said. "What happened was—"

But in mid-sentence, there was a ping or a zip, and he ceased his talking. A line of blood dribbled out of the side of his mouth. He threw a confused look in my direction and hurtled to the ground.

A vortex spun, time and space whooshed away.

And I fell to the ground beside him.

By the time the police and the ambulance arrived, Star's body was already cold. It must have been fifteen minutes. Maybe longer, maybe shorter, I couldn't tell. Dayva came out of the house first, clutching her hands to her mouth and moaning in horror and sorrow, and soon thereafter the old man appeared, stumbling across the lawn in his walker—as always, swathed in his Red Sox hat and sweatpants. He stopped near his son and did the last thing I expected. His face curled up and he leaned over toward the ground and started blubbering like a baby. Dayva went over and put her arms around him.

Bruce Gormley appeared and walked Douglas slowly back inside. Dayva stayed outside with me. She said she'd witnessed it all and asked if I had caught a glimpse of the shooter. Of course, I hadn't.

After the medics confirmed that Star was deceased, the police took me aside, frisked me, and asked me what I knew. After I spoke, Dayva joined us and confirmed that she'd been watching out the window and that I had, in fact, been engaged in a conversation with Star at the time. She said the shot seemed to have come from somewhere in the woods. Soon after that I was released on my own recognizance.

As I was preparing to leave, someone called to Dayva in a desperate voice and she ran inside. A few minutes later, a second ambulance roared up to the house and Quentin Douglas was carried out on a stretcher. Dayva saw me across the lawn and mouthed the word, "stroke."

I trudged back down the beach in a dream and found my way to the Jeep. It wasn't until I sat down that I realized I was shaking all over. I leaned forward, buried my head in my arms, and sobbed uncontrollably.

About an hour later I was able to drive back to the newsroom. I shadow-walked inside. Stefanie saw me come in and lifted her hand in acknowledgement. She had a tissue in her hands and was dabbing her eyes.

"Are you all right?" she asked as I flowed up to her desk. She stood up, came around, and gave me a hug.

"Who the heck knows anymore," I replied.

"I can't believe this happened—" she began, but pulled back and stopped as tears overtook her. She gestured to me to sit down. "I can't help it," she said, as she took her seat again. "I always thought of him as a good friend."

"I'm sorry," I said, and added that I hoped it wasn't my fault. She told me it wasn't; a killer was on the loose and no one was safe anymore. She just wanted to be sure I got any help I needed. I was grateful that she chose not to remind me I'd visited the Douglas place without authorization, and in fact in violation of her directions.

You can trust her, the voice said. *She understands your struggles.*

"I know," I said out loud.

"You know? You know what?" Stefanie asked.

"Sorry," I said. "Sometimes a little voice talks to me. Maybe a wire is loose in my head, it's probably just my own thoughts."

She shook your head, "It's your spirit guide. I have one," she told me.

"It is?"

"Do you trust what it says?"

"Always," I replied.

"It's your spirit guide. Don't ignore what it tells you. You're lucky to have one."

"Does yours help you?"

"Only when I need it the most."

She tapped me on the arm and asked me if I wanted to go home, and I said no. If it was all right, I'd rather remain in the newsroom. She said that would probably be for the best. As I returned to my desk, she bought me a cup of coffee. From time to time, when I looked over at her, she was still in tears. I had to pat my own face now and then.

Late that afternoon I got an unexpected phone call. Beatrice was on the line, wondering how I was. If I didn't want to be alone that night, would I like to come stay with her and Eileen?

That sounded perfect, and I spent the night in their spare bedroom (after the three of us polished off two bottles of Meursault). On either side of me on the bed, the newly washed Chewbacca costumes sat at attention like twin guardians.

Detective McGuane called me in first thing the next morning and wasn't so solicitous of my feelings.

"What gave you the right to pay a surprise visit to my prime suspect?" he began.

I told him I still wasn't convinced that Star was the one, and I went there to get something, anything—to dig down deeper if I could.

"They'll be digging deeper all right—six feet under."

When I bowed my head, he relented a bit. "Okay, this wasn't your fault. But I need to know what happened. Tell me everything."

I told him about walking down the beach, coming up the path to the lawn, and finding the personalized diamond-studded metal tool, which apparently was something golfers used to repair greens. I described how Star took me by surprise, which meant that he had probably been out for a walk, and I told him that Star and I talked.

"Anything unexpected in that?" McGuane asked.

"Yeah, there was," I replied. "Star was about to tell me why the will was being changed, why his father had been living in fear, and why he'd ordered Chester Danville to dig up some of the gold, when—" I paused for a breath.

"Well, I'll be," he muttered. "You were about to break the case."

"It was headed that way."

"Or maybe Star was making something up on the spot."

I agreed that was possible too.

He grunted. "Well, at least we know one thing. Whoever shot Star had been tracking him on his walk. By the way, I hope you aren't blaming yourself for this, Christie," he continued.

"I guess I am. The only reason he stood still was because I was there."

"That's no issue either way. A good shot can hit someone who's walking, it's not even an issue."

"For real?"

"For real."

I nodded.

He shook his head. "You didn't do any damage, Christie. And maybe, in your unconventional way, you've given us something to go on. By the way, have you heard anything more about the old man?"

I said I'd heard it was a stroke, and he shook his head again. "It was a seizure. He's resting still in the hospital, he'll need a day or two more, but he's expected to recover fully. At least as fully as any ninety-year-old-plus can recover. Maybe he'll be able to tell us something next week. Something to shed a little light on this."

He let out his breath in a rush. "A son murdered, a daughter almost murdered." He saw my reaction and added, "Speaking of which, we got back the analysis. It was like we thought, rat poison. Strychnine. Enough to take down a 130-pound human."

I wondered if there were any prints. No, he said. Just mine and Dorothy's.

"What's next?" I asked.

He said he didn't know. He gazed off into the distance. "I do have one question. If the murderer wasn't Star, how in the world did his fingerprints get on that bat?"

On the way to the newspaper, I stopped at a coffee shop. And when I came out, who was sitting in a red pickup truck, chatting, but Bob Brown and Steph Sylvan. Sylvan was in the driver's seat.

Brown pointed a finger at me like a gun and, as I flinched, he rolled down his window and gave a rough laugh.

"There he is, the man of the hour," he commented. "How's it feel to be famous?"

"Not so great, if you want to know the truth."

Brown turned to Sylvan. "This guy was standing right next to Star Douglas when he got shot."

"This guy was there?" Sylvan asked through his big dark beard. "This guy?"

"Yeah, they were chatting about the weather or something," Brown said. "That's what I heard from my buddy at the station."

"The weather. That must've been one scintillating conversation," Sylvan observed.

"I guess it was," I acknowledged.

"That poor jerk, Star. Never had a chance in life," Brown said.

"What do you mean?" I asked.

"No one liked him growing up. He was the rich kid no one wanted to play with."

"I heard he was a good ballplayer," Sylvan put in.

"Didn't help him any. Girls didn't like him, he was creepy and needy. Guys thought he was a loser. He tried to buy his way to get friends, but everybody stayed clear of him."

"He seemed okay to me," I said. "Maybe he had his demons, but he was honest about a lot of things."

"Are you saying you knew him?" Sylvan asked. "He told you his secrets about the lifestyles of the rich and famous?"

"No, not really," I replied. "I never got to know him much. I'm not even sure he was that honest. It's just a feeling I had about him." Even to myself, my thoughts weren't making any sense. Was this PTSD?

"We all have feelings," Sylvan agreed.

"You know, Christie, in the past few weeks you've had two close calls," Brown told me. "Death by water—check. Death by gunshot—check. What's next?"

"Death by fire," Sylvan quipped.

"Nothing, I hope. Thanks to you, the water didn't get me. And as far as yesterday, I don't know if I was in danger—"

"You were standing right next to him. Could of been you."

"I guess you're right. I've been lucky," I offered.

"Maybe the Douglas kid was *unlucky*. Maybe they were trying to shoot you and they missed," Sylvan suggested.

His voice was so cold and unsympathetic, I turned toward him in annoyance. But he started laughing and raised his hand and flapped it at me. "Hey man, don't get all bent out of shape. Just trying to inject a little humor into this for you."

Brown gave him a shove. "You need an injection yourself, you turkey. Something to quiet your evil little mind."

"Who's the one here with the evil mind?" Sylvan came back. "Wouldn't that be you, Bobby Brown? Our Lord Shiva, savior of skinny scallopers and death of fat cats?"

"You keep running your mouth and I'll be the death of you, you freak!" Brown told him. They were still arguing as they drove off in the old red Tacoma with the bumper sticker you saw everywhere now, *It used to be nice on the island.*

The prime suspect was dead and Bob Brown, the alternate suspect, was so full of himself and his self-regard and his hodgepodge of opinions that it seemed unlikely he could have found the time to murder anyone. Had the pool of suspects run dry?

Not yet, I realized. It had only seemed to run dry because I'd let someone fall off my radar.

Anthony Dyer.

How could I have lost sight of that flash of anger behind his eyes? We all know that revenge is the simplest and cleanest of all motives. It was certainly enough to explain the death of Chester Danville. True, there was no clear path to connect Dyer to the attack on Luna and the murder of Star. But one peripheral detail did match: He was slender enough to have been the person in the wolf suit.

What motive could he have had for taking out Luna or Star? After all, they'd had nothing to do with his wife's affair. Unless . . .

What if Dyer thought they'd been in on it somehow? As friends of Danville—maybe even as enablers?

It was possible. But where was the evidence?

Then it hit me.

The metal device I'd found on the lawn, the tool for repairing divots on golf greens. Earlier in the month, when Dyer came to the apartment to look at the Morso stove, didn't he finger something in his pocket and take it out—and didn't it sparkle, sort of like the tool I found on the lawn?

In our brief encounter a minute or two before his death, Star took the tool from me and acted like it was his, but was it really? He'd told me he had chronic frozen shoulders. If so, how could he still be playing golf?

If the metal piece belonged to Dyer, it wasn't just a coincidence that it had ended up on Douglas's lawn.

Maybe Dyer had come earlier in the day, seeking revenge. And maybe, without knowing it, he'd dropped the divot tool. I'd seen him pull it out of his pocket for no reason, it might have been a habit of his. It could have tumbled to the soft turf on the Douglas lawn without his realizing it.

And there was one more piece of supporting evidence. Dyer was the captain of a shooting club. He must be a decent shot with a gun.

But how could Star and Luna have helped Danville in his affair with Jenny Dyer? By all accounts, the two lovers had been off on their own, blissfully entangled in the stacks of the Historical Association Library.

There was someone who might have an answer.

Dayva opened the door just wide enough to peer out at me.

"You again?" she asked.

"Yep. It's me."

"What now?"

"I'm trying to figure out what happened."

"Yeah? Join the club."

"Would you mind if I ask you a question?"

Maybe the near brush with death had given me some standing in her eyes. Her eyes narrowed the slightest bit. "Go ahead."

I asked if she thought Star or Luna could have been involved in any way in greasing the wheels for the affair between Jenny Dyer and Chester Danville. He was a relative, a friend, the family lawyer—had they enabled the relationship somehow? Maybe by providing a meeting place for the two lovers, for instance?

She pulled me inside and closed the door.

"Star found a room for them," she said in a quiet voice. "It started after Anthony Dyer learned of the affair. Chester and his lady couldn't go on as before, they needed somewhere new. At the time, Chester was helping out Star and Mr. Douglas with something big. What it was, I have no idea," she added, in response to a look I gave her. "And in return, Star let Chester and Jenny use a bedroom in the basement."

I wondered if Luna had also been involved somehow. "That wasn't very likely, was it?" I asked. "Didn't she keep her distance from her father and everything he represented?"

That was true, Dayva replied. But Luna was a longtime friend of Jenny's, and sometime in late summer she began to chauffer Jenny to the house, with Jenny crouched down in the back seat, dressed up like a teenager. Like Dorothy.

She gave me a look. "You're not gonna cause any trouble about this, are you?"

I promised her I wouldn't. "Just getting to the truth," I said.

"Uh-hu," she replied.

Stefanie shook her head. "You have no real proof. I wish you would believe me, it's not Anthony." A few days had passed since the latest murder. Her eyes were dry, and it seemed like she'd made a conscious effort to return to her starchy, professional comportment.

"There's some pretty suggestive evidence." I ran down the list.

"I don't buy it. He's not the type. Too brittle."

"Revenge. It's the classic motivation."

"Let Anthony be," she told me. She adjusted her glasses. "Not that you ever obey me anymore." The look in her large eyes was almost sympathetic. But weary.

"I can't do nothing," I protested.

She brightened up a bit and told me she'd read and approved the two stories I'd written. They were quite good, she said. The first was the main story—a report on the murder and its continuing aftermath. The second was an eyewitness account, which she'd suggested I could try if I felt up to it. As it turned out, I found the act of writing to be strangely liberating. But I wasn't sure how the island would react to it.

As I climbed into my cold bed late that night, I was still thinking about Anthony Dyer. There was one thing that didn't add up. Did Dyer really seem like someone who could have written the poems and the messages? Yet what else did I have to go on? In the morning, I would press forward.

But I couldn't do it alone.

CHAPTER FIFTEEN

A Second Murder Stuns the Island
Murderer still at large
BY PETER CHRISTIE

November 6 Star Douglas, one of two children of the retired commodities trader Quentin Douglas, was murdered this week on the lawn outside the stately waterfront mansion that belongs to his father. Death came with a single shot and was thought to be fired by a sniper who was sequestered in the surrounding woods.

This is the second murder on the island in the past month, and local police say they are working around the clock to solve the cases. In some quarters, Star had been discussed as a possible suspect in the first murder—of lawyer Chester Danville—but police now claim those rumors were never taken seriously. But with the death of Star, the investigation seems at least temporarily stymied.

According to local health care providers, anxiety in the town is rising to dangerous levels.

[See a related story below for an eyewitness account of that event. Warning: The story contains graphic details of a violent crime.]

Stefanie wasn't the only one whose eyes regarded me with weariness.

"What is it, Christie?" It was a look someone might give a brother-in-law who was asking for a personal loan.

I asked McGuane if he agreed it was time to reassess who was the main suspect. A muscle twitched in his jaw but he said nothing. As he listened in silence, I laid out the evidence that pointed toward Anthony Dyer.

"The divot repair tool is interesting," he commented after I finished. He asked me again to describe where I'd found it and where it was now. I said Star had dropped it into his pocket, so maybe it was with his personal effects at the funeral home.

"The coroner is working on this now. Caliber, type of rifle, etc. All his personal stuff will be over there."

He acknowledged that the information from Dayva was also of interest. Depending on the identity of the murderer, someone who'd assisted in the smooth operations of the affair could conceivably be a target for revenge. He said Dyer was a crack marksman and agreed that his size and frame matched my description of the figure in the wolf costume.

But he, like Stefanie, said he didn't see how Anthony Dyer could do something like this.

"Stress. People do strange things when they're in agony," I argued. "None of us is immune."

McGuane's face looked fleshier and paler than I remembered. He too was under stress.

"What do you suggest? That you and I visit Dyer in his workshop and ask him if he committed two murders and just missed pay dirt on a third?"

"Something like that," I replied.

Then he surprised me. "All right, get in the cruiser." He glowered at me.

Star's body lay large and lifeless on a table off to the side of the wide, dingy room, and the coroner was sitting at a desk, pecking away at his typewriter. He and McGuane talked a few minutes, after which the coroner took McGuane off to the side and handed him a plastic bag containing the divot repair tool. McGuane nodded at me to get back into the cruiser.

On an island this small, everybody knew where everyone else worked, and McGuane was able to drive us right to Dyer's shop.

It was a big garage-like building with a metal front door. Inside, row after row of work tables bristled with every imaginable kind of saws and drill presses and lathes and some other machines I didn't recognize. Tools were hung along the walls with scrupulous care and a consummate sense of order: hammers, screwdrivers, carpenter squares, levels, drill bits, super-sharp metal hole punchers, hand saws, pliers of every description, shears, and rulers. I was reminded of my father's shop, in his heyday as a builder and designer.

Dyer stood at one of the work tables. He didn't seem surprised to see McGuane. "Good morning, Rick," he said, with a curt nod. It was the first time I'd heard McGuane's first name said out loud. Dyer then tossed his head in my direction. "Why's he here?"

"He's helping me," McGuane said.

"Helping you."

"That's right."

"Doesn't he write for the paper?"

"This is off the record. For the time being, he's my assistant."

Dyer's eyes washed over me and left a residue of sticky disgust.

McGuane pulled something out of his pocket and tapped it down on the work table. "So, Anthony, tell me about this," he said.

Dyer picked up the plastic bag and examined its contents. "That's my divot repair tool. I wondered where it was."

"It's a nice one. Is that a diamond?"

"Sure is. The Club gave it to me for being a commodore for twenty-five years."

"Nice of them. You wanna know where we found it?"

Dyer said he did.

"On the Douglas lawn. Right on top of the treasure that was dug up last month."

"How in the world did it get there?" Dyer wondered.

"I was hoping you'd tell me that."

Then it returned: the flash of anger in his eyes that I'd seen a few weeks earlier. "What are you getting at?" he demanded.

McGuane shrugged. "Nothing much, I guess—if you can tell me something more."

Dyer turned toward him and his throat seemed to swell like a lizard's. "There's nothing for me to tell. I've been missing this thing for over a week now."

"Come on, Anthony, help me out here. Why'd we find it in Douglas's yard?"

"I have no idea," Dyer replied.

"Were you walking around there the other day, maybe? Like you went for a walk in town, and somehow you ended up on the Douglas lawn?"

"No. I haven't been there in . . . in weeks."

"In weeks. When were you there last—and why?"

"A month ago. You know why."

"Anthony, let's be real. Two people were murdered there. Your diamond-studded divot repair tool happens to be sitting in the exact spot of the two deaths. Am I supposed to believe that this is just a coincidence?"

"Like I said, I know nothing about it." Dyer tried to turn back to his work.

"Did the tool hop out of your pocket when you were on the links and walk on its two stubby legs over to the Douglas property? Is that what you expect me to believe?"

"I'm telling you I don't know anything about this," Dyer said. "And I'm telling you to leave my premises now. And I mean right now. Because this is all a frame job, and I'm getting a lawyer before I talk to you again."

McGuane gave me a look. Let's go.

On our way out, I spotted a gun rack in the corner. Seven or eight rifles of various sizes, stashed as neatly as stalks of corn.

We drove most of the way back to the station in silence. Finally McGuane grunted and said, "Poor guy."

I asked him what Dyer had meant when he said McGuane knew why he'd been on the property several weeks earlier.

"Sometime before the first murder, Dayva Johnson made a 911 call. An intruder on the lawn. It was Dyer, he'd figured out what was going on inside that house. When the cruiser pulled up, he admitted to what he was doing and agreed to leave. He was crying his eyes out, the guys felt sorry for him. No charges were pressed."

"Not a guy who looked like he was out for revenge?"

"Not at that time."

"He sure has a nice assortment of rifles in the corner of the shop."

"Yeah, well, we have to wait for the report from the coroner. Once that's in, we can take a look at the rifles if we need to."

When we were almost to the station, McGuane told me there was something he'd been wondering about. What about the literary side of things—did Dyer strike me as somebody who could compose a poem in the British hero style?

I told him I'd been wondering the same thing, and I thought no. But so far, that was the only piece that didn't seem to fit.

"Maybe it's not as important as I once thought," he commented.

On that, as in so many other things, reality was about to weigh in.

An early evening visit to a grocery store on a small island is more than just a shopping trip; it's a time to reconnect. And it shows the good and the bad of small-town life.

In the produce section I ran into Beatrice and Eileen, who were looking over the baby bok choy and discussing whether or not it looked healthy enough. They thought the color looked artificial; it was a darker green than the bok choy they usually purchased at the organic store. Since I'd stayed with them so recently, there wasn't much need to catch up. Instead, Eileen and I had a quick and friendly exchange, a debate about which was better, Saint-Aubin or Meursault. She still favored the former and I the latter.

In the dairy aisle I came upon Bruce Gormley, picking out a quart of low-fat milk and scowling. A nod of hello from me, a grunted hello howyadoin' from him. I refrained from making any references to the pleasures of wingless air travel. This encounter, though quite brief, led to a surprise. Being next to him gave me a new and different view of him. He wasn't just a big slab of a man. There was something radically untrustworthy about him, something that could spawn betrayal in several different directions, maybe even at the same time—if my intuition was to be trusted.

And then, at the meat counter, I found Luna and Dorothy discussing the quality of some chicken that was on sale. Since Star's murder we hadn't seen each other, and Luna looked pale and stricken. She gave me a big hug and said she'd been worried about me. I told her I was doing okay and asked how she was. She just shook her head and gazed off to the side. Her ice-blue eyes had melted toward watery. Dorothy hopped over and gave me a hug as well. She held on longer than I expected, and when I pulled back, I found I was face-to-face with someone new: Bob Brown.

His breath smelled of liquor and his eyes, small and crafty, spoke of trouble. "Well, looky who's here," he exclaimed. "It's the drowning duo."

"The drowning duo?" Luna returned.

"And the loser who wouldn't get out of the basepath," he added with one of his patented smirks.

Dorothy pushed right up to him. "Don't you call my mother a loser."

"You be quiet, little girl. Maybe I shouldn't have saved you."

I asked Brown if he would mind cooling it, we're all just here to shop. He gave me a quick, insinuating look. "The peacemaker, huh? Is that how you see yourself?"

"There's worse things to be," I said.

"Your breath stinks," Dorothy told him. "And you stink too." Luna pulled her back and established herself in front of Brown.

"Well, look out people, Momma Bear is here," Brown observed.

"Darn right I am," Luna replied. The expression on her face was turning dangerous. "Don't you dare come a step closer."

"I do what I want," he came back.

"Not when I'm here you don't."

Brown waved a dismissive hand toward her. "You people are as crazy as bedbugs. And not even half as cute." He lunged past Luna and chucked Dorothy on the chin. "Except for you, sweetheart," he lisped. "You're not so bad." Dorothy let out a yowl, and Luna jumped onto Brown. And that's how the fight began.

In less than a minute it was over. Brown was a big, strong guy, but Luna was a fury, and before you knew it, she had Brown pinned on the ground, with her arm around his neck and one of his arms twisted painfully behind him.

"You're not getting up till you apologize to my daughter," she seethed.

"Not gonna happen," Brown muttered. She wrenched his arm farther and he groaned in pain.

"Say you're sorry," she repeated. "Tell my daughter you're sorry."

"I'm sorry," Brown murmured.

"Tell her you won't violate her space ever again."

Brown remained silent, and Luna tightened the torture one more notch.

"I won't violate her space," he spat out.

Luna released him and stood up over him in a wide stance. "You better believe you won't. And you'll stop bullying the women of this island—or next time you won't be getting up because next time you'll be dead."

Bob Brown took an inventory of his body parts and raised himself to his knees. From there he leveraged himself onto his feet.

"Look around you—there's witnesses all around. You just assaulted me. And then threatened to kill me. And you wonder why the whole island is saying that you're the murderer." He looked like he was going to say something more but Luna took a step toward him and he shut his mouth, turned, and limped away.

The bullet in Star Douglas was a close enough match to Anthony Dyer's collection of rifles, and the next day McGuane ordered them all brought in for testing. I found myself thinking more about Dyer. He'd seemed genuinely surprised to learn that his divot tool was found on Douglas's lawn. Was he telling the truth when he said he hadn't been there in several weeks? How else could it have gotten there?

That left me wondering about another matter that McGuane had brought up recently. Star Douglas's fingerprints had been found all over the bat that was tossed in through Clara Danville's window. But with Star's death, he was no longer a suspect, and the murderer was clearly still at large. So what were Star's prints doing on the bat?

On my lunch break I looked up the number of a local accounting firm and placed a call. Someone picked up after one ring.

"Ramos Accounting."

"Hey, Rozzie, it's me, Peter Christie."

"Peter Christie! Star third baseman! I've been thinking about you. You've had quite a time of it recently, haven't you?" She asked me about the near-fatal scalloping outing and then, a bit more gingerly, about Star's death. We talked a while and then I said, speaking of Star, I had an odd question to ask. Did she know if he'd ever come to any of the softball games this season?

"You wonder if you ever met him before?"

"Yeah, something like that."

She said Star had been known to show up at games sometimes, in fact he was a sponsor of one the teams. "I think it's the Great Whites," she said. "Oh yes, it is the Great Whites. If I'm remembering this right, he made an appearance before one of the games earlier this fall, but once the game got going, he disappeared. You may have heard, for the past several years, seeing Star was like seeing a ghost."

"He was an outstanding ballplayer in high school, I guess."

"In his day he was a heck of an athlete. Even this season, people were still asking him for batting tips."

"And I guess Luna was also a star athlete. Lacrosse?"

"That's right."

"The Douglas blood must contain some serious athletic genes."

"Maybe. I hear the old man still gets around pretty good, despite everything."

I asked if she had heard about Luna and Bob Brown getting in a fight in the grocery store, and she said she had. In fact, she'd tracked Brown down afterward and told him in no uncertain terms that he had come to a crossroads. If he wanted to have anything like a life, there was only one course of action open to him. Get some help. Stop drinking. Immediately. She doubted he would follow her advice, though. She added that she thought of him as a friend despite everything, but this behavior simply could not continue.

Our conversation was coming to an end. She mentioned that she was already looking forward to next season and did I expect to be on the island still? I said I hoped I would be. I suspected she was wondering about Haddie and me but was too polite to ask. And anyway, what could I have said?

Later I tried to figure out what, if anything, it meant that Star had come to one of our softball games. Probably not much. It probably had nothing to do with his prints on the bat.

Some things simply didn't add up. Star's prints being on the bat. Dour, unimaginative Anthony Dyer writing the poem and the messages.

When I got back to the office, Stefanie called me over. "Two things. First, in case you haven't been told yet, about an hour ago they brought in Anthony Dyer for questioning."

"They did?"

"They didn't arrest him, they let him know he's a person of interest. Meaning he *could* be a prime suspect. They questioned him and released him. He's none too happy about it."

"I'll bet."

She kept going. "Second thing. I just talked to Detective McGuane, and I'm taking you off the story."

"You are?"

She nodded. "My fault entirely. I misjudged our readers when I asked you to write that eyewitness account. My judgment must have been thrown off by my own personal grief. Twenty-five subscribers have already canceled. They said details like that don't belong in a public newspaper."

"I'm sorry."

"Like I said, this is on me, and anyway it's not the only reason I'm reassigning you. You've gotten too close to the case—you've somehow worked your way into becoming a sort of informal assistant for McGuane. He said in fact you've been very helpful. So don't think of this as a punishment."

"It feels like a punishment," I said with a shrug.

She patted me on the arm and told me to hang in there.

I wasn't about to give up my interest in the case, and asked what she thought about Dyer being brought in for questioning.

She said she understood why they had to do it, but added, "That poor man has been to Hades and back. I don't know what he did to deserve all this, and yes, I still believe he's innocent." Her eyes burned behind her horn-rims.

She emphasized that she was moving me on now to other stories: summer rental regulations, waterfront issues, a controversy involving the high school principal and a young teacher he'd accused of insubordination. "And Christie, try not to get anyone thrown in jail, okay?" she pleaded.

I told her I'd do my best.

The meeting of the Summer Rental Workgroup was loud and agitated. Half the people in the audience were year-rounders who claimed they'd have to sell their homes and leave the island if they weren't allowed to keep receiving the income they made renting out their small cottages or basements in the summer. As it happened, Anthony Dyer was a member of this group, and he spoke strongly in favor of property rights and the freedom to rent. The other half of the audience—a well-heeled crowd, men in expensive suits and women with Hermes handbags—claimed that summer rentals were destroying the island. The rentals attracted disrespectful, disruptive tourists who clogged up the streets in summer and stressed the infrastructure. The summer rental opponents talked about losing the sense of community that was so integral to island life. Interestingly, most of those complaining the most about "sense of community" seemed to be seasonal residents, not year-rounders. My take on it was that the year-rounders were struggling to make ends meet and were renting out homes to help keep their finances afloat, while the other faction was flush with cash and simply didn't want to be bothered by the annoying little people who rented.

I knew there was another side to the story. Haddie had mentioned once that she and her family—year-rounders for several generations—were dead set against the explosion of summer rentals. They didn't have anything against people who rented for a month or longer, but they hated the churn of all the frequent turnovers every week—cars parked in the streets loading and unloading, the ferry jam-packed with vehicles all summer. To make things worse, year-round homes were being converted to rentals, exacerbating the shortage of housing for locals.

Both sides had good points to make. The question was, could a solution be found in the middle—maybe by limiting rentals somewhat but not completely? A solution like that looked doubtful.

As I was leaving the building someone strode up past me, turned, and positioned himself in front of me on the sidewalk.

"You piece of garbage," he said.

"A good evening to you as well. Anthony."

"They brought me in for questioning."

"I heard. I'm sorry that happened." I'd realized I'd used that word a lot recently.

"You're sorry?"

"I'm sorry if it caused you distress."

"I came and looked at your stove for free. I didn't charge you a cent. I was just being a good neighbor."

"Thank you for that."

"Is this how you reward me? By convincing McGuane that I was a murderer?"

"I didn't convince him of anything, Anthony."

"Give me a break."

"I told him about the divot repair tool. He's the one who put it together. That and the rifles."

"And you think you know why I did it."

"I don't think I know much about that," I said.

"Horsefeathers. All your talk about 'catastrophes.' That night in your apartment. You think I didn't know what you were getting at?"

I paused. "Yeah, I can own that."

"You can 'own' that? What kind of elitist talk is that?"

I took a deep breath. "Look, Anthony, I've been known to make a mess of my own life," I told him. "So I know people make mistakes. It doesn't mean they're evil."

"You're saying I think Chester Danville was evil?"

"I'm talking about someone else."

"You have no right to talk about her."

"Okay, but I just want to say, give it time. Sometimes people wise up, they ask for another chance."

"Who the heck are you to tell me that?"

"Because like I said, I'm someone who screwed up big time."

He shook his head and shifted his weight from one foot to the other. "Tell me something, Christie. Do you think I did it? Do you think I killed two people?"

"Do you write poetry, Anthony?" I asked.

"Do I write poetry? What's that got to do with it?"

"I'm just curious."

"Why do you wanna know?"

"Just tell me. Do you write poetry?"

"Of course not. I hate poetry," he said. "They made me read Robert Frost in high school and I hated every word of it. All those roads he didn't take. All those deep woods. What a fraud."

I watched him carefully. He was speaking from the heart.

"No, Anthony, I don't think you did it. And I wish you the best, I really do."

"Get out of my face!" He gave me a shove and stalked off into the night.

CHAPTER SIXTEEN

Early that evening a call came. With a stab in my heart, I saw it was Haddie.

"Hey," I said.

"Hey. I'm here with Luna and Dorothy. I've been spending most evenings with them these days."

"Oh, that's nice."

"Yeah," she continued. "So we just came upon a quote and Luna says you might be interested in it."

"A quote? What quote?"

"'I smell you and I feel your air.'"

It felt like something had struck my chest. "You found that quote? You know where it's from?"

"I do. For a while now I've been reading *The Hobbit* to Dorothy. And tonight when I was reading, Luna stopped me and made me read a section out loud again. She said that's the quote you were looking for."

"So it's from *The Hobbit*! Is it Gollum?"

"No!" Dorothy interjected, from the background. "*Smaug* says it. He says it to Bilbo. He senses someone is sneaking into his tunnel, trying to get at his treasure, but he can't see who it is. So he calls Bilbo a thief and says, 'I smell you and I feel your air.'"

I thought back to the softball game. The conversation on the bench with Steph Sylvan. "Of course, that's where it's from." A swirl of ideas took flight.

"I guess it's not from porn after all." Luna's voice in the background.

"Mom, shut up." Dorothy's voice.

"Peter, will this help you?" Haddie asked.

"It helps big time," I told her. "Thank you."

I must have put too much emotion in my voice, because hers sounded a bit confused when she replied. "Well okay, I'm glad we could help."

I tried to dial it down a notch. "You really did. You guys have a nice evening."

"We will," Dorothy promised. "And let's go scalloping. I have a half day of school Friday, and the low tide is at 2:00. Can you go with me then?"

"Sure," I replied.

Luna said they'd be at the cottage and I could pick up Dorothy there. "Just one thing," she said. "No going out deeper than your waist."

"That's a promise," I said, and forgot to hang up.

Steph Sylvan, newly disclosed aficionado of Hobbit lore and language.

I cradled the phone in my hand. Hobbit lore. Hobbit language. Why did that seem so important?

You already know the answer, the inner voice said. As the voice nudged me toward a solution, I was beginning to think my intuition was correct: it was the distilled wisdom of my great-great aunt.

A piece of the puzzle spun in my thoughts, looking for a place to land. Then, with a strange sense of a missing key fitting perfectly into a lock, it found its place of rest.

That poem. The poem found in Danville's pocket. I'd called it "British heroic." But it wasn't just British heroic.

It was *Tolkien*-heroic.

In fact, wasn't there a poem in *The Hobbit* or *The Lord of the Rings* that was quite similar?

In one corner of the apartment were several boxes full of old books that hadn't managed to find their way onto the bookshelf I'd constructed out of cement blocks and pine boards. *The Hobbit* was nowhere to be found, but as I shuffled through I did find a small boxed paperback set of *The Lord of the Rings*. It was worth a look.

I skimmed through the pages . . . the comical opening that described Bilbo's birthday party, the inception of Frodo's heroic journey with Sam, the mystical meeting with Tom Bombadil, and the arrival at the inn in Bree when Frodo and Sam meet a mysterious stranger by the name of Strider. The owner of the inn, Mr. Butterbur, gives Frodo a letter that Gandalf has left for him, warning of the increasing danger they face.

And there it was. The letter with a poem beginning:
All that is gold does not glitter.

"All that is gold does not glitter . . . All that smolders isn't seen."

The similarity was impossible to ignore.

The poem found in Chester Danville's pocket must have been written by someone obsessed with Tolkien. Probably the same person who told a hot young bartender, "I smell you and I feel your air."

In other words, Steph Sylvan.

But there was no evidence that would make Sylvan the prime suspect. And there was a major problem: what was his motivation?

All that was known was that there'd been a conflict involving his scallop boat, which he kept moored in front of the Douglas place. Early in the mornings, the boat's noisy motor had disturbed Douglas's sleep. That was the extent of it. It hardly seemed enough to drive someone to commit murder.

Still, this clue had to mean something.

For starters, Anthony Dyer was no longer the only person of interest.

Where was Steph Sylvan now? Probably in the shanty, opening the day's catch of scallops.

From somewhere, I heard a series of musical beeps. It sounded like someone dialing on one of the new button phones that had begun to replace rotary phones. To my surprise, I saw the receiver of my phone was still in my lap.

A tiny voice was coming out of the speaker on the receiver. A woman's voice. "Hey, are you there or what?"

Puzzled, I called down to the phone, "Oh, hi. Yes, I'm here."

"I called you because . . ." the woman paused half a beat. "I was thinking maybe we could get together for lunch on Saturday."

"Um . . . that sounds great," I said. Even though the voice was tiny, I recognized it now.

"Are you sure you'll be in from the Point by lunchtime, Jeff?" Haddie asked.

"Uh, sure, I think so," I said, and hung up.

What was that all about? There was no time now to figure it out. I had to find Sylvan and shadow him.

I looked at my watch. 6:30. He might still be at the scallop shanty, dropping off his day's catch.

Back to the Jeep.

I was in luck. Sylvan's red Toyota Tacoma sat outside Souza's shanty. He was probably inside, finishing up the difficult and messy task of opening, or "shucking," his five bushel-boxes of scallops. My luck held. In less than ten minutes he strode outside, rubbing his hands together as if he had just washed them. He was done. He climbed into his truck and drove off with a rumble.

At a discreet distance, I followed in my Jeep.

Sylvan drove up to Atlantic Lumber Yard, parked in the almost empty lot, and walked inside. I parked nearby and sauntered in after him. I actually had a reason of my own to be there. With the weather turning colder, it was time to buy some real firewood. The bits of sticks I'd found along the road, augmented by scraps of lumber donated by friends of friends, no longer did the job; the temperature was falling into the low thirties most nights and sometimes into the twenties. On many mornings when I woke up, my half-frozen breath hung over me like a cloud. For two or three mornings now, I'd had to force myself to climb out of bed and take a shower.

I paid for the bundles of firewood and kept a watch out the window. No sign of Sylvan yet.

But when I trudged out with the firewood in my arms, he was already there. In the orange light from the streetlamps, I saw him folding back a blue tarp in the bed of his pickup and loading in some pieces of construction wood. They looked to be one-by-four trim pieces, pre-primed. He placed them next to a ragged assortment of long bumpy cylinders of metal, repurposed window weights I thought.

It made sense that Sylvan had a stockpile of them for his commercial scallop rig.

"Hey, Steph," I said.

At the sound of my voice, he almost jumped. He gathered himself and turned to face me. Behind his thick black beard, his smile was friendly but wary.

"Well, if it ain't the famous Peter Christie," he replied. He looked at the bundles in my arms. "Cold nights, eh?"

"Yeah. But geez, firewood is expensive on this island. Ten dollars for this bit of wood. Precious, I guess." I watched him carefully. He seemed to take no notice of Gollum's favorite word.

He tapped the pieces of wood he'd just placed in his truck. "Redoing some door trim," he offered.

We talked a bit about trim work and I mentioned that my father had made a career of restoring old houses. We talked about different types of wood—pine, mahogany, maple, poplar.

I peered in a little closer. "Hey, are those what I think they are? Old window weights? I'm guessing you use those for your dredges?"

He said that was right and recited what I'd heard before about the reuse of the weights.

"Waste now, want not?" I prompted him.

"That's right." He cracked another wary smile.

I leaned closer and saw that one of the weights had a coating of a reddish orange stain in the gullies created by its bumpy surface. "Looks like they get rusty out there in the water," I said, not knowing why I bothered to mention it.

"Those old things, they do," he said. He shook his head. "It's the salt in the water. Gets to 'em over time. No matter how you much you try, you can't get the rust off." He swished the tarp across the truck bed, covering it all up, and secured it with a bungee cord.

"Well Christie, we'll be seeing you around," he said. He slunk around to the driver's side of the truck and got in. His old truck lurched off down the road.

He'd seemed nervous, edgy, suspicious of me and of why I was there. It was easy to think this was the behavior of someone with something to hide.

Maybe. But if I looked at the situation dispassionately, I was getting a bit too far over my skis. I could be talking myself into a scenario that existed only in my own mind. Because the truth was, there wasn't anything here that would incriminate anyone.

A poem that Sylvan might or might not have written wouldn't stand up in a court of law, much less in the office of one Detective McGuane—who already seemed to believe he had his suspect. McGuane had once thought there might be a literary clue hiding in the poem, but recently he'd stepped back from that. "Maybe it's not as important as I once thought."

At one point, confusing some terms, he'd called it a literary illusion.

And an illusion was all it might be.

The tiny voice on the phone, the surprise. Haddie's voice. When I climbed into bed that night, I couldn't ignore it any longer.

The best I could figure, after the phone call with Haddie, when she told me where the quote came from, I must have forgotten to hang up. A few minutes after that, thinking we were disconnected, Haddie tried to dial another number. A number that belonged to a guy named Jeff. She was calling to invite Jeff to meet her for a lunch date. The way she talked to him—the little pause in her voice as she asked. The hesitation might have been for a number of reasons, but it was impossible to overlook this one: she was highly interested in seeing the guy and was hoping he'd feel the same.

A young woman, smart and principled and moving forward in her life. You can't expect time to stand still.

At least Dorothy and Luna liked me still.

The next morning I paid a visit to McGuane, who welcomed me with a grunt and said he was glad I'd been taken off the story, I could help him with any new clues that came in through me without fear of a conflict as a reporter.

There was more news on Dyer. One of Dyer's rifles, a Winchester Wildcat 22 caliber, was a match to the bullet that was found in Star. This rifle, the Wildcat, was very popular on the island with hunters and precision shooters, so the evidence was by no means conclusive. But it was enough to identify Dyer as a person of interest—a suspect still in the on-deck circle, you might say.

I told him about Sylvan and the quote from Tolkien and said I was convinced that Sylvan had written the poems. As I spoke, his eyes grew sleepier. "Sylvan. Interesting guy. But where's the motivation?" I admitted I had the same question. But I reminded him that we both doubted that Anthony Dyer could have written the poems.

He said he knew he'd been asking me for help with the literary stuff. He hadn't given up entirely on that, but for now he thought we should leave the poems aside. Things had changed. I'd been a close witness to two murder attempts, one of which had succeeded. He wanted me to write down every detail I could remember from those two events and see if any pattern emerged.

I went home and wrote them down and no pattern emerged.

Instead, a pattern emerged somewhere else—back in the literary realm. Precious metals, golden treasure. Was it a mere coincidence that there was treasure buried in the Douglas lawn and there was treasure buried in Smaug's cave? It seemed to implicate Sylvan in some way, but how?

Was Sylvan obsessed with treasure as much as Smaug was? Could that be the motivation that drove him? But if so, what need had there been for the murders? Couldn't he have just snuck in some night, dug up some treasure, and carried it off to his own version of a cave?

I puzzled over that as I drove out to the West End to pick up Dorothy and go scalloping. In the week or two since I'd been to the cottage, the vegetation had died down, and a pale grey wash spread over the dunes sloping off to the Creek. But if you looked closely, there were still some subtle undertones of color: the viburnum branches showed red at their thin tips, like the red claws of female blue crabs.

Dorothy stood in the driveway with her waders on, holding her rake at her side, like an old-time farmer grasping a pitchfork. On the ground beside her hunched the bushel basket shoved into its inner tube. Luna helped us load the gear. The scallop rakes were too long to fit into the Jeep, so we had to get Dorothy situated in her seat and then push in the rakes from the back, situating them so the handles jutted out the open window beside her. "Have fun, kids," Luna told me. For a woman in her late forties, she looked pretty darn good.

Shawnee Point was quiet that day. No family scallopers. Only a few commercial boats out on the water. The harbor was glassy, a pale silvergrey like the shadows that fade into the east at dawn. I thought the stillness had an eerie quality—as if the world spread before us were an inflated image of itself, something that could be punctured and tossed aside like an old balloon.

It seemed possible that my mind was a bit out of whack from all the stress and all the worry. I told myself to relax, to try to enjoy my time in this lovely setting.

Dorothy and I were soon side by side on the water, our rakes bouncing along the bottom in front of us. The reassuring rhythm helped restore my belief in the solidity of the world around us. Then, out of nowhere, the question came.

"Do you love Haddie?" Dorothy asked.

"Yes, I do," I replied immediately. "She's very special to me."

"I thought so. I told her you do."

"Thank you."

"I don't think she loves you," she offered.

"Oh. Well, that's too bad."

"But I think she *should* love you. Because you're a good guy and you're as smart as she is. And nobody else really is."

"Maybe you can put in a good word on my behalf," I suggested.

"I have. I do. But I don't think it makes any difference."

We stopped and lifted our rakes out of the water. They were heavy with pebbles and seaweed and green crabs and hermit crabs—and also adult scallops, twenty or twenty-five of them in each of our rakes. We got to work separating the scallops out from the junk and dropping them into the basket. The harbor spread around us like a bedsheet pulled tight at the corners. There was no time and no end or beginning. We were here, and that was all. A commercial scallop boat chugged by, its culling board and metal frame edged against the beige sky. The guy at the wheel looked like Sylvan, but I couldn't be sure. A minute or two later the boat's wake, a gentle series of waves, washed over us with a swish like the beginning of the world.

We started off on another push. Again and again.

Our bushel basket was almost full as we headed back to shore, and a cold wind rose out of the north and blasted across us as we made it to shore. The viburnum bushes waved and shivered, the late-afternoon light seemed to scatter like sand. An early winter storm was coming. We loaded the scallops and gear into the Jeep and headed back to the cottage.

"You're one of the best friends I have," Dorothy told me.

"I feel the same about you," I replied. Luna greeted us when we drove up and lifted out the basket of scallops, promising to bring me some the next morning once they were shucked.

It was dusk by the time I made it home. The temperature was already below freezing, and the wind was growing stronger by the minute.

Two hours later, it was the coldest night of the year. Temperature hovering just above the single digits. I'd run out of the store-bought firewood. It was a Friday night. Everything on this little island was closed.

The stove was chewing weakly on a few pieces of construction byproduct. I sat near it, pounding my chest for warmth and brooding over my wreck of a life. With waves of nausea, I reviewed my life. How I'd been unfaithful to my wife, doing the very things that I'd hated my father for doing. The ensuing fall from grace, the loss of a wife I loved and a career I'd cherished. Leading me, after some time, to this lovely but distant island, where I'd come to a dead end once again.

I'd fallen so far, I couldn't even keep myself warm in my own apartment.

I had no friends close enough to approach this late in the evening for stray pieces of wood. Forget about going to McGuane or, for goodness sake, to Bob Brown. Haddie was barely talking to me. And even if she was, I didn't want her pity.

I deserved every bit of my misery.

I was down to my last piece of salvaged wood, a tough gnarly old stump that seemed like it could produce a lot of heat and get me through the night. But it was too big to fit into the stove. I had to split it somehow. But what did I have for tools?

Nothing really. No axe, no wedges.

You do have some tools, you know. Under the bed.

That was true. I had my father's old toolbox, stashed away under the bed. But why would my great-great aunt know about that?

I slid out the toolbox and creaked open its metal top. As always with things that reminded me of him, I felt a queasy sensation in my stomach. I fiddled through the contents of the toolbox. An array of ancient wooden-handled screwdrivers, drills, shears. A squarish wooden hammer that reminded me of Thor's hammer. A slim chisel.

Among the whole assortment, only the chisel was designed to split wood. It didn't look large enough to do the job, but it was worth a try.

I put on coat, hat, and gloves (wooly with a few holes in them) and carried the big chunk of wood, the chisel, and the wooden hammer downstairs and out into the frigid air. In the light from the garage, I set the wood up on its end in the gravel, held the point of the chisel to the wood, and tapped it with the hammer. The chisel bounced off with the first few strokes, but soon it penetrated down into the wood, opening a slight crack to either side. I tapped and tapped. The chisel went deeper and deeper. The slight crack spread. The chisel went as deep as it could go.

But it wasn't nearly enough. In fact, the tough, knotty wood hardly seemed to feel its presence. The slight crack on either side should have spread in both directions, opening up a deeper crack that would split the wood in two.

It wasn't even close.

I went inside, took off my gloves, and blew on my hands. The tips of my fingers smarted from the frost. I could feel the cold deepening in the apartment.

I looked through the toolbox again.

My father's screwdrivers were a special set of wooden-handled tools that were probably antiques. It seemed possible that I could pound them into the crack and expand it farther along the length of the wood—far enough, maybe, to split the chunk into two usable pieces. I'd have to smash down onto the screwdrivers' wooden handles with the big hammer—which would probably damage the screwdrivers and possibly destroy them.

There seemed to be a grim justice about it.

I picked up one of the screwdrivers, examining it more closely. About ten inches long, with the metal blade accounting for half of that. The wooden handle bulged out to about an inch in diameter, and there were grooves cut across it, probably to enhance the grip. A nice design feature. It was an elegant and useful tool, something my father surely valued and enjoyed. When it came to his building projects, he'd had an innate sense of style, an understanding of the ways the physical world was structured. There was an aptness, an appropriateness, to his tools and his actions.

How different that was from his behavior toward my mother—the affairs, one after another, and of course the violence.

I spun the screwdriver in my hand and felt a strange satisfaction.

I knew one screwdriver wouldn't be enough to help, but perhaps two or three? Or why not all of them? When combined with the opening from the chisel, they might be able to extend the crack far enough along the log to split it in two.

I pulled on my work gloves, grabbed all six screwdrivers and the large wooden hammer, and started back down the stairs.

A frigid wind blew off the Atlantic. The frigid temperature took my breath away. Though it was well below the freezing point, somehow at the same time the air was full of moisture. And the moisture in the wind seemed able to work its way right through every layer of clothes and into my bones.

I set the chunk of wood on its side. There was no sense in working any further from the top end, as I'd tried to do with the chisel. The screwdrivers wouldn't reach down far enough. I'd have to follow the crack along the side of the wood, working along it as I went.

Thwack. The first screwdriver blade entered the wood. A microscopic crack spread farther, but only a tiny distance, down the side of the wood. *Crack.* A bit deeper. The screwdriver felt the impact. One side of its handle slivered and fell off. Yes, a sense of grim satisfaction was filling my soul. *Cra-ack.*

Forty-five minutes later, the wood lay on the ground in two roughly equal pieces. Beside the wood lay the remnants of six antique screwdrivers. I shoved them into my coat pockets and carried the chunks of wood, one by one, upstairs. There was just enough life left in the coals to coax a flame. I set one of the pieces of wood into the stove. It was bone dry and began to crackle with that happy sense of release. After a few minutes, a thin breath of warmth started to spread through the room.

I poured a glass of wine, took the screwdrivers out of my coat pockets, and arranged them on the dining room table. They looked like refugees from a war. Handles shattered in varying degrees, blades bent this way and that. We were all refugees, I thought. Even the famous Agatha Christie had found herself a refugee for a time in her own house.

The screwdrivers hadn't been intended for this job, but they had been good enough, they had done it. They'd given up their lives doing something for which they'd never been intended.

Just as Agatha Christie had used her rickety old Morris as a tool for which the car had never been intended: as a doorway to her own death, a plunge down a scenic cliff in Surrey Hills. But when the Morris snagged in the bushes, that doorway closed off. Instead, the Morris accomplished something completely unexpected: it gave her the opening to a new identity and a new life. Fresh hope after the failure of her first marriage.

The temperature in the apartment slowly rose toward comfort. It was odd, I reflected, the way things in our lives find uses for which they'd never been intended. How sometimes, they might even help us break out of the mental prisons we create for ourselves.

Another thought, a connection, was stirring somewhere in my mind, but I couldn't retrieve it. Like a word you can't put your hands on.

Don't give up. You know what this is.

As I got up and poured myself some more wine, it came to me. The window weights—those long cylinders of rusty metal.

They too were being put to a use for which they hadn't been intended: as a weight for the dredges that commercial scallopers towed behind their boats. That seemed significant. But why?

My success with the wood was easing my thoughts in new directions. Hadn't I seen a few of those weights recently? In the back of Steph Sylvan's pickup at the lumber yard?

When he pulled back the tarp, one of the weights had revealed an orange tinge in the gullies beneath the bumps. It's rust, Sylvan had said, waving his hand at it. Those old things.

Something about his tone of voice had raised a flag.

That oblong shape of metal had changed its life in mid-career.

Was it about to change its career again? Was it on its way to returning to a window? Probably not—Sylvan said he was repairing a door. Besides, he still needed the weights for his scallop dredges. The commercial season was a long way from being finished.

But if it was being returned to a window—at this time when it was most needed on a scallop dredge—that was significant. That old thing. That rust. Was it really rust?

By now the apartment was warm and toasty. I raised my glass of wine to my father's ruined screwdrivers and said thank you.

I wasn't proud of the destruction I'd caused. Yet in an odd way, I was glad I'd done it. It wasn't just that they'd allowed me to get through this, the coldest night of the year. It was that they'd found themselves a new career that was unique and helpful.

And in some odd way, it was helping me to put *him* in the rearview mirror.

Changes. People always had a reason for changing careers or changing locations or changing their identities. Sometimes it was to find new opportunities. But sometimes it was to hide their past, their secrets.

What secrets were hidden in Sylvan's window weights?

CHAPTER SEVENTEEN

Early the next morning I drove back to the parking lot near the Douglas estate and made my way down the cinder path to the harbor. The intense cold took my breath away. I started along the beach until I came opposite a distressed-looking house with a red Tacoma pickup in the drive. There was no doubt whose house this was. He was known to be the caretaker there during the offseason.

There was no path to the house, just a thick growth of bushes and small trees between the house and the beach.

I pushed through the bracken and small trees, the scrub oak and pitch pine. As I came closer I could hear a noise like a small woodpecker. The sound was irregular—it would stop and start—sometimes in quick percussive strikes, sometimes little taps more evenly spread out. In the cold air the sounds were as clear as crystals of frost.

Closer still. The taps were louder, coming from a room on the first floor. *Tap tap tap.*

Sylvan had said he'd be repairing a door, but these taps sounded too close to be from an inside wall where a door would be found. They were coming from the outside wall.

I was now within fifteen feet of the house. It looked to be a classic Cape Cod three-quarters house, typical of the island, with an offset chimney, simple windows, and a steep roof. Not typical for the island, it showed signs of decay: rotting corner boards, cedar shingles that were split in half and bulging off the exterior walls, a sagging roofline.

I crouched behind a pine tree and peered through the branches, wiggling my fingers in my gloves to warm them. Sylvan's profile was there in the window. He was working on the window. He was nailing a piece of trim in place.

Why window trim?

I thought about what Bill Barnes had told me. The window weights were suspended in the channels and then covered over by a piece of trim.

Steph Sylvan was doing one of two things. He was opening the windows to take out more weights that he could use in his dredges. Or he was putting a weight back *inside* the window for some reason.

But for what reason?

I could figure out which of these he was doing. I slipped through the trees and bushes and came up behind his pickup truck. Looking around carefully to make sure no one was around, I crept out into the open.

A sudden sound. A rattle or a scratching. I collapsed to the ground.

The sound returned. From where I crouched, I saw the source. It was just two branches on a scrub oak, rubbing against each other in the wind.

I stood up, walked over to the back of the pickup truck, and lifted up the blue tarp a few inches. The window weights were there, covered by a layer of frost.

Or were they? Most of the weights were there. But one of them was missing. The one with rust on it.

The one with the 'rust' on it.

Slipping back into the trees and bushes, I knelt down on the frozen ground. Despite the cold, a sticky sweat covered my skin. I remembered so clearly how it felt, hiding in the woods so long ago. The emotions were there, stored just beneath my skin. I took a few breaths. This was different, though, in one way. This time I wasn't fleeing the unspeakable—I was trying to discover it. But what had I found?

I reviewed what I knew.

Early this morning, Sylvan had retrieved the rusted weight from the back of his pickup, threaded a cord on it, hung it back into a window channel, and was now covering it over with a piece of trim.

Why?

You know why.

The reddish stain wasn't what he'd said. It wasn't rust.

It was the blood of Chester Danville.

The window weight had been the perfect murder weapon. Because after the murder, it could go right back onto one of his scallop dredges, out of sight of the world.

Why hadn't he left it there?

For the past few weeks, Sylvan had used the weight in the dredges, no doubt expecting that the salt water would wash away all signs of the blood. But as it turned out, it didn't work. There was blood still embedded down in the gullies between the bumps. There was no way to wash it off. So Sylvan decided to go with Plan B: hide the window weight forever out of sight, safely ensconced in a window channel where no one would ever think to look.

I still didn't know why. His motivations were unknown, but *what* he'd done was indisputable.

As Danville lay there on the lawn dying, Sylvan had taken a baseball bat and touched it to the gushing head wound, giving the bat the blood it needed to become a piece of evidence. Sylvan would then use that bat to frame Star Douglas. Later he must have found a way to get Star's fingerprints on the bat, probably at one of the softball games that Star visited. Maybe he asked Star to show him a new batting stance.

It was all a perfect plan. Except for one thing.

Someone had stumbled onto the truth.

The *tap-tap-tapping* had come to an end. Sylvan had completed his work. I edged my way backward through the scrub oaks and viburnum bushes. And not a moment too soon. Sylvan walked outside, climbed into his truck, and drove off.

I found my way to the beach and continued down the path and back to my Jeep.

I reached the apartment just as Luna and Dorothy arrived with a bowl of the most plump, succulent scallops you've ever seen. I invited them inside. Why's it so cold in here, Dorothy wanted to know.

"We have to get that window weight out of the window," Luna was saying. "They'll need to test the blood on it. It's the only way to prove he's the one. And then they can arrest him."

Shortly after inviting them inside, I'd revealed to them what I'd just discovered. They both agreed with my thinking.

"How are we going to get that window weight?" I wondered.

"Wait till Sylvan goes out scalloping. And sneak inside and take the window apart," Dorothy said.

But Sylvan wouldn't be scalloping again until Monday. It might not be wise to wait that long. Sylvan had shown he was poised to strike again at any moment.

"Tell McGuane. He can get a court order. They can go in the house and search for evidence," Luna suggested.

That could take a few days also, I pointed out. And today was Saturday. Would the courts even be open?

"We have to do it ourselves," Dorothy insisted. "And get the sample to McGuane right away so it can be tested immediately."

"How can we do that when Sylvan's home?" I asked.

Luna asked if he was home now.

I said maybe not. About half an hour earlier, I'd seen him drive away from the house. Dorothy asked, could he be in his boat now, scalloping? No, Luna answered, the commercial scallopers aren't allowed to go out on Saturday or Sunday. And it was too cold anyway today—below twenty-eight degrees, which was the minimum temperature allowed for commercial scalloping.

Luna said she had an idea. She picked up my phone and talked to someone—waited a few minutes—talked again. She hung up and told us she'd been talking to Dayva, who had walked out to the shore and confirmed that Sylvan's boat wasn't on its mooring. That meant he was probably cruising the harbor, scouting out new scallop beds for next week.

Sylvan was on his boat in the harbor.

We looked at each other and a flash passed between us.

"What's that thing they always say—there's no time like the present?" Dorothy asked.

I grabbed the last few tools from my father's toolbox: a pry bar, a cat's paw, a hammer, a nail set, and a handful of finish nails.

We left Dorothy stationed near the driveway, hidden in the bushes, bundled up in a down coat and a wool hat and gloves. She was our warning system. If she saw the red pickup approaching, she would race over to the window and let me know.

We'd left the Jeep in the same parking lot as before and pushed through the trees toward the house. Luna sequestered herself outside the window, close by in case I needed help. "Don't freeze," I whispered to her.

I approached the wall. A piece of the wooden gutter hung like a drooping moustache. The shingles were paper thin, curling back at the edges.

At the window I came upon a bit of good luck. Probably focused on the task of hiding the window weight, Sylvan hadn't locked it shut. The lower sash slid easily open and held its position, and I climbed up and through. I took my position inside and laid out the tools on the floor.

The room showed multiple signs of neglect: discolored shadows under both windows that spoke of water leaks, cracks in the plaster, missing chunks of ceiling. An old fan with a frayed cord lurked in one corner.

By contrast, the recently replaced piece of trim, a vertical slab on the right side of the window, looked naked and new. The wood had been primed but not finish-painted, and the nail holes were still clearly visible. Picking up my father's surprisingly heavy, all-metal hammer, I tapped the nail set to punch the nails in farther. The nail set had a thick yellow handle and a long, thin snout, round and blunt on the end, roughly the diameter of pencil lead. Like a woodpecker inserting its beak into bark to dig out bugs or grubs, the snout was able to chase the nail deeper and deeper into the wood and even out the other side of the trim. This tool had seen a lot of use; the handle was striated with stress lines and riddled with bumps from errant blows.

Once the nails were most of the way through the wood, I inserted the tip of the pry bar under the edge of the piece of trim and rock it back and forth, gently dislodging it. I tapped the pry bar in farther, levered it, and the trim popped free.

And there it was: the window weight, feigning innocence, hanging in a dusty channel three inches wide and two feet high. Even where it hung in the shadows, you could see the reddish hue between the bumps. I lifted the weight a few inches so the line went slack and started to untie the slender white cord where it was fastened through the top. The knot was tough and tight but finally came free.

The window weight felt surprisingly heavy in my hands.

I pushed open the sash, but without the weight to counterbalance it, it banged down shut. Pushing it open again, I held it in place with my head and called softly to Luna, and she hurried up to the house and took the weight from me, clutching it to her chest and retreating into the bushes. Her breath made clouds of white. I lowered the sash, which despite my efforts fell pretty hard onto the sill.

After tucking the cord into the empty channel, I nailed the piece of trim back into place using the same nail holes.

Argh, I realized. I should have brought my camera and taken a picture of it hanging there in the channel.

A voice outside the window. "He's here," Dorothy urged. "Get out!"

I knew that meant Sylvan would soon be inside the house.

One more nail to set.

A crunching in the driveway as the truck rolled to a stop.

Done. I pushed the sash open and reached down for the tools. The sash slid closed.

Somewhere outside, a truck door opened and whooshed shut.

I lifted the sash again, held it with one hand, and reached back with the other hand to grab the tools one by one and toss them outside in the grass, as Dorothy retrieved them. I worked feverishly, but it seemed to take forever. Finally I scurried through and let myself fall to the ground. The sash fell shut behind me. The three of us slipped into the bushes. The front door banged shut. I wormed my way forward into the woods and we started our journey back to the Jeep.

We were most of the way back to the shore when we heard the scream.

We didn't talk till we reached the Jeep. Dorothy's face was flushed from the cold and her eyes glittered. "Who was screaming?" she asked.

"Sylvan," I said. We climbed into the Jeep. I backed it up, turned it around, and headed down the dirt road—slowly, cautiously, trying not to call any attention to ourselves, trying not to stir up too much dust. No one spoke. The seconds piled up on top of one another, heavy and slow. We came back onto the main road and headed with a bit more speed toward town. At the edge of town, I pulled us into the anonymity of the parking lot at the grocery store and turned off the engine. The cold wind rocked the Jeep, and we drew our jackets closer around us.

"The scream," Dorothy repeated. Her voice was breathless and quiet. "What was that all about?"

"It was Sylvan," I said.

"Why did he scream?"

"I guess he realized the weight was missing."

"How did he know? Didn't you nail the trim back in place?" Luna asked.

I told her that yes, I had nailed the trim back in place. But Sylvan had found out somehow. Maybe he tested the sash to make sure that the weight was still moving properly in the channel, that the hiding place was secure. And what did he find? When he pushed up the sash, instead of staying open as he expected, it slammed shut.

"Maybe it fell on his fingers," Dorothy suggested.

Sure, I said. But it was more likely that Sylvan screamed because he knew he'd been found out. The sash wouldn't fall unless the weight had come untied or someone had removed it. He knew the knot had been good. That meant someone had broken in and taken the weight.

"Then Sylvan knows we're onto him," Luna said.

"Does he know it's us?" Dorothy asked.

I thought of the encounter outside the lumber yard. His edgy nervous manner as we talked about scalloping and window weights.

"Probably not you. But I think he knows it's me," I said. I explained our encounter.

"Don't go back to your apartment," Luna warned. "We all need to go somewhere safe now." She glanced nervously around the parking lot.

"I wonder where that might be," I replied. But first, I said, we had to go to the station and hand in the evidence. I called McGuane. He didn't sound all that happy to hear from me on a Saturday, but he agreed to meet us at his office.

It wasn't until we were parked at the station, about to climb out of the Jeep, that I looked at the floor and took an inventory of the tools that lay there. Pry bar, cat's paw, hammer, a few finish nails.

No nail set.

I'd left the nail set back at the house, under the window. I pictured it lying there like an exotic yellow woodpecker, all body and beak and no wings.

No wonder Sylvan screamed so soon after he arrived.

McGuane listened without interrupting. His eyes had never looked less sleepy.

"If you're right about all this—" he waved his hand at the window weight, which was resting on a towel in a cardboard box—"you've done a good piece of detective work. And you've also put yourself and these fine folks in some real danger." He gestured toward Luna and Dorothy, who stood with me beside the desk.

I told him I knew about the danger for me. I hoped Luna and Dorothy were less in peril. "But I had to do this. I promised someone I'd figure this out," I added awkwardly.

McGuane didn't say anything, but he watched Luna and Dorothy exchange a glance, and his eyes emitted a photon or two of light.

"I'll get this to the lab pronto," he promised. He told us where we should hide out in the meantime. And he said he was sending someone out to keep a lookout on my apartment and on Luna's cottage.

Dorothy spoke up. "So, Detective, I understand why you think Peter is in danger. Sylvan knows Peter saw the window weight in the back of the truck. It would be logical for Peter to be the one who went to Sylvan's house and took it out of the window." She gestured toward the window weight. "But why would my Mom and me be in danger?"

McGuane explained that Sylvan might have security cameras on his house and in the yard. They were a new invention, but people like Sylvan were likely to have them. Sylvan would have seen me on the camera and Luna as well. Maybe even Dorothy near the driveway, depending on how extensive his security system was. On top of that, he certainly knew about Dorothy going scalloping with me. And if he had been the guy in the wolf costume on Halloween, he would have seen the three of us together then.

Not to mention, he added, that Luna was the last living offspring of Quentin Douglas, which could put her life doubly in danger.

Dorothy reached over and hugged her. Luna shook her head grimly.

Before we left, McGuane took me aside and said he no longer considered Dyer a person of interest. But he planned to bring him in for more questioning on Monday, if only to make it look as if they still suspected him. "I'll make it up to Dyer one of these days," he added. I told him about the encounter outside the town building, and he nodded but didn't comment.

The police had found two empty bedrooms in the barracks for us. Dorothy, Luna, and I spent the afternoon playing game after game of Monopoly and Parcheesi and other board games. It was no surprise to find that Dorothy was a whiz at the games and won almost every one. She was especially adept at Monopoly, making strategic choices about when to buy houses and hotels on her properties, and she seemed to have a seventh sense about when Luna's or my token would land on her properties. Unlike Luna and myself, she seemed for the time being to forget her worries.

That evening as we were falling asleep, a series of sirens rushed down South Valley Lane, past the cemetery and toward the center of the island. It was morning before we found out what had happened. My garage apartment had burned down to the ground overnight. A complete loss; nothing was left of it but the chimney and the Morso stove. The initial report from the Fire Department said it appeared to be the result of a malfunctioning wood-burning stove with a major crack in its frame. A stove that should have been condemned months earlier. Of course, I knew the stove couldn't have been the cause; the ashes had been cold for a day or two.

Earlier that evening, the police detail had detected someone skulking around Luna's cottage. They fixed a spotlight on the figure, and it slipped off into the underbrush and didn't return. The police remained at the cottage the rest of the night.

At the time of the fire, no one had been available to monitor my apartment.

After lunch we drove out to see what was left of the apartment.

There wasn't much more than a burned-out depression in the ground, a brick chimney, the stove, and some charred lumber. Plumes of smoke still wafted up from the ground like the spirits of the departed. Around the edges of the yard, some shreds of scorched paper drifted in the air above a random tatter of clothing and a fragment of a picture frame.

The fire had consumed everything that belonged to me. A favorite chair. My clothes. All my notebooks with notes for stories. My typewriter. The only photographs I had of my mother. A few letters from her. Some baseball cards and Marvel comic books. My passport. My diploma from Brown and my journalism grad work at Tufts. A few awards I'd been given in high school and college. My wedding ring and license, my divorce papers. My books, which totaled several hundred. My collection of LPs, both classical and pop. The Beatles, the Association, Bob Dylan.

Basically everything but my wallet and the Jeep. Oh, and a few fragments of a metal box: my father's tool box.

Dorothy gave me a hug and said she was really, really sorry.

While we were there, McGuane stopped by and expressed his condolences about my stuff. He pulled me off to the side and said they'd found traces of Danville's blood in the gullies between the bumps of the window weight. They were closing in on Sylvan but weren't ready to arrest him yet. For the moment, they were still extremely concerned about everyone's safety. They had two police stationed at the Douglas mansion and had more officers available at various places around the island. Outside Beatrice's apartment on Main Street. Near Luna's cottage. And at the barracks. By the way, he said, the three of us should return to the barracks and stay there until we heard otherwise.

Dorothy came over and nudged me on the arm. "Ask him why they don't arrest Sylvan now," she whispered to me. I told her she could ask him that herself. She turned to McGuane and put the question to him.

McGuane replied that it was a tough call. They wanted to catch Sylvan in the act—of something. They wanted to be careful not to spoil the case.

"You have the window weight," Dorothy countered.

McGuane said that was true. But unfortunately, they didn't have any prints on the window weights. It was what you called circumstantial evidence. They had nothing that directly implicated Sylvan.

"What does that matter?" Dorothy almost screamed. "Peter saw the window weight sitting in the back of the guy's truck. Peter ripped open the window of his house and rescued the weight from where he'd hidden it. What more do you need?"

It was one person's word against another's, McGuane explained. Sylvan could claim that Peter had made it all up.

But why wouldn't he tell the truth? Dorothy asked. There was a long pause, and McGuane replied, "We all wish the world were like that, don't we?"

We all let it go at that.

Back at the barracks Luna took a phone call and talked for a long time. After a while she called me over and handed me the phone. "It's Haddie," she mouthed.

"Hey," Haddie's voice greeted me. "I'm so sorry about the apartment. And your stuff." We talked a while and she said Luna had filled her in on all the work I'd been doing. She thanked me for digging so deep. For figuring out who the monster was that was responsible for all this. She said we must all be in shock, and she thought maybe she was too.

As she spoke, I had an odd image in my mind: balloons and how, over time, they lost their air. For a few months, I'd lived with a goal that filled me with its urgency and motivated my every step. But now that I'd chased it down, it felt less important, maybe even inconsequential. Had I really helped Haddie? The whole thing was sad. Her grandfather was still gone from this world, his legacy tainted. Star, her second cousin, was dead. Luna's father had just been released from the hospital. In the process my apartment, along with all my possessions, had been obliterated. Everywhere you looked, the power of hatred and decline had seized the upper hand.

Haddie did her best to sound appreciative and grateful, but a finely woven formality weighed down the cadence of her words. It occurred to me that this was one way that relationships ended. The oxygen withdrew from the room, slowly, relentlessly, until the flame wavered and gutted out. It was very different from the end of my marriage, but every bit as painful, in fact more so in a way because I thought I'd been getting somewhere, I thought I was finally learning how to fight back against my flaws.

But the truth was, I had a long way to go. I was still impulsive and probably still immature in many ways. As evidence of that, I had to exert every bit of willpower left in me to withstand a perverse impulse: to ask her how she'd enjoyed her lunch with—now what was that guy's name? Oh yes—Jeff.

I checked myself and assured her that this nightmare would soon be over. She said she hoped so too. Before I knew it, we had said goodbye.

Luna took the phone back from me and gave me a steadying look with her steel-blue eyes. She understood me, I told myself. Too bad she was fifteen or twenty years older than me. No, that was something none of us wanted.

Stefanie called around lunchtime and asked how I was. She had heard about the fire and was hoping I was alright. I explained that a lot had been going on. Naturally I couldn't give her all the details; we were in it deep and felt we might come out the other side sometime soon.

"Peter, if your life is really in danger you should get out now," she urged. "Get off the island. You don't have to go through this." I told her I appreciated her concern but I felt safest now right where I was.

Stefanie pushed back and said this whole thing was moving into a very troubling phase, a time of extreme danger. A new message had arrived for me at the office, and she didn't like at all what it said. She read it to me: THE OLD MAN, HIS DAUGHTER, HIS GRANDDAUGHTER, HIS STAFF, HIS BURGLAR—GUARD THEM WELL, FOR NONE SHALL SURVIVE. FIRE IS THE LEAST OF THE MANY WEAPONS IN THE ARSENAL OF A DRAGON.

"*Burglar*. That's interesting," I said. There was a definite Bilbo Baggins-Smaug quality to all of this.

"It's not interesting at all," Stefanie replied. "I find this terrifying, Peter. By the way, are you the burglar?"

"Probably. It beats *rat-hound*, don't you think?"

"Gallows humor will do nothing to help you at this moment, young man. You need to get serious and keep yourself safe."

"Thank you, Stefanie. I agree." What I didn't say was, nothing and nowhere felt safe to me anymore.

That afternoon Luna and I tried to figure out what Sylvan had been trying to accomplish with all this violence. He'd neutralized the lawyer who, according to Dayva, was doing "something big" for Quentin Douglas and Star. That probably meant Danville was in the process of making a change in the will. Sylvan had also murdered Star, who was one of the two children, and he had tried to inject Luna, the other child, with a deadly dose of poison. We discussed McGuane's comment about Luna being doubly at risk as the last living offspring of Quentin Douglas.

All this seemed to point in one direction: inheritance. But what did that have to do with Sylvan?

Were there any other clues that we'd overlooked?

Luna said she hadn't seen any, but admitted she might easily have missed them. Her task early that fall of chauffeuring Jenny Dyer to the house had caused her distress and had probably made her less aware of what was happening around her. She might not have noticed clues that were right in front of her eyes.

What about the clue that you heard from Dayva?

I told Luna I did recall one piece of information that could be important. In our first meeting, Dayva had mentioned to me that there had been an unusual visitor toward the end of summer, and Quentin Douglas was visibly upset afterward. Could that be that significant, I wondered.

Neither of us could make much of it. How could that have had any effect on the will or the inheritance?

Dorothy was listening in and asked us to explain how wills work. We told her what we knew. People with offspring usually created a will that gave most of their estate after death to "their children." Sometimes the provisions of the will set aside a portion for friends or other relatives, or in some cases for charitable causes. If there had been a history of extensive conflict or estrangement within the family, the parents might choose to disinherit some or all of their children and bestow their estate elsewhere. But disruptions like that were, for the most part, rare. The vast majority of the time, the estate went to the children.

The explanation left Dorothy unsatisfied, and she asked to see some tangible examples. We looked through a set of encyclopedias in the barracks library and found some formal descriptions of wills and the generally accepted practices that guided them. One passage stated, "In most states in America in the twentieth century, a reference in a will to 'my children' refers to all offspring, including nonmarital offspring, unless the will is drawn up to explicitly exclude nonmarital offspring."

Dorothy looked puzzled. "What are nonmarital offspring?"

Luna told her it meant children who were born outside of a conventional marriage.

"Was I born outside of a conventional marriage?" Dorothy wanted to know, and Luna confirmed that she was. Dorothy then asked if Luna intended to exclude her from inheriting anything. Absolutely not, Luna assured her. "Everything that is mine will be yours. Now and always."

"Is that how your will is written—'my children?'" Dorothy wanted to know.

It was, Luna confirmed.

What about grandfather's will? How was that written? Dorothy asked. And with that question, the clouds parted.

What provision had Chester Danville been in the process of changing in Quentin Douglas's will? Why was he changing it? And how would the change benefit Quentin Douglas or his offspring?

We began with the assumption that Quentin originally had a conventional will, one that left his estate to "my children." Despite the series of estrangements in the family, such a will was probably acceptable to him. As far as we could see, he had nowhere else to leave his estate. He wasn't a philanthropist and showed little desire to fund any charitable causes. After his death he was probably content to let his money flow to his children and salve their emotional wounds, knowing it might improve their opinion of him in retrospect.

But this past summer and fall, two events had changed everything.

The first was that Star came home for some visits and made a sincere effort to reconnect with his father. That may or may not have been welcome to Quentin Douglas. And it would have had little or no effect on the will except for the second event.

The second event was the key to it all: Quentin Douglas learned of the existence of another child, a son . . . a nonmarital offspring.

The son had been living on the island for several years, keeping a low profile. He found a rental home near his father's mansion. He worked hard, teaching himself to be a successful commercial scalloper. He joined a softball team. He became friends with a fellow outcast. He was biding his time, waiting until the right moment to announce himself.

You know what can happen when hope turns to bitter disappointment.

That time came late this summer—so he thought. He presented himself at the Douglas mansion and introduced himself to his father. What he asked for or demanded will always be a mystery. Whatever it was, the meeting did not go well. Words were exchanged and he was escorted rudely out, no doubt, by Bruce Gormley.

But this much was certain: Steph Sylvan was the "unusual visitor" who left Quentin Douglas so distraught afterward.

It all fit, every bit of it, even the small wound that Dayva tended to on Douglas's arm after the visit. Sylvan was making use of a new and emerging science: DNA testing. Before leaving, the visitor gathered a sample of Douglas's DNA to confirm what he already knew: he was a blood offspring. A proven member of the *flawless bloodlines.*

After that failure to connect, the son's tactics underwent a sea change. A 180-degree turn. He nursed his wounds and prepared to exact revenge on a world that failed to recognize what was rightfully his. Perhaps he had always been resentful and sly, but now, in his anger and disappointment, he cultivated hatred and payback. As vengeful as a dragon hiding in its lair.

After the meeting with the unusual visitor, Quentin Douglas felt tricked and bullied—two things that he couldn't tolerate. He called in Chester Danville and ordered him to alter the will so that it explicitly excluded any and all non-marital offspring.

Somehow Sylvan found out. Somehow—but how? It wasn't Dayva who told him, it wasn't Star Douglas, it definitely wasn't Quentin Douglas or Chester Danville.

That left just one person. Gormley. I thought back to the meeting in the dairy aisle of the grocery store, the sudden insight that came to me as I stood next to him. The sense that Gormley was capable of betrayal—in several different directions at once. For reasons of his own, Gormley could have revealed the secret to Sylvan. Maybe they'd met in one of the island bars and bonded. Or found each other somewhere else. The origin of their bond was unclear. But it had to be Gormley.

When he learned of the impending change in the will, Sylvan knew he needed to buy himself more time. He dreamed up the perfect crime, with a murder weapon that no one would ever be able to trace. He amused himself by writing poetry that would amaze and astonish the world. His sense of grandiosity swelled like the pool of blood inside a tick.

He surveyed the Douglas property around the clock, and when Danville appeared on the lawn one night, shovel in hand, he saw that his moment had arrived. He secured his weapon, gathered up his poison, and returned to the Douglas place and committed the murder that shocked the island. He left the poem in the victim's pocket, part warning, part braggadocio. More important to him, Danville's death put on hold the changes in the will.

In his deviousness, Sylvan brought a baseball bat to the murder; he dipped the end of it in the blood of the victim and found a way to get Star Douglas's fingerprints on it at one of the Great Whites' softball games. Then he tossed the bat through Clara

Danville's window, strengthening the evidence against Star. It was to his advantage to widen the circle of suspects a bit further, and he figured out that Anthony Dyer might also be a possibility. He got ahold of Dyer's divot repair tool (maybe by tracking him at the golf club) and he planted it on the Douglas lawn. His sense of power and competence increased with each and every action.

Sylvan's ambition was growing like a cancer; he hungered now to increase his share of the inheritance. So he went after his two half-siblings.

He had to accomplish all this in secret and beyond detection—so as not to be excluded from the inheritance—and eventually he would need to see to it that Quentin Douglas also met his fate. Luna and Quentin were the challenges that still lay ahead of him; they were his unfinished business.

Once all that was taken care of, he would innocently present his DNA evidence to the world, as proof that he was the one living offspring of Quentin Douglas, the wealthiest man in the Commonwealth of Massachusetts. If the court accepted this evidence, his work would be done.

There were some things we still didn't know and couldn't know for now. Who was Sylvan's mother? How had he transformed himself, so quickly and completely, into a ruthless killer? Had he shown those tendencies earlier in life?

But it wasn't hard to see that Sylvan had done all this with a chip on his shoulder the size of Jupiter and with a self-infatuation that bordered on the insane.

To this point in time, with each and every task on his list, he had experienced success.

But now that he had been found out, Sylvan must know that his hopes for a large inheritance were a shipwreck on a rocky shoal. That only made the situation more dangerous for the rest of us.

The game was up, and all that remained now was the prospect of utter and final revenge.

CHAPTER EIGHTEEN

It was quiet that night at the barracks and across the whole island. No fires, no break-ins, no murders. I slept through the night in a stupor of exhaustion.

But we were up bright and early the next morning, wandering about and trying to figure out what we were doing. Was there a breakfast to be had? Coffee or tea? Finally, a kindly female officer came by with some food for us. And over cereal and toast, Dorothy spoke the words that would change our lives.

"I'm worried about grandfather."

Luna explained that the police had two officers stationed on the property to guard him, but Dorothy wasn't mollified. "We should be with him," she stated, in the tone of voice of someone who wouldn't take no for an answer.

"Dorothy, it's been fourteen years since I stepped into your grandfather's house," her mother reminded her.

Dorothy replied that wasn't her fault. Wasn't it time to let bygones be bygones? How long were the divides in the family going to last?

Luna replied that this wasn't just her doing. In fact, he'd ordered her never to come back.

"But he's in danger now," Dorothy argued. "He needs us there. And you need to forgive him."

"You'll understand when you get older."

"I hate it when people say that."

"We all have to accept things for what they are. It's part of growing up."

"I hope I don't. Because that won't mean I've grown up. It'll mean I've *given* up."

Luna recoiled almost imperceptibly. "I hope you never give up, honey," she told her daughter. The ice blue in her eyes was approaching the watery phase again. She hugged her daughter.

Dorothy pushed a strand of her brown hair back from her face. "You don't have to give up, either, Mom."

Luna turned to me. "How do you feel about this, Peter?"

"I think we should go there. He's vulnerable."

"You only met him once," Luna told me.

"Twice," I corrected.

Dorothy wondered what Sylvan was like when he was young. Was he the type of kid who pulled the legs off of crickets? "How does someone get to be such a monster?" she asked. "If we only knew who his mother was, maybe we could find out more about him."

We talked about why some people became monsters. Was it a lifetime's buildup of rage and resentment? Was someone born that way? Did it all go back to Adam and Eve?

That was only a myth, Dorothy replied. She'd been thinking about evil and she was pretty sure it came from the places in people's hearts that hadn't healed. We were all born with wounds in our hearts and then we got more wounds as we grew up when people hurt us or ignored us. Sometimes those wounds didn't heal. And that was when evil came along. It was the pus in a wound that didn't heal.

We sat in silence, pondering that.

After a few minutes Luna washed out her cereal bowl and spoon and said, "All right. Let's get ready."

I called McGuane to let him know where we were going. He said okay, he understood why Luna and her daughter would want to check in on the old man. There were officers there, but it was a danger zone still. We should be careful. He said he would come over there too.

Dayva pulled open the door and a bell chimed deep in the house. As she let us in, she nodded politely toward Luna and gave me a semi-friendly hello. Dorothy received a quick squeeze on the arm.

"How's grandfather?" Dorothy asked.

"He's in the back resting."

"Did they confirm that it was a seizure?" Luna asked.

Dayva's manner grew more formal as she addressed Luna. "A seizure. Yes, that's correct. He's tired but he's fine. He's resting."

"I can't wait to see him!" Dorothy exclaimed.

"He lay down for a nap a few minutes ago, but he should be up at the top of the hour," Dayva replied. "I know he'll want to see you."

"I can wait, I guess. C'mon, Mama, I want to show you my room!" Dorothy took Luna's hand and led her up the luxurious marble spiral staircase to the second floor.

There was a commotion somewhere far off, a rustling, a rattling of wheels, the wheeze of breathing.

And he was there, at the opening of the hallway onto the spacious expanse of the living room.

"What are you doing here?" Coming from a wizened old man in a walker—someone who had been released from the hospital only a day earlier—the voice was strangely resonant and powerful.

"Good afternoon, sir."

The eyes twinkled darkly. "You're the reporter, aren't you. The one I threw out a few weeks ago."

"Yes, that's right." I squared my shoulders, turned, and faced him directly. Let him try to throw me out now. There was no running away this time.

He showed no fear. He took a step closer to me in his walker. "And now you've taken it on yourself to come back unannounced to murder me. Or, it may be, to solve the murder and make yourself a hero."

"It's nice to see you again," I replied. "Hard to believe, this is already the third time."

"'The third time.'" He seemed to be remembering something. "It wasn't very nice the last time you were here, was it?"

I could feel Dayva watching closely, monitoring the interaction.

"I was here on that awful day. I'm very sorry for the loss of your son, sir. I wish I could have done something to prevent it."

He chose to ignore the expression of sympathy. "Did you come alone? I thought I heard others."

"You did. Your granddaughter Dorothy is here. With her mother. Luna."

He drew up straighter in his walker and turned his gaze toward Dayva. "My daughter Luna is here?"

Dayva nodded. "She is, Mr. Douglas."

He glanced around the room. "Well, where are they?"

Dayva took a few steps closer. "Luna is upstairs with Dorothy, Mr. Douglas. I told them you were resting. When she heard that, Dorothy took her mother up to see her bedroom."

"Ah, yes. Of course. Mothers and daughters and their rooms. A home and its land are extension of women's own bodies, in some way, so I've read."

"I expect Dorothy and Luna will be back soon," Dayva added.

"So Luna is in the house. Well, I'll be," the old man commented. He frowned and gazed out the window toward the woods. "I wonder what she's like now. She was such a petulant little teenager. Quite disagreeable most of the time. Do you know my daughter Luna?" he asked, turning to me.

"A bit," I said.

"Well, what's she like?"

"She's a strong and sympathetic person. And a wonderful artist. Fabrics."

"A wonderful artist," he repeated. "Can you remind me, why are you here today?"

"I guess you could call it a friendly visit from the three of us."

"The three of us . . ." he repeated. It was meant as bait—or more accurately, a command. I was required to explain the relationship.

"We're all just friends," I continued. "Brought together by circumstances, nothing more. But in any event, I was hoping to talk to you."

"Hoping to talk to me." There was something curious in the voice. Though he was fragile and small and solitary, it wasn't fear; it was closer to a musing wonder that someone would have the effrontery to suggest such a thing. "And why is that?"

Recently the words of the evil old dragon Smaug had been in the forefront of my mind. It seemed that Sylvan associated himself with the wicked old monster. But for all his violence, Sylvan was more of a shadow figure, closer in essence to another villainous Tolkien character: Gollum.

Here, in the crafty, probing questions of this rich old recluse, was the real Smaug: a cunning and covetous creature of formidable power and perception.

"Why are you here?" he repeated. "And why do you wish to talk to me?"

Now was the moment. There would be a brief opening before the others came back.

"Well, you see, I wanted to ask you about Steph Sylvan," I said, in a quiet, measured voice.

His eyes registered nothing. "And who is that?"

"Uh, well—I think he paid you a visit this summer." I glanced over at Dayva.

She took another step forward. "Mr. Douglas, that was the man who upset you last summer."

A shadow crossed over his face. "Oh. That man." He scowled at the floor and lifted his head again. His eyes had a strange glow, almost humorous, but his mouth looked like it had tasted something horrid. "He claimed he was my son. Can you imagine that? My son!"

"He was just making that up, then," I replied. "Spinning a story out of nothing?"

"He told me the name of his mother. I knew her. Long ago. A very coquettish thing. Not nice at all. We had some fun together, a few nights, she as much as I." His mouth worked like a primal creature, tasting, testing, remembering.

I saw Dayva clasp her hands together. A sound of knuckles cracking.

"Then perhaps Steph Sylvan is your son?" I asked.

The look was purely bewildered. "If so, I never knew it."

"But surely, your knowing or not knowing wouldn't change the truthfulness of his claim—if it's true."

The old man swung toward me and looked me up and down. "You are very bold in your statements."

"Not bold. Just simple and transparent," I came back. "Life is hard to predict. Sometimes things happen, there can be a mistake or a malfunction of one thing or another, and the unexpected comes into our lives."

"'The unexpected comes into our lives.' You have an odd way of expressing yourself."

"The point I'm trying to make is, the man known as Steph Sylvan seems to truly believe that he is your son, and I'm guessing that he came to you to claim what he thinks is due to him."

"He's a thief. A con man. He has no proof of anything."

"He might have evidence now. DNA," I told him.

"That's still an unproven science." His brows drew down over his eyes. "He wounded me."

"I heard."

"You seem to know a lot for someone who is just a 'friend' of the daughter I'm about to see for the first time in twenty years."

Their footsteps sounded above us, their voices echoing in the high ceiling as they came to the stairs.

"I don't know a lot," I allowed. "But it does seem possible to me that Steph Sylvan murdered Chester Danville and shot your son Star."

Quentin Douglas set his mouth grimly. "Yes, I thought as much. But why?" Again his face registered genuine confusion.

"Revenge, I think. Though he may have begun with other goals."

"He probably thought at first that he could hide his involvement in the murders and step forward with his claim once we were all out of the picture, as it were."

"I think that's right."

"But I suppose by now he's blown his cover, hasn't he?"

"He has. Big-time."

He shook his head. "Too bad for him. He'll get nothing now. No matter what he does." He shook his head again. "The fool."

Dayva took a step toward the window. "Mr. Douglas, I think someone is outside."

There was a knock on the door. Someone large stood outside, a wool hat, floppy windbreaker. "Oh, it's the detective," Dayva said, striding over to the door. As she welcomed McGuane inside, footsteps pattered down the marble staircase, and the old man reached into his bathrobe.

"If Sylvan comes back, do you think you might shoot him for me?" he asked. "I have a pistol. Here." He pulled a small handgun out of the folds of his bathrobe and caressed it between his hands. "You didn't expect this, did you?"

"Certainly not," I replied, shying away.

"Gramps! Put that gun away!" Dorothy called. She was traipsing across the floor toward him.

Quentin Douglas waved the gun around—in the process, pointing it directly at me several times, which was quite alarming—and beckoned me over. I accepted the gun from him, stepped away, and placed it off to the side on a table just as Dorothy ran up to him and threw her arms around him.

"Gramps!" she called. "I was so worried about you."

Still holding on to his walker, he accepted her hugs with a pleased expression on his face. Then he drew back and looked at her. His face beamed with concern and affection.

"It's wonderful to see you." For a second or two he looked almost boyish, eyebrows relaxing rather roguishly. "You've grown even in the past week or two. You look very healthy and well-tended-to."

"You do too, Gramps," she said, smoothing the thin white hair on his head.

This was unexpected. It wasn't just that she elicited a different side of her grandfather. She seemed to have elicited a different person entirely. While the rest of us saw an angry, selfish, resentful old man, she saw a champion, someone who could recognize her for who she was, someone who was an ally and a confidant. And it wasn't that he projected a false image of himself to her, I saw: when he was with her, he really *was* that person.

The focus in his eyes was all on her now, no longer directed inward on himself and his pleased certainty of self-worth.

"Am I to understand that you brought your mother with you?" he asked Dorothy.

"That's correct, Dad. I'm right here." Luna stood before him, arms at her sides, fixing her ice-blue eyes on him.

"So you are," he said. The face returned to a studied neutrality. "So you are."

"It's been a while, hasn't it?" she added.

He didn't respond at first. He just looked at her, his pale blue eyes searching for something in her face. "I cared for you more than you realized," he said finally. "I was more concerned about you than you knew. But your mother and I . . . it was no good."

"I know that, Dad."

"When she left, you left with her," he said, looking at the floor.

"That's right. We moved to the Cape while I finished high school."

He raised his eyes to her. "What in the world happened to her after that?"

"The year I went to college, she moved out west to a small town in Wyoming, and she disappeared from the map. No one knows what happened."

"She was quite beautiful in her youth. But then so were you. And Dorothy is as well."

"Thank you, Dad. I guess."

"Your mother had issues of mental health, so they said."

"That's difficult to assess, Dad, isn't it?"

One of his hands shifted on the grip of the walker. "Star came back to see me. He hasn't had an easy time of it. *Didn't have*, I should say."

"That's right, Dad," Luna agreed. "He didn't."

He shook his head. "I guess I made a mess of it all. And now I fear it's too late."

Luna took a step toward him. "Don't say that, Dad."

Dorothy traipsed up to him and put her arms around him again. "I love you, Gramps. You're the greatest."

His mouth made one of its strange small-animal motions, and he gazed out at Luna.

"There are things I still don't understand—" he began.

The voice of Detective McGuane interrupted them. "Someone is sneaking around out there."

"Who is it?" Dayva asked, striding over to stand beside him at the window.

"I think it's Sylvan." He looked closer. "Oh man. Looks like he's taken down the two guards out there!"

"Have Gormley take care of him," Douglas ordered Dayva.

"Bruce Gormley left this morning," she revealed to him.

He looked stunned. "There are so many things I don't understand," he commented. "But this above all: how did that villain come back into my life?"

Luna threw me a questioning glance, and I told her quietly, "Your father and I talked while you were upstairs. He knows about Sylvan."

"I suppose this is all about the will," the old man speculated. "But what they don't know about the will is—"

His voice was cut short by a massive explosion outside. But it wasn't simply an explosion, it was an ongoing frenzy of sound, a rushing gashing whooshing inferno—a jet engine blasting off, a waterfall bursting to life, a tornado whirling up toward the clouds. And it showed no sign of stopping.

Dorothy screamed and grabbed her grandfather tighter. Luna and I ducked down and scurried over to the window, coming up beside McGuane. Dayva was nowhere to be seen now. McGuane pointed toward the underground propane tank. The manhole cover had been removed, and a blast of gas was gushing out of the opening of the pipe. It was white and billowy and had already spread its noxious rotten-egg fumes around the grounds.

"He had a sledgehammer. He broke the pipe. He broke it open!" McGuane exclaimed. "I don't know where he is now, I don't see him!"

"Is that gas dangerous?" Luna asked.

"Deadly. One spark, and the whole tank goes. The entire house. Us included."

"We have to get out the back!" Luna exclaimed. She hurried over to Dorothy and her father. "Quick—out the back! All of us! Where's Dayva?"

Dayva was still nowhere to be seen. I noted in passing that the handgun was still lying on the side table where I'd placed it.

Quentin Douglas pushed down the hallway first, with Dorothy, pale and silent, at his side. McGuane and Luna followed and I brought up the rear. McGuane was on his phone.

Toward the back of the house the frenzy of sound was still loud, but more subdued at this distance, like the dull roar of a river rapids.

McGuane stashed away his phone and finessed his way up to the front of the line. He stood to the side and pushed the door open.

"Careful! Sylvan might be back there!" I called.

And even as I spoke, a bullet whizzed down the hall, splintering a vase of flowers on a side table. With a deft move, McGuane slammed the door shut.

"It's a trap!" he announced. "Stay low! Move to the center of the house."

"What if the tank blows?" Luna asked.

"We have to take that chance."

As if to emphasize his point, two more bullets tore into the ceiling. Our fractured dance line swiveled around and retreated to a room in the center of the house, a windowless storage room that looked to be full of canned goods and oils.

Dorothy was holding on to her grandfather and trembling. "Won't he come in here after us?"

McGuane gave her a little wave. He was in the doorway, holding a handgun of his own. "I called. Help is on its way," he said.

I now had a moment to reflect on what was happening and what we might expect.

From what I knew of Sylvan, he had an over-the-top baroque aesthetic. A penchant for diabolic complexity that seemed to meet some need inside him. He developed his plans in exquisite detail, and he favored multiple redundancies that would guarantee success. For instance, the first murder: a window weight, used on a scallop dredge, that would never be suspected and, if it was, that could be hidden back inside a wall. His tortuous teasing clues, framed as poetry in the style of an author who had given the world one of its most vengeful villains—and all the more appropriate in this case because of the oblique reference to mounds of buried treasure. Numerous other distracting clues that implicated other possible suspects: a baseball bat with the fingerprints of Star Douglas, a divot repair tool belonging to Anthony Dyer.

And now—after his lust for wealth and recognition had imploded in the furnace of his excesses—now, for his moment of revenge, he had concocted a superfluity of death and destruction. Multiple means of death, destruction on a scale difficult to imagine.

Hence the gas eruption—the release of the deadly vapor that with a spark or two would blow the remains of the Douglas mansion into the harbor. But that wasn't enough. To heighten the panic and terror before he set the blast, he devised a clever mousetrap: he knew we would try to flee out the back, and thus he stationed himself there, rifle in hand, ready to open fire at those foolish enough to show themselves. We were lucky that he had failed to take any of us out at that point.

But he wasn't done. He had, after all, built in redundancies. Now he knew that none of us would dare to try to escape again out the back.

That meant he had returned to the front of the house and was preparing to carry out Plan A, the detonation of the Douglas mansion and everyone inside.

I turned to Luna. "I'm going out front. See what I can find."

For a second, they all stared at me. "Do what you have to, and don't fail," Quentin Douglas advised me.

"Be careful, Peter," Dorothy whispered.

I darted down the hall, paused for a moment in the great room to snatch the handgun off the table, and slipped up to the front door.

I knew this was the moment of peril. As quickly and silently as I could, I eased myself over the railing, tumbled down, and landed on the same bare patch where I had found my camera a few weeks earlier. I crawled to the end of the steps, hidden by the arbor vitae and the slats of mahogany, and looked out.

Steph Sylvan was there, dark beard, slender body, quick focused motions, farther away than I expected. He was at the far edge of the lawn, kneeling in the space between several small cedars, his rifle on the ground beside him. He was fiddling with another device that looked like a short, fat rocket launcher. He checked a few things, peered through the sights, and set it on the ground. He then picked up a small object, roughly the size and shape of a ping-pong ball. He rummaged around in a backpack and pulled out something that looked like an oversized hypodermic needle.

Someone else was in the yard as well. Dayva had found her way to the elm tree and was hiding behind the far side of the tree, leaning carefully out from time to time to follow Sylvan's actions. A few yards away, wreaths of gas swirled around the raised platform, where the rope was still tied in place. For better cover, Dayva slipped farther back and crouched down behind the wooden rope platform.

What was Sylvan up to? This wasn't a traditional gun, and the ping-pong-sized ball was not a bullet. What could it be?

Of course. It was an incendiary device. Sylvan was going to make his way onto the lawn, close enough to aim accurately but at a safe distance from the gushing propane, and loft a flaming ball into the inferno of gas. He would turn and run and probably dive to the ground to be sure he kept himself completely out of harm's way. Behind him the burning device would set off an explosion that would rock the island and leave a crater the size of a basketball court. For weeks afterward, bits of the Douglas mansion, blackened shards of wood and plaster, would wash up on the shores of the harbor.

I had a handgun with me, but there was no way I could aim well enough to shoot Sylvan, even if he came closer. For that matter, I wasn't even sure the gun was loaded (though knowing Quentin Douglas, it seemed likely that it was). Alternatively, I could run toward Sylvan and try to distract him, but that promised to accomplish little. Sylvan still had his rifle and had shown that he was an excellent shot. And so, there being nothing else to do, I stayed in my hiding place.

And watched.

Crouching low to the ground like a combat soldier, Sylvan made his way across the lawn toward the elm tree with a barely perceptible limp. He looked about cautiously, confirmed that no one was watching, and took his spot, lowering himself onto one knee, raising the device to his shoulder. But no, he decided, not close enough. He stood up and moved forward some more until he was just a few feet from the tree.

Dayva was now behind the rope platform hidden from Sylvan's view, and when she peeked around the edge, she caught sight of me. She gave a small waggle of her fingers. And in that moment, as Sylvan moved forward and slowed to a stop beside the tree, I saw a new possibility. I half stood up and waved to Dayva to get her attention. Then I raised my hand and made a motion like a ticking clock. She clasped her hands together soundlessly in front of her face. She understood.

Sylvan found his final spot and eased himself down onto one knee. He took the hypodermic needle and injected something into the ping-pong ball—probably some sort of incendiary catalyst—and then he dropped the ball down a plastic tube that was mounted onto the barrel. He raised the device to his shoulder and brought his face closer to the sight.

By now, Dayva was up on the platform, rope in hand. A brief delay was called for, and it was important for Dayva to have cover—there had to be something, anything to keep Sylvan from noticing her as she launched herself. I stood up, threw my arms into the air, and called out a big hello to Sylvan.

"Over here, Steph! It's me, your friend! The burglar!"

He spun toward me, dropped the incendiary device, and reached for his rifle. "You!" he snarled. I fell to the ground. Several bullets whizzed overhead.

A second later a rope must have swung out into the air carrying a person of great strength and skill. There was a deep thud, a cry, a muffled yell of outrage. I jumped to my feet and picked up the handgun and looked about wildly.

Dayva and Sylvan were on the ground, rolling about. The rifle and incendiary device lay nearby, off to the side. They fought silently and intently. It was an even match and seemed likely to go either way. Dayva was strong and agile, but Sylvan had a sinuous, cagey fury. I held the revolver in front of me, pointed at the ground, desperately trying to figure out how to disable the lock.

Sylvan broke free of Dayva, jumped to his feet, and immediately let out a sound like someone being struck in the stomach by a football. Did I really hear the *huff* of his expelled breath a split second before the blast of the gun? It wasn't possible, but it's what I thought at the time.

I guess I'll never know for sure. But what was indisputable was this: McGuane had stealthily made his way outside, and with one shot from him it was over.

The sirens arrived less than a minute later, and the men and women of the island Fire Department spilled out of two trucks, training their hoses on the cloud of escaping propane, wetting it down and coaxing it back into the ground. Once there, the noxious gas—like the spent force of thwarted revenge—would slowly dissipate into the dirt and be absorbed into the eternal elements from which we all spring, and to which we are said to return in time.

CHAPTER NINETEEN

That night Luna and Dorothy remained at the mansion with Quentin Douglas and Dayva Johnson. Dayva had performed the most heroic act of the afternoon, carrying it out with great courage, but afterward she just wanted to be alone. Luna and Dorothy stepped up to feed and care for the old man. As I left the house, Luna stood beside Quentin Douglas, and he was holding her hand like a child reaching up to grasp its mother.

Detective McGuane tended to the removal of the body and various other tasks. Before he left he told me, "Not bad, Christie, you lived up to the standards set by your great-great aunt." He asked if I'd like to stay at the police barracks again. No, I replied, thanks, I'm good—thinking that I would go back to my apartment and sleep.

For some reason I drove back to the office—now deserted—and sat alone at my desk in the eerie glow of fluorescent light. It was a good fifteen minutes before I remembered that my apartment was no longer in existence. Oh well, I thought, and slumped back in my chair. Something would come up. And something did. Beatrice and Eileen guessed that I was at the office and called and invited me to stay in the guest room of their Main Street apartment. When I arrived, they recommended nothing but a strong red Burgundy. Eileen brought out a dusty old bottle of Gevrey-Chambertin. I didn't take much note of the nose or the finish, but it did have the proper effect. After consuming most of the bottle myself, I felt like a hot air balloon that was slowly nodding and bumping back to Earth.

Later in the evening Beatrice called me over to the phone. "It's for you," she said. I picked up the receiver and Stefanie's voice asked how I was. She said she knew I must be experiencing many different emotions but she hoped the main one I felt now was relief. She added, when I felt good enough to come back to work, we would talk. If I wanted to return to this story and put it to bed myself, she would be honored to print whatever I wrote. For now she just wanted to send her support. And to encourage me to take the advice of my spirit friend—whatever it told me. I thanked her and promised to talk again soon.

No sooner had I hung up than the phone rang again, and thinking that Stefanie had called back by mistake I answered it myself and said, "I didn't mean *this* soon!"

"Oh," a voice replied. A woman's voice. A lovely, quiet quality. "Hello?"

"Peter?" the voice continued.

A pause. "Yes."

"I thought you were there. I'm just calling to say, I hope you're okay. And to thank you."

"Thanks," I said.

Beatrice and Eileen gave each other a quick look and cleared off a few things and left the room.

"It sounds like you went through a lot today. A whole lot."

"We're all okay," I told her.

"I know now's not the time to talk."

"No." I worked to catch my breath.

"Dorothy told me everything. Everything you figured out. Everything you did, for—well, for us all."

"We all played a part in this." By now, the day was retracting over me like the roof of one of those baseball stadiums that can close out bad weather. And the wine was lowering the lights toward the evensong.

"It's finally over," I added.

A pause from her. "Okay. Take care and get good rest."

And that was it.

I made my way back to the guest room and sat down on the bed. Before I could begin to process what Haddie and I had just said to each other, someone else spoke up.

Yes, it's over. You did it.

That voice. Why now? I wondered.

You proved to yourself that you aren't running away anymore.

"Yeah—finally," I said out loud.

You never really were, you know.

"I wish I could believe that." I pictured a young boy standing alone and afraid in a hallway, about to place his hands on a door knob. Behind that door was chaos, pain, and the suffering of someone he loved.

The door was locked. He always clicked it locked. You did everything you could.

For a moment I lost my breath again. Time took a tumble.

"Is that you, Mom?" I finally asked.

You didn't know?

"I thought it was my imagination. Or maybe my great-great aunt."

The voice laughed gently.

It was me all along.

"Oh, Mom, I'm sorry. I'm sorry for all you suffered. I'm sorry I couldn't stop it."

I was stronger than you realized. And I had to protect you.

"And you did," I said. "You did it in spades."

As well as I could.

"Better than anyone else ever could have. You were a hero, Mom."

I did what I had to. And you will do what you have to. The violence you saw when you were little—it disrupted your life. For years. It's time for you to put your life back together again.

"I know."

And you will, Peter. You will.

"I'll give it my best."

I'll always be with you if you need me. But for now, I'm saying goodbye.

"Goodbye?"

You learned the lessons you had to learn. You showed how resilient you are.

"I hope so."

My love for you lives on, it will always be inside you. Don't forget.

"I won't forget. Ever. Thank you. I love you."

I love you.

"Love you forever."

A tap on the door. "Peter, are you okay?"

"I'm okay," I replied.

"Who are you talking to in there?" Beatrice asked.

"Just talking myself to sleep."

"You sure?"

"I'm sure."

"All right. Sleep well."

"I will."

Footsteps crept off down the hall.

That night I slept in a deep and still pine forest, a place I recalled from somewhere long ago, a haven, a realm beyond time.

Over the next several days, events moved forward and more knowledge came to light. Betsy Cranmore came forward with an apology. The morning of the murder she'd noticed activity at Steph Sylvan's house, but she thought he was getting ready to go out commercial scalloping. She'd forgotten that the commercial season didn't begin until November first.

Luna called to tell me that we'd been correct in most of our guesses about her father's will. After the meeting with Steph Sylvan that August, Quentin Douglas had ordered Chester Danville to revise the will to exclude any and all non-marital offspring, and Danville was preparing to draft those changes at the time he was murdered.

About a week before his death, Danville asked and then insisted that he be included in the will himself. But the old man categorically refused. As rumored over the years, Douglas was leaving most of his money to family as well as a significant amount to Dayva.

What about Danville digging up the bags of gold and silver? I asked. Was he really following the wishes of Luna's father?

He was partly, she replied. He was supposed to dig up one bag of gold and one of silver so her father could store them in the massive safe he kept in his bedroom. But Danville dug up two extra bags of gold—each worth several hundred thousand dollars—apparently to give to himself and to Jenny Dyer, and as I had speculated, he brought bags of quartz rock to bury in their place.

Detective McGuane revealed that Sylvan was born Alonso Shepardson; his mother, Naomi Shepardson, was a waitress and massage therapist. Growing up in Tulsa, Oklahoma, he had no idea who his father was. He was an excellent all-around athlete and an all-state soccer player. He was also a gifted if erratic student who loved to read, especially heroic tales and fantasy novels. His favorite author was J.R.R. Tolkien, the great master of heroic fantasy.

During his teenaged years, he began to get into trouble—shoplifting, burglary, then assault and battery. After being accused of participating in a murder that may have been gang related, he served a year in prison.

During a prison visit, his mother finally revealed to him who his father was. An uber-wealthy selfish SOB who cared nothing for him or for her and deserved to suffer as a result.

Once Alonso got out of prison, he assumed a new identity, changing it a few more times over the course of his life. He became Steph Sylvan shortly before moving to the island.

Once Sylvan saw that Douglas had no intention of welcoming him into the family, the smoldering injustices of the past burst into full flame, and he lurched from one act of retribution to the next, wreaking pain and destruction to spectacular effect. *Fate ignites its glorious fire.*

McGuane offered one final thought. He said he'd been correct at the beginning about the importance of the literary insights I might have into the poems. Those connections, it turned out, had helped me figure out that Sylvan was the guy.

It had taken me a while to identify the origins of Sylvan's poetic sense, but one thing had always been beyond doubt: the overwhelming sense of revenge.

About a week after the death of Steph Sylvan, Haddie called and invited me to take a walk with her.

Pawtuck Swamp was less than a mile from Shawnee Point, but it couldn't have been more different from the familiar shoreline defined by salt and sand. The swamp was a freshwater oasis, protected by an overarching bower of tupelo and black oaks, with ferns scattered around the forest floor (dried up and shriveled at this time of year) and—most surprising of all—a clear stream that ran like a ribbon of light through its heart.

Haddie walked in front, showing me the way, wearing a windbreaker, jeans, and waterproof boots that were necessary for the muck that greeted us each time the path approached the stream. Somehow, as usual, she managed to look both sensible and unconsciously stylish.

"What do you think of this swamp?" she asked.

"I had no idea such a place existed on the island. Or that it could exist."

"I love the island for its shoreline, the shore birds, the salty brine, the shellfish. But this is my favorite spot of all."

As we delved deeper into the woods, the water pressed up closer to the path and created a true swamp, and the trees changed to species I didn't recognize—ones that apparently could grow up to their knees in water. After a while the path climbed back to higher ground and to a simple wooden bridge over the stream, where Haddie took a seat, dangling her legs out over the water. I sat down not far from her.

We began to talk, first about little things and then, as we both knew it would, the gravitational pull of the unspoken brought us back to that morning at the newspaper office, when she learned of the death of her grandfather.

"What happened then, Peter?" she asked. "Why were you so distant?"

I did my best to explain the wall that had formed in me decades ago, silently and beyond my ken. Over the years I'd sensed the existence of the wall but had never really understood it till recently.

"You were trapped in your own cocoon?"

"In a way, yes."

I said it had occurred to me that Steph Sylvan had probably undergone something similar in his life—though much more extreme. Similar in that he felt that anything he did was justified, that he had the complete right to do it. More extreme because of the horrific measures he felt fully entitled to take in order to redress the injuries he'd suffered.

"Could that be why you were able to understand him ahead of anyone else?"

That was likely, I replied. I pointed out that unlike Sylvan, I'd never deliberately tried to hurt someone. But I'd still found ways to do harm—to my wife, to my marriage.

It was strange, I added, that I shared with Sylvan the fact of being a non-marital descendent. I reminded Haddie of my great-grandmother and my great-grandfather Harry Miller, the beloved brother of Agatha Christie, and pointed out that my grandfather was the out-of-wedlock result of their union.

That coincidence was perhaps of little note, but there it was.

We fell into silence and began to drop bits of leaves into the water and watch them float away down the current, spinning like tops when they came to the whirlpools where the streambed deepened and sped up at a curve a few yards downstream.

She touched my hand. "What's going on with the walls now, Peter?"

I told her, oddly enough, that I thought they'd been largely washed away in my brush with death out on the water.

"When you and Dorothy were scalloping?"

I nodded. "After that happened, I felt different. A rebirth, in a way."

"A rebirth?"

"It might sound ridiculous. But the descent into the water, into the underworld—well, it changed something. Can a wall be washed away? Not really—nothing ever disappears entirely."

"When I visited you in the hospital, I thought you did look different somehow. But I told myself, you were probably just exhausted and probably terrified."

We agreed how strange it was that Bob Brown, of all people, had been the one who waded out and saved me. Haddie said she'd heard he was somewhere in the Midwest now at a rehab center and was doing everything he could to get out.

She sighed and said, "And then there's Jeff."

I went on full alert.

She continued, "Jeff is a college kid who's taking time off to work as an intern, and for the first time in my life I'm a supervisor." She went on to say that she found the whole situation very trying. Jeff didn't do what he was supposed to, he didn't show up when he was supposed to. She felt insecure about being his boss. The other day she made a lunch appointment with him and left her post early to meet him at the coffee shop, but he never came. He forgot. He was so maddening she didn't know what to do.

"That's too bad," I commiserated. I knew, sometime soon, I'd have to let her know that I was the voice on the phone.

Another period of silence. Then I said, "I need to tell you something about the end of my marriage. I was unfaithful to my wife."

"I see," she said. "I wondered."

"But I want to tell you something else. That will never happen again."

She patted my hand again, just once, almost a small slap. "We're getting ahead of ourselves, aren't we?"

"Okay. But one more thing. An apology. I wasn't there for you when you heard about the loss of your grandfather. I let you down, and I'm sorry."

Our eyes met. She squeezed my hand and released it. She let out a big sigh that floated out over the bridge in a white cloud. "I can't believe what he did. And how he treated my grandmother." She fixed her gaze on something on the forest floor, a squirrel or maybe a pheasant. She took out a tissue and dabbed at her eyes, and I reached over and put an arm around her. She leaned against me, but soon pulled away and said we should go back.

I followed her down the path as it wound through the dusky twilight. That night, as I slept between the Chewbacca twins in the guest room in Beatrice and Eileen's apartment, the musky odors of the freshwater swamp played in and out of my dreams.

CHAPTER TWENTY

Island Returns to a Stunned Sense of Peace
Murders solved but questions linger
BY PETER CHRISTIE

November 20 As Thanksgiving approaches, and people on the island express gratitude for their loved ones and for their many blessings, an event that may be mentioned more than most is the resolution of the violent murders that tore apart the fabric of the community.

With the death of Steph Sylvan in a dramatic face-off with police and other community members at the waterfront estate of Quentin Douglas, a frightening chapter in the life of the island has come to a close. [See a related story below for an eyewitness account of that event.]

The end of this case is cause for celebration and relief. As Reverend Brenda Gonzalez of the First Congregational Church put it, "a wound has been lanced, and the healing can begin."

But according to Gonzalez and others, it also raises additional questions about the island and the great disparities of wealth and poverty that are found here and have dramatically increased over the past few decades. "The murders were cruel and senseless, but what do they reveal about the underlying problems and tensions in our society?" Gonzalez recently asked at a community forum. "How do we reach the hearts of those who have no hope in their lives?"

Some community leaders are calling for . . .

I had no plans myself for Thanksgiving. Beatrice and Eileen were headed to New York to see some friends; they said I was free to stay in the apartment but hoped I wouldn't spend the holiday alone. It wasn't until the Monday before Turkey Day that I received an invitation.

The voice on the phone was young and eager. "Hey Peter."

"Hey yourself, Dorothy," I replied.

"My mom and me want you to come over for Thanksgiving."

I told her I'd love to come. And she said, "Well, someone else is coming too. I bet you can't guess who."

"Hmmm, no. I can't guess," I said.

"It's Haddie, you nincompoop," she told me.

That was so Dorothy: so intelligent, so lacking in social knowledge.

"That's great," I replied. "Of course, I'd love to see her."

"I don't know what she thinks about seeing you. I'm still trying to convince her what a good guy you are. I think you two should get married. But she refuses to commit."

"Well, that's all right, Dorothy. People need time, you know."

"Are you refusing to commit too?"

"Everything at its proper time, right? You can't hurry someone like Haddie. She has her own ways and her own wishes."

"I wish she didn't."

"People don't always conform to our wishes."

"Well, you do. Pretty much anyway. Oh, there's one more thing."

"What's that?"

"We're stuffing the turkey with scallops. Haddie and I are going to Shawnee Point on Wednesday afternoon to get them.

But she wants you to come over that evening to help shuck them. She says it's time she taught you how to open scallops."

Something was dancing in my heart. "Let me know when, and I'll be there."

Late that night I sat down and wrote a letter to my ex-wife, expressing some of the thoughts I'd been unable to say back then, during the breakup. I was sorry for my faithlessness. I was sorry for the pain I'd caused to her and to our marriage. I knew I was responsible for what had happened and I didn't expect anything from her now. I merely wanted to say I would hold her in my heart and I wished her all the best.

I wrote the letter out by hand, folded it into an envelope early the next morning, put on a stamp, and drove to the old brick post office downtown, where I slid it through the brass mail slot. A sense of walls breaking up and crumbling.

Now it would be up to me to find better days.

It was the Wednesday evening before Thanksgiving.

"Peter Christie," Haddie declared. She was wearing some sort of yellow waterproof gear and was standing at a tall wooden table in the shed out behind Luna's cottage.

"That would be me," I agreed.

"Are you ready for a difficult challenge?"

"Always ready," I confirmed.

"Is it true that you have sometimes been grossed out by wet slimy stuff?"

"Guilty as charged. As least in my errant youth."

"And in your non-errant present state?" she questioned.

"We shall see," I replied.

"Well, there's nothing messier than what we have right here."

She gestured toward the pile of scallops that rested on the table in front of her, next to a few blunt knives and some pots. On the floor rested two big trash barrels.

"Historically, I've had some issues with neatness and fastidiousness," I acknowledged. "But I've begun a new chapter."

"I see," she replied. "As you know, tonight's topic is opening scallops. Would you like a tutorial?"

I said I would, something perhaps along the lines of the tutorials she'd once received on mic-drop endings and good ledes.

"Very similar," she said. "Though less focused on words and—as you'll see—more experiential." She took my hand, placed in it the wooden handle of a scallop knife, and closed my fingers over the handle.

"This is how you start," she said. "Turn the shell over, so that the square edge is to your right. Insert the blade into the shell close to that square edge and cut the muscle inside. Cut it as near the top as you can. Leverage the top shell open and flip it back. Now comes the tricky part. The gooey part. The part that will challenge you. You see the dark mass of guts there? Square up the blade of the knife directly behind those guts, and pull them forward, over the top of the scallop muscle, or "eye," as you might pull a sweater over your head." She completed the maneuver, then flipped the cleaned scallop into a pan and turned to watch me.

I did as directed, positioning the shell correctly and leveraging it open. I squared up the blade of the knife. On my first try the guts pulled forward, over the "eye" of the scallop, just as she said they should. By now my hands were suitably slimy and messy.

I lifted my right hand and wriggled my fingers to show I was fine with it.

She remarked, "Not bad. You show some potential."

"Give me time," I told her. "You'll see, I'll only get better."

As I flipped the cleaned scallop into the pan, she gave a little laugh, gentle and delightful. We both picked up another shell and got to work, and I prayed in silence to the voice no longer inside me, the inner voice that had guided me and protected me through years of missteps and stumbles. I gave thanks for the love and care that had sustained my heart for better days ahead, for moments such as these.

THE END

ABOUT THE AUTHOR

James Sulzer lives on Nantucket, Massachusetts. A graduate of Yale University, where he was a Yale National Scholar, he is the author of a novel about Emily Dickinson, *The Voice at the Door*, and a novel about John Keats, *Writ in Water*. Other published works include the novel *Nantucket Daybreak* and a trilogy of middle grade novels for children, *The Card People*. He has produced countless "Sonic id's" for Public Radio, and in his early years on the island, he labored as a commercial scalloper. He and his wife Barbara have three grown children.

A free ebook edition is available with the purchase of this book.

To claim your free ebook edition:

1. Visit MorganJamesBOGO.com
2. Sign your name CLEARLY in the space
3. Complete the form and submit a photo of the entire copyright page
4. You or your friend can download the ebook to your preferred device

Morgan James BOGO™

A **FREE** ebook edition is available for you or a friend with the purchase of this print book.

CLEARLY SIGN YOUR NAME ABOVE

Instructions to claim your free ebook edition:
1. Visit MorganJamesBOGO.com
2. Sign your name CLEARLY in the space above
3. Complete the form and submit a photo of this entire page
4. You or your friend can download the ebook to your preferred device

Print & Digital Together Forever.

Snap a photo

Free ebook

Read anywhere

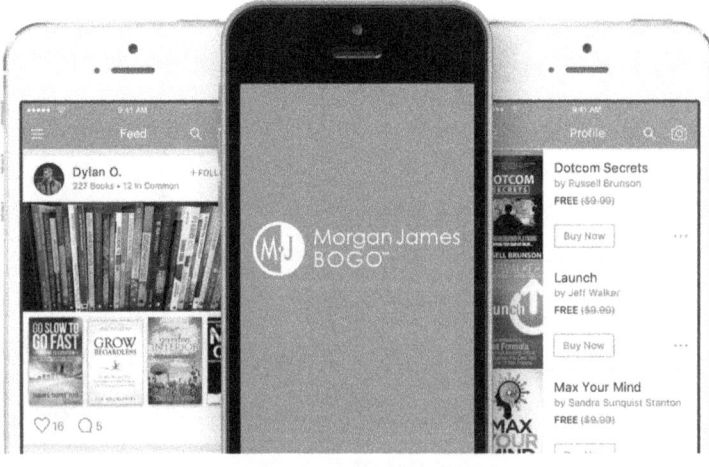

www.ingramcontent.com/pod-product-compliance
Lightning Source LLC
Jackson TN
JSHW021511310126
97585JS00007B/33